shadow **boxing**

sherie **posesorski**

COTEAU BOOKS FOR TEENS

Edited by Alison Acheson
Cover images, "Girl Crouches in Cardboard Box," by Amy Guip, Photonica Collection/Getty Images, and "Textured Scroll Background" by Sam Alfano, iStockphoto
Cover and book design by Duncan Campbell
Printed and bound in Canada by Friesens
This book is printed on 100% recycled paper

Library and Archives Canada Cataloguing in Publication

Posesorski, Sherie
Shadow boxing / Sherie Posesorski.

Mixed Sources
Cert no. SW-COC-001271
© 1996 FSC
FSC

ISBN 978-1-55050-406-4

I. Title.

PS8581.O758S43 2009   jC813'.54   C2009-901295-2

10 9 8 7 6 5 4 3 2 1

COTEAU
BOOKS
FOR TEENS

2517 Victoria Avenue
Regina, Saskatchewan
Canada   S4P 0T2

Available in Canada from:
Publishers Group Canada
9050 Shaughnessy Street
Vancouver, BC, Canada   V6P 6E5

The publisher gratefully acknowledges the financial support of its publishing program by: the Saskatchewan Arts Board, the Canada Council for the Arts, the Government of Canada through the Book Publishing Industry Development Program (BPIDP), the Association for the Export of Canadian Books and the City of Regina Arts Commission.

In memory of my mother
Dora Posesorski

and for Jodi Button

chapter**one**

I stood on the side of Dufferin Street with my thumb out again. I hardly ever had to hitchhike. But when I did, it was always truckers who picked me up, and never those scared suburbanite rabbits in their armoured van suvs.

And really, I was as far from scary looking as a sixteen-year-old in 2004 could get. No piercings. No tattoos. No black eyeliner and purple lipstick. Not a whiff of the goth about me. Well, on the outside, anyway. No exposed midriff. No exposed anything, other than my face, neck and calves. I was wearing a long-sleeved yellow t-shirt. I always wore long sleeves; but I had a reason for that. In the bulging pockets of my cropped cargo pants were a bottle of water, my wallet, sunglasses, a hat and a half-eaten granola bar.

I wiped the sweat off from under my bangs. If some trucker didn't pick me up soon, I'd be too ripe to get into any vehicle with anyone with a working nose.

It was so ugly here outside the city limits of Toronto. There were patches of new housing developments containing cookie-cutter townhouses, a few strip malls, gas stations and donut shops, and that was it. Not enough people living in the spotty subdivisions to justify a bus route. The rest was empty land, stretches of parched yellow grass and trees that had given up the fight and remained leafless, even in the summer.

After breathing in the visibly thick and smelly fumes of the speeding cars for another ten minutes, finally a trucker delivering bottled water pulled over.

"Want a lift, huh? I'm going as far as Newmarket," he shouted.

He swiped at the sweat running down the sides of his face with the back of his left hand. As far as I could tell, this balding, beefy, middle-aged trucker seemed like a guy just doing his job, and me a favour. And not like a serial rapist/killer trolling for fresh prey. So when he opened the passenger door, I climbed in, dragging up my duffel bag, trusting he was what he appeared to be, and not a prospective client for my criminal lawyer father.

"It's been a long time since I've seen a hitchhiker," he said, glancing over at me as he drove off the shoulder of the road and back into traffic.

Probably a really long time. I had yet to see anyone else when I'd had to hitchhike.

"What's in the bag, and where you headed?" he asked.

"A couple flowerpots, some bulbs and seeds, a spade, a blanket, a prayer book and stones," I mumbled. "I'm going to Pardes Shalom Cemetery to visit my mother."

"Oh yeah, that Jewish cemetery out in the middle of nowhere," he said.

"The Jewish cemeteries in the city are almost all filled up. So all the synagogues and Jewish organizations banded together to buy a plot of land huge enough to bury another century's worth of Toronto Jews," I explained, speeding through the explanation, recalling how hideously my father and I had fought when he'd informed me just how far away my mother was going to be buried.

He had the pull to get tables in restaurants reserved for weeks, tickets to sold-out plays at the Royal Alexandra Theatre, seats on overbooked flights, but hadn't put much effort into getting my mother a burial plot in the downtown cemetery where her parents lay. I still believed that, despite the onslaught of what he called explanations, and what I considered feeble excuses.

"It's a hike, huh, to see your mother?"

I shrugged. I didn't want to say more.

"I'm Joe, by the way," he said, sticking out his right hand.

I shook his hand. "I'm Alice."

"Don't you have anyone to drive you?" he asked.

"Usually my cousin Chloe drives me, but she's taking a summer course." I could almost hear the question he was too polite to ask. How come there was no one else?

"It's so isolated on this stretch of Dufferin. Aren't you afraid?" he asked, giving me another assessing look.

"Some."

"You should be," he said. "For your own good."

I knew that. Assault. Rape. Kidnapping. Murder.

After all, the only programs I watched on TV were crime series, and I was more familiar than I cared to be with my father's caseload and clientele.

And you didn't have to look and dress like the latest hot celebrity star or model, which I certainly did not. More like Hamlet actually, if you viewed my cropped pants as pantaloons and my dark blond, short, shaggy hair as a Prince Valiant type hairdo.

Was I leaving something off the crime blotter? Robbery. Not much to steal off me unless you were into gardening. Okay, I was being flip.

The truth was I wasn't afraid enough, not if that's what it took to get to the cemetery every week.

After some hemming and hawing, he spit out, "Are you sure you can't find someone to drive you? It's a no man's land here."

I stared down at my picked-raw cuticles. Then I made myself look up. On one side, there were grassy knolls and sand traps, part of a golf course in mid-construction, and on the other side, four cows grazing on waist-high grass near a barn.

"Your father?" Joe said, clearing his throat.

Right. In the six months since my mother had died, my father had gone to the cemetery only after running out of reasons why he couldn't make it "today." Have to meet a client. Have a summation to prepare. It's snowing too hard. It's raining too hard.

When he did take me, I'd sit down, as I always did, next to the gravestone, while my father would pace behind me. I swear I could feel him calculating how long he had to be out there before he could announce, "I'll meet you in the car," and walk off. His behaviour disgusted me. Instead of being able to think about my mother, all I could think about was how repulsive my father was. So I'd stopped asking him to drive me.

I could have asked my aunt Leslea, the provider of the potter's field style flower bed display before my mother's gravestone. Right. As a showy gesture of her "caring," she'd offered to pay for the gardening. And she'd chosen the bargain basement selection consisting of a few geraniums dead from the get-go, surrounded by wizened, sickly brown shrubbery on its deathbed. It was the most wretched of all the flower bed arrangements I'd come across in the cemetery.

I'd complained about it to my father, who'd done zilch. Next I'd offered to pay for the gardening, but he wouldn't allow it. He said it would shame his dear sister. Shame her? How? She was shameless.

She was rolling in alimony payments from Chloe's father, who'd hit the road when Chloe was two. She got "pocket money," as she dubbed it, in a cutesy voice, from her "prestige" jobs working as a real estate agent for an agency that dealt only in luxury residences and as a prop decorator for American movies filming in Toronto.

When Chloe had gotten her driver's licence two months ago, it had solved the lift problem and the flower problem. Chloe said we should do the gardening ourselves.

"I didn't mean to pry," Joe said, with a loud gulp, signalling as clear as an ambulance siren just how uncomfortable he was. "Sorry. It's none of my business."

"There's no one except my cousin," I said, sounding abrupt although I didn't mean to. Not that I was embarrassed on my behalf. I was, though, on my mother's. It made it seem as if she didn't have many people who loved her.

"You know what," he said, breathing so hard I could count each breath. "Passing by that cemetery always brings back the memory of my best friend in high school. He was killed instantly crossing the road when this asshole speeding driver ploughed into him. And ever since then, I can't step foot into a cemetery without getting the shakes," he said, flushing.

Feeling totally guilty about being the Grim Reaper in the guise of a teen hitchhiker, I tried to lighten the mood with a choice story about Leslea. Last week she had been showing a couple a pricy condo at the too appropriately named Granite Place. When the couple had gone out onto the balcony, they'd noticed it overlooked a small cemetery. My aunt told them, not to worry, it wasn't a particularly "active" cemetery.

"Therefore, only the occasional gravedigger and open grave when you sit out on the balcony drinking your morning java," Joe said, groaning.

Determined to make the sale, Leslea hadn't given up. Restful, she'd tried, peaceful, I continued, mimicking my aunt. I knew the whole story, thanks to Chloe, who loved passing on tales about her mother that further fed our conviction that she and my father just didn't get it. Chloe had gone along because she and Leslea had one of their gazillion beauty appointments afterwards.

Joe hooted at that. "Peaceful? For whom? And you can't know that unless you're some damn psychic claiming you can communicate with those who 'have passed over,'" he added.

That was the problem exactly. Maybe if I knew my mother was truly at peace, maybe then I wouldn't feel so haunted.

Joe stopped in the entrance of Pardes Shalom. I turned to him and thanked him, then hopped out.

Lugging my bag, I headed up the hill along the curved roadway to my mother's gravesite.

chapter**two**

Most definitively, Pardes Shalom wasn't a Mount Pleasant style cemetery. Mount Pleasant was as much a park as it was a cemetery, with its flowering dogwood and magnolia trees, paved pathways, sculptures, waterfalls and elaborate gardens.

And people treated the midtown cemetery as they would any park. In good weather, it was full of walkers, joggers, cyclists, mothers with strollers and teachers, like my history teacher who'd taken us there last spring on a tour of the graves of the famous dead buried in the cemetery. Prime Minister William Lyon Mackenzie King was buried there, as was pianist Glenn Gould.

To me though, a cemetery was a cemetery, no matter how pleasant and park-like. When I have kids, I won't be pushing them in strollers through a cemetery. Their exposure to the dead can wait, thank you very much.

There were never walkers or baby strollers in Pardes Shalom, a strictly utilitarian cemetery. A humongous hunk of land divided up in sections, it resembled a parking lot for the dead. There were barely any trees, no gardens, scarcely any benches and not many visitors.

It was a five-minute walk up a hilly gravel road to the section where my mother was buried. I shifted my duffel bag from shoulder to shoulder; it was heavier than I'd thought. When I reached my mother's gravestone, I had to sit down right away. Suddenly my legs felt too wobbly to stand.

Feeling semi-revived after slugging down a bottle of water, I stared at the flower bed. It would be pretty next year when the bulbs and seeds we'd planted bloomed.

I dumped everything out of the duffel. First, I put a stone on top of the gravestone, and recited *Eil Malei Rachamim,* the prayer for the dead. Then I grabbed a chamois cloth and polished the gravestone, careful to remove any dirt embedded in the engraved letters of my mother's name and inscription.

Ellen Borenstein Levitt. June 15, 1959 to January 4, 2004. Cherished daughter of Leon and Rivka, loving wife of Eric, devoted mother of Alice and aunt of Chloe. Forever in our hearts. May she rest in peace.

I polished until the granite shone as brightly as a mirror. Then I lined up the pots containing full-blooming impatiens and geraniums. I dug out the withered flowers and began replanting.

Chloe was so much better at this than me. The flower decorator, she nicknamed herself, but it was more than that. For Chloe, the flower bed was a canvas where she planted flowers by size, texture and shape in an unexpected pattern that seemed perfect after she finished. I didn't have her eye or her green thumb so I kept to the arrangement she'd made.

After plucking off the yellowing leaves on the shrubbery, I was done, and sat back on the blanket. Next should be the scene that occurs all the time in movies and books where the person at the gravesite relates everything new in her life. That scene never happened when I was alone at my mother's gravesite. Neither had the famous deathbed scene where the dying person and the people she loves all get to say everything in their hearts in tearful, mushy, eloquent-as-Shakespeare farewell speeches. One sentimental lie after another, that's what those deathbed scenes were.

The last few days of her life, my mother had been too doped up with morphine to be able to speak in the palliative care hospice my father had shipped her off to. Palliative care. Right. Palliative care *really* means no food, no water, nothing but drugs, and nurses circling like death vultures.

My mother had drifted in and out of consciousness, and our last exchange was a look. She had the most anguished, frightened, sad expression I'd ever seen on her face as she stared up at me. I couldn't stop seeing that expression on her face.

If Chloe was here with me, she'd go on and on, reciting all her good memories of the times we'd had with my mom. Last Sunday Chloe had reminded me of a vacation we'd taken in Fort Lauderdale during the Christmas holidays several years back. Leslea was off with some boyfriend skiing and my father was preparing his defence for another one of the scumbags he'd gotten so rich defending. Or at least that was what he claimed.

My mother, who loved Christmas, as did Chloe and I, had driven us to Lantana, where the offices of *The National Enquirer* used to be located. Every year just outside their offices, the tallest and most beautifully decorated Christmas tree in the United States was on exhibit.

The crowd was immense. Yet my mother somehow squeezed us right to the front of the tree. On the drive back, we went through the neighbourhoods listed in the local newspaper as being the most spectacularly decorated. It was amazing to see those small rinky-dink bungalows decked out with lights, Santas, reindeer, Toylands and Christmas scenes to the nth degree. I never saw anything like that in Toronto, where a string of lights passed as Christmas decoration.

Later, we joined Chloe's dad, who was in Miami Beach for a couple days for a business conference, at Rascal House, this Jewish deli renowned for its mammoth portions of every Jewish delicacy from pancake size latkes to matzoh balls, floating like tennis balls, in a vat of chicken soup.

Uncle Samuel's parents had been born in Poland and they had immigrated to Canada, meeting up and marrying in Montreal. Like my mother, he spoke Yiddish and loved old country Jewish food. I swear he had much more in common with my mother than Eric ever had. As Chloe and I were trying out all the different dishes, they yakked away in Yiddish to each other, occasionally interrupted by us asking them to translate what they were laughing over.

That was a good memory, one I was grateful to Chloe for reviving.

And also the story my mom always razzed Chloe about. When Chloe was three years old, she'd grabbed some change Leslea had left on the coffee table, and swallowed the coins. My mother rushed Chloe off to the emergency, leaving two-year-old me with a neighbour. Where was Leslea? Good question.

The ER doctor ordered an x-ray of Chloe's stomach and there was the change . . . three dimes and four pennies. For a week, my mother had to comb through Chloe's shit until she collected, as she joked, the exact amount of change. Where was Leslea once again? The smell of shit made her sick, so the job became my mother's. She'd done most of the changing of Chloe's diapers.

After Chloe shared her good memories, she then told my mother all her news, even when I made faces as she went on about Kevin. She called him her boyfriend. He called her his "friend with benefits" – a phrase he'd picked up from some newspaper article on teen sex, and repeated endlessly until I wanted to smack his mouth shut. In other words, he got sex and Chloe got the "benefit" of dreaming he was her boyfriend.

This would be followed by me rapidly mumbling my way through stuff. My talk was short, kind of like those banner news sentences running on CNN. If Chloe knew what I was really feeling about doing this, she pretended not to know, not wanting to make me feel even worse than I did already.

Without Chloe, I didn't have to pretend. I just said out loud what I always said.

"I love you. I miss you so much. I'm so sorry you died alone."

Without Chloe, I had to struggle to retrieve any good memories. All I ever seemed to remember at her gravesite, in overabundant detail, were the last weeks of my mother's life. In the only vague conversation any of us had had with my mom about her dying, she'd asked not to be taken to a hospital. What she was saying was that she wanted to die at home.

My father hired a nurse to look after my mother during the day. Chloe moved in and when we got home from school, we took over for the nurse. We fed my mother. Gave my mother her doses of pain medicine. Sponge bathed her. Changed her diapers when she became too weak to get out of bed to go to the bathroom. At night, we took turns sleeping. One of us would sit up watching over my mother while the other slept in a sleeping bag on the floor. I, the machine of work – the only trait I was grateful to share with my father – would do my homework and assignments while keeping an eye on my mother.

We waited for those blessed minutes when my mother would be her old self, affectionately teasing and questioning us just as she always had. She would ask one of us to bring her some makeup and a hairbrush so she could make herself look presentable, she'd say, and then we would gab. Inevitably though, she would fade out, and return to just lying there, answering questions when we asked, but mostly silent.

Sometimes she'd call out, "Help me, help me!" We would hold her hands, and try to reassure her. But we couldn't give the reassurance she really wanted to hear, that she wasn't going to die.

Where were my father and my aunt during this time? Leslea floated in and out, full of trite rationalizations and insincere apologies. She would give my mother a quick air kiss on the cheek, sit far away from the bed and then rush off.

And my father. So many cases. So busy, busy, busy. Like his sister, he too would float in and out, full of his stock rationalizations and oily apologies. On the weekends he would sit in the bedroom with us, offer to help, but he was useless. If he fed my mother, he did it too fast, making her choke, or he dribbled food all over her.

Dr. Chen, the palliative care doctor who came every other day to check over my mother, was a great help. He advised us to spend as much time as we could with my mother, and to say everything we had to say to her. The first part Chloe and I did as best we could, but the second part, no. We couldn't say goodbye when my mother didn't want to acknowledge she was dying.

The weekend before she died, instead of Dr. Chen, this obnoxious palliative care nurse came to see my mother. With our bad luck, Leslea and my father were there doing their obligatory in and out visit. The nurse started tsk-tsking about how this wasn't the place for my mother. Naturally she knew just the place for her – a hospice where she worked part-time in the boonies of Richmond Hill, an hour's drive (and that was in the lightest of traffic) from our house. The hospice was dependent on government funding for upkeep and salaries, and had zero patients at the time. Which meant zero salary for that fat-ass nurse.

Of course this information was music to my father and Leslea's ears. At long last they'd met a medical professional who saw things as they did.

Fat-ass then stuck her face into my mother's and asked in a false cheery voice, "Do you like me?"

In that last flash of being her old self my mother replied, "So far."

Chloe and I burst out laughing at my mother putting her right in her place. The nurse got all huffy and waddled out of the bedroom.

A victory for us, we thought. What it really was though was the kind of pyrrhic victory my grade ten English teacher had pointed out in Shakespeare's plays when it appeared that Macbeth, Richard iii and Hamlet had triumphed over their enemies. They had, but it was a victory with defeat built-in, the same way a thief was triumphant after a robbery just before being caught by the police.

In other words, while we were gloating in the bedroom, the nurse was all the more determined to make the sale to my father and Leslea. After she left, my father and Leslea called us into the kitchen. It would be better at the hospice for my mother, they insisted. Only better for them, Chloe and I insisted right back.

On Monday, when Chloe and I came back from school, my mother was gone, exiled to the hospice.

I would never forgive my father for that. Ever.

My mother lived another five days there. Since Chloe only had her Level One beginner driver's licence then, we were dependent on my father or Leslea to drive us there.

The two nurses who worked with fat-ass were even worse.

By then my mother hardly spoke. And the few times she did, she said only one word, *vaser* – that was the Yiddish word for water, because they weren't giving her any food or water.

It was hard to choose which of the three was worse. One imitated the gasping sound my mother was occasionally making as she struggled for breath. Chloe and I were afraid to tell her to knock it off in case she took it out on my mom when we weren't there.

Another one showed her complete absence of empathy and decency in the moment my mother gave me that terrible anguished look. Chloe had gone out to McDonald's to get dinner for us. The nurse started telling me what to say to my mother. She said it was evident (evidently apparent only after confabs with my father and Leslea), that my mother wanted to die but didn't want to leave me. And that I was the cause of her pain. So I should tell her it was okay for her to go. I would be okay.

I didn't want her to let go of me. And I didn't want to let go of her. But I parroted the nurse's words. Then the nurse gave my mother another shot of morphine, to get rid of her fear, she claimed. And that was the last time my mother was conscious.

On the Friday morning of that week, the vice-principal summoned Chloe and I out of our classes. There was my father in the hall. One of the nurses had called to say my mother was going to die within hours. We raced to Richmond Hill, but she died minutes before we got there.

That anguished expression and the sight of her lying there on the bed, already cold and so white, that was what I remembered first and most.

I got up from where I'd been sitting next to the flower bed, sprinkled the rest of my bottled water on the flowers, stroked the tombstone and left her by herself again.

chapter**three**

Rushing along Queen Street West, dragging my duffel bag, muttering I mustn't be late, I mustn't be late, like a dirty, sweaty imitation of Alice's rabbit, I had to say I fit right in. Not with the goths and the grungers, but with the regulars who lived on the street, their lives in the bags they hauled around with them. During the day they rested their backs against the bags as they sat asking for change. In the evening I'd often see them sleeping, snuggling their bags as if hugging a loved one.

I paused and took a deep breath before opening the door to Atticus Antiquarian Books. I'd been working there part-time since April. I liked the job, I liked John Atticus, and since the list of what I liked wasn't long even in the best of the times, I didn't want to lose the job

What was the worst John could say or do? Fire me? Blow a gasket and yell at me? Shake his head and say, "I thought you were responsible."

Of one, two or three, option three would do the trick. Anger didn't work on me. You could scream until the blood vessels in your eyes burst and it wouldn't do a thing to me. I stayed calm, my heartbeat sure and steady. But make me feel guilty, boy, that would do the job, and how. I'd be twisting in remorse like a contortionist.

Ahh, cool air. John kept the window air conditioners blasting in the ground floor section, especially on humid days like today. Humidity was bad for the books. And bad for John, considering how he wore a three-piece suit and bow tie every day.

"I suit the place and the place suits me," he would kid, loosening his Trenton, New Jersey accent like some men loosen their ties when the boss isn't around.

John's bosses were those rich book people willing to spend big money on first-edition books. And those sometimes snotty book people believed only a guy wearing a suit and speaking with perfect diction like Alistair Cooke, the host of *Masterpiece Theatre,* was someone they could trust to know books. John's natural voice, which sounded like his nostrils were stuffed up from allergies, was similar to that of the Bronx bus driver Ralph Kramden from *The Honeymooners.*

I wasn't familiar with either of those ancient TV series before I started the job. John, though, was a big, big fan and had lent me tapes of the shows. He was a pack rat. Like my mom. Another reason to like him. I liked both series too, maybe *The Honeymooners* more.

John had this way of knowing exactly what someone would like. That, of course, made him do as well as an antiquarian bookstore owner could do. But it wasn't just a selling tool; it was the way he was. I had been working here three months and he already knew my tastes better than my father did. Better than I knew them. The era of the gift card was a godsend for my father. Before the gift card, I swear it was as if he grabbed the first thing he saw in any store.

The air conditioning was blow-drying my sweat. At least I wouldn't be obviously spotty when John saw me. I heard his voice.

He must be on the phone in the little office in the back. There was lots of valuable stuff to steal, but it was under lock and key. Tastefully, of course. In lord of the manor mahogany bookcases fronted by leaded glass and museum-type display cases. So even if John was on the phone in the office, there wasn't anything to steal quickly and effortlessly unless you planned to haul out the red leather wing chairs and matching loveseat.

As a joke, I asked John if he modelled the décor of the bookstore after the English manor library in which Alistair Cooke sat in a wing chair introducing whatever classic English novel had been made into a TV movie for *Masterpiece Theatre* and, to my astonishment, he said, "Yup!"

I heard him talking rapidly. It was the New Jersey voice. He probably was speaking to his wife Eileen. I scanned the shelves. The books were an interesting mishmash. There were kids' books like *The Tale of The Flopsy Bunnies,* 1909 autographed first edition, by Beatrix Potter, and *You Don't Look 35, Charlie Brown!,* 1985 edition, by Charles Schulz. Both $1500. The price rose after Schultz died of colon cancer.

The second rule of antiquarian bookselling (after, logically, the first rule which was that dead authors were the bestselling authors, outselling books by living authors), was that prices skyrocketed when an author died. Right after Mordecai Richler and Carol Shields died, John said, the store had been as crammed as a department store holding a Boxing Day sale, every first edition he owned of theirs grabbed and gone, and at inflation prices.

It was the old, old dead that sold the best. An 1865 first edition of *Our Mutual Friend,* by Charles Dickens. $4,000. An 1831 third edition, with illustrations, of *Frankenstein,* by Mary Shelley. $12,000. Robert Burton, *The Anatomy of Melancholy,* 1624 first folio edition. $7,000.

Once a week I dusted the insides of the bookcases. First time in my life I looked forward to dusting, because I got to touch books by my favourite authors, like Dickens and Schulz. I'd rest a hand on them, like people did in court when they swore an oath to tell the truth on the Bible. When I touched the book, I felt as if I could feel the author's spirit. I did this a lot. And not just with books. All things.

I heard John put down the phone. Now I had to get ready to explain.

When John had interviewed me for the job the first thing he'd asked was if I was dependable and willing to work hard. He'd had lots of very pleasant workers who behaved as if they didn't know what a watch was and treated the bookstore like their own personal library, and some who, when they weren't reading, were napping. Snoring even. I'd laughed at that and promised I didn't snore, and that I was dependable.

I worked upstairs in Atticus's Attic where John sold second-hand books and remaindered paperbacks and hardcovers.

I could have dressed casually like Randy Weinstein, the other clerk, did. Instead I dressed in what John called my Catholic school uniform, a long-sleeved white oxford shirt, pleated black skirt, knee socks and black oxfords, even though upstairs there was only one sputtering window air conditioner and a constant layer of dust, no matter how often Randy and I dusted. It was as if the walls and ceiling were shedding. Although John sometimes moaned that Randy was using the attic as his own personal *Playboy* mansion, he liked Randy, who somehow was able to work really hard and work the space for date bait. I liked him too.

Randy was friendly with everybody, easygoing even with the hardest-to- please customers. Despite presenting himself otherwise, from our talks I realized he was actually longing for a real girlfriend and a real relationship, and not hookups.

"Alaace," John said.

Before he could say anything about me being late and looking like a dusty, dirty, and I prayed not too awfully smelly, Pigpen, I burst out, "I didn't have time to go home and change. It was a choice between being really late and clean or a little late and dirty. It won't happen again, I promise, I do. I know I . . ."

I suppose I could have told him the whole truth about hitch-hiking thirty kilometres each way to visit my mother's gravesite, but I didn't want to use that as an excuse. I didn't want his pity or sympathy.

John knew. Chloe once told him, but he wasn't the type to ask Nosy Parker questions. I mean, if I'd started talking he would have listened; he was a good guy. Since my mother died, I've have more than my share of run-ins with gossipy gore hounds who wanted to know all the awful details, who wanted me to do a weepy "soul bar-ing" performance because that was the only kind of grieving they got. As if they cared. Yeah, right. As if people rubbernecking a car crash "cared." I used to talk about my mom's illnesses to my friends when she first got very sick. However, I promptly learned that peo-ple wanted you to talk just so much, and not much more.

They didn't want you to turn into a snivelling mess in front of them.

They didn't want you to obsess and obsess about it.

I didn't feel relieved after sharing. I felt ashamed and alone. So I'd stopped talking about it with anyone except Chloe.

I was so preoccupied with my mother's illness and care, I didn't have the concentration, energy or time to hang out with friends, so my friendships fizzled out.

"Alaace," John said. "You know you can look me in the eyes. Lateness isn't a grand felony. I've seen you dressed better and smelling sweeter, but it's fine."

I did look him in the eyes then, and he gave me such a kind look, smiling a little but looking concerned, his forehead all creased, the lines at his eyes accented. He had the nicest face. Not handsome by a long shot; he had a beaky nose and a really long face, and his hairline had, well, receded, retreated, he wisecracked. There was no better word to describe his face. Nice.

"Go forth and dust the whole joint, tables and all. Do the cataloguing tomorrow," John said, with a wave. "To the moon, Alaace!"

That was what Ralph Kramden always said to his wife Alice whenever she got on his case. John had said that to me as a joke once, but it stuck and now he would say it to me whenever he wanted me to go upstairs to the attic pronto. So, dragging my duffel bag, that's where I went. To the moon.

chapter**four**

I stashed my bag behind the cash register, and looked around, trying to choose which area to hit first, armed with a duster, and a sweeper for the floor. God, it was hot up here. It truly was an attic, with a pitched roof and exposed rafters, arched windows and a creaky, scuffed oak floor. The room was jam-packed with tables, and bookcases lined the walls. The one-of-a-kind books were shelved, and the paperbacks and remaindered books stacked by subject and genre on tables.

The light from the window was hitting the table overflowing with World War ii books, making the dust visible. That seemed as good a place to start as any.

The books on the Axis countries were separated from the books on the Allies; the books on the Western theatre were separated from the ones on the Pacific battlegrounds.

Then there were biographies of the leaders. Churchill cheek by jowl with Roosevelt; Stalin and Hitler isolated on either edge of the table. I lifted each pile, careful to keep the order, dusted the table and then each individual book before returning the piles.

I got into the Zen of dusting and wiping until I hit several piles of books on the Holocaust. My grandparents, on my mother's side, were Holocaust survivors from Poland.

I had these tiny fragments of memories about them. I wished memories were like full scenes I could replay as I did numbered selections on a DVD. But mine weren't. They were like torn-up pieces of scenes. Flashes of images and a couple of sentences. And that was it for the memory.

Bubbe and Zaide, that's what I had called my mother's parents. My father's parents were too Canadian for that. They insisted on Grandfather and Grandmother. I didn't see them much, which was fine with me. They had retired and settled in Phoenix because of Grandfather Levitt's asthma. I got the occasional letter from them and – like son, likewise parents – gift cards on the appropriate occasions.

My mother used to speak Yiddish to Bubbe and Zaide when we visited. That I remember. I used to try too, which had pleased them.

My father seldom came along. He didn't have much tolerance for their heavily accented English, their speaking half in English, half in Yiddish and their rambling stories. They were too Jewish for him.

For years Chloe and I had talked up the ins and outs of my theory that my father had modelled himself after fashion designer Ralph Lauren, a.k.a. Ralph Lifshitz, the boy from the Bronx who transformed himself (and those buying his clothing) into the image of a picture-perfect wealthy WASP.

My father dressed like one of those immaculately groomed, über-Christian male models in Ralph Lauren ads – the ones looking as if they are waiting for their manservant to bring in the hors d'oevres and the predinner cocktail. He was secretly (and not very secretly at all, as revealed by that irrepressible smirk on his face) complimented when people thought he wasn't Jewish.

Now I could say that John did the same thing with his Alistair Cooke take-off. But for John, it was just a role, a uniform he put on just as a doorman did, he once said. He made fun of himself. My father, on the other hand, took himself and his American idol seriously.

When I was younger, my mother used to cook Jewish-style food on a regular basis: the staples like borscht, chicken soup, farfel, potato kasha, knishes, boiled beef flanken and gefilte fish. My father put a stop to all that, only allowing her to cook them on Jewish holidays. She fought back at the beginning, as she continually did. My father eventually wore her down though. He had that winning ace in the hand – she loved him. Since she loved him, she gave in. Until she gave up. On everything. I didn't want to think about that.

Luckily for me, three customers came up just then. Unlike the big chain bookstores, where you either needed to hire a detective to find a clerk or you had one breathing vapour on your neck as you browsed, here we – we meaning me and Randy – had been drilled by John in the Atticus's Attic rules of customer engagement to act like book butlers, like Jeeves. We were supposed to watch browsing customers at a respectful distance, and offer suggestions and assistance only when asked.

Customers one and two, a couple I guessed, asked me for help in finding some of the books for a summer course they were taking at the University of Toronto. That was a treasure hunt, and it took twenty minutes to find all of the Victorian novels on their reading lists. They were happy with the cheap editions and I was happy, as usual, about being too busy to think. By that time customer three had left and was replaced by customer four.

She gave me the uppity look people give waiters when they want service immediately, and I went over.

"Is there anything I can help you with?"

From her raised eyebrows and the way her nostrils were turning in like they were trying to shut out an unpleasant odour, it was evident she was sorry she'd asked me. I glanced down at my clothing. Hard to believe but I was now even filthier than I had been when I arrived. There was even a cobweb hooked onto the pocket of my cargo pants.

"I'm searching for coffee-table art books . . . for gifts," she added, as if the attic wasn't good enough for books for her, but only as a source of gifts that looked like they cost more than they in fact did.

"Alice," John called from downstairs. "Chloe's on the phone for you. She says it's important."

I used to carry a cell phone when my mother was sick. After she died, I told my father to cancel it. Each time it rang, it reminded me of the calls I'd receive, telling me to hurry home.

I directed the woman to a table filled with remaindered coffee-table books, and went downstairs to John's office.

"Hey Chloe, what's up?" I spoke softly. John was with a customer.

I heard her sniffing. "Chloe, what happened?"

"I'm in trouble. Can you come now?" she said, clearly trying not to cry. "I'm at school and something just happened in Parnell's class. With Kevin."

On another day, I would have asked John if I could leave early. "I can't leave," I whispered. "I came late from the cemetery. Can you hang in till I finish in an hour or so?"

"Yeah, yeah," she sighed. "See you soon."

I put down the receiver, and John gave me a questioning look. I shrugged and went back upstairs to the cranky customer who was so cranky and demanding I didn't have a second even to think about Chloe until I got on the subway heading towards school.

At this point in the afternoon, the subway line was nearly deserted. I stretched out in the middle of three empty seats, placing the duffel bag next to me. Damn! I'd finished the Joseph Conrad novel *The Secret Agent* I'd brought with me to Atticus's this morning, which gave me nothing to do but brood about Chloe.

Chloe had failed two of her classes last year. Unlike me, the work machine, she hadn't been able to focus enough to do her work while my mother was dying. And the result was that she was in summer school for the next eight weeks, taking an art class. That wasn't so bad, I kept telling her; it could have been biology, with the fumes of formaldehyde toxically mixing with the body odours of thirty sweaty students.

Frigging Kevin. He was such a user, but Chloe just didn't want to see it.

Unfortunately for Chloe, she shared her mom's obsession with men. Leslea was never without a boyfriend; the seat next to her was still warm from the ass of her last boyfriend when she managed to corral a new one.

Leslea looked (with a lot of paid help) like one of those glamour babe models in some Vogue magazine photo layout. She had reddish wavy long hair (enhanced with dye, highlights and lowlights) and one of those Barbie hourglass figures – big boobs (supplemented with saline implants), a tiny waist and not a centimetre of loose flesh thanks to hours of Pilates, hot yoga, exercise machines and regular Botox and collagen injections.

Though Chloe felt disloyal and guilty, she did yearn to resemble Leslea instead of her father. She had his mass of thick, curly, brown hair, though hers was currently dyed scarlet with gold streaks. She was short, maybe five foot two, had the same round face with chubby cheeks, and the weight problem. It wouldn't be so noticeable if Chloe didn't pack herself into clothes you had be a size 2 to look good in.

She had his nose – a pug nose – but was still refusing her

mother's offer of a nose job, and her dad's best feature: big, expressive brown eyes with the longest lashes.

Uncle Samuel was a hotshot financier. Since the divorce he'd been working for a multinational stock brokerage company in Hong Kong.

She stayed with him for a couple of weeks either in late summer or during the winter school break, and met up with him in various American cities when he was on business trips. Occasionally he used to drop in on our family vacations.

He seemed as if he would be a good father to Chloe. Who knew what had happened between him and Leslea, but their breakup and divorce had been so ugly he hardly ever came back to Toronto. Chloe used to joke, though it was no joke really, that it was as if Leslea was as deadly for her father as kryptonite was for Superman; hence he stayed far, far away.

For years after the divorce, Leslea had fed Chloe a load of lies about her father. The lies and distortions (your father doesn't love you, but I do; your father doesn't want you, but I do; if he loved you, wouldn't he be around; he abandoned us) had been finally, at long last, exposed for what they were. Still, like poisonous weeds yanked out, they had already done their damage to Chloe.

My mother had reunited Uncle Samuel and Chloe five years ago when she'd invited him to join us on a winter vacation in Miami Beach. Since then he'd been hounding Chloe to live with him. And she would have – in a finger snap – had he not lived in Hong Kong. They had grown closer; but no matter how much she had come to love her father, she wasn't willing to give up her life here, her friends, the familiarity. Why didn't he just move back, I thought, but never said to Chloe. I didn't want to ruin things between them; yet, she must have thought that too.

Chloe talked to her dad two or three times a week and emailed him daily, but his presence was really, bad pun or not, in the presents. The Sony Vaio notebook computer. The video cell phone. The BlackBerry. The iPod. The digital camera. The flat panel plasma television. To list just the recent presents.

She often had this puppy dog gaze, so eager for attention, with Uncle Samuel, her boyfriends, even Leslea sometimes. That gaze broke my heart. She wanted so much to be liked.

I saw the tail end of the sign that said Museum. My stop. I jumped up, and just barely made it through the closing doors. I had to yank my duffel bag free. I stood panting for a second, wondering with a sick feeling about what kind of trouble Chloe had gotten herself into now.

chapter**five**

n the heart of the Annex, Emerson High School was your typical decaying downtown high school. Three stories high, its arched leaded windows were streaked with decades of grime, its red bricks caked brown with dirt and the churchlike massive oak double doors at the main entrance chipped and scratched. Yet its academic reputation was as good as the ritzy private schools nearby, and it had a similar population of rich and privileged students.

When my parents had bought their home on Tranby Avenue in the Annex, the Victorian row houses were selling at the bargain price of $50,000. The same houses, even without complete renovation jobs, were currently selling for over a million. Mostly counterculture types and academics used to live in the area (the University of Toronto and Ryerson University were in the vicinity), but now the prices said it all – it was people with money, and lots of it.

Since artists living in the Upper Annex above Davenport and theatre people performing in the neighbouring small theatre circuit frequently lectured and taught courses at the school, Emerson had especially good arts classes.

The art classroom was on the second floor at the north end. I hurried up the stairs and down the hallway. I yanked open the door to the classroom studio and saw Chloe sitting on a chair in the far corner near the window, her head dropped down so all I could see of her was a mass of red hair with streaks and shoulders slumped forward in a give-up-on-everything posture.

Ms. Parnell's back was to me. She was standing in front of an easel, a clipboard in her hand, evaluating some student painting. Neither noticed me standing in the doorway. When Parnell was concentrating on a piece of work, she concentrated, hearing nothing, seeing nothing, thinking about nothing except what was in front of her. Parnell had to be able to do that, working as she did in a big room with students noisily slogging away on stuff that was supposed to pass as art.

There were a handful of talented artsy students, but a good number were not even interested in art, taking it only because they thought it was an easy credit. Good luck! Parnell was a tough marker, knew her stuff and expected you to know it too. She didn't expect you to paint as well as Emily Carr or Georgia O'Keefe, or sculpt like Louise Nevelson — the trinity of art goddesses she worshipped, and that she resembled in bits and pieces . . . in their later years. As sinewy as a yoga instructor, she wore her nearly waist-length silver grey hair in a tight bun that accented her oval face, had a prominent Roman nose and had skin that was creased by years out in the sun sketching and painting. Parnell didn't expect her students to be artists. However, she did expect them, in her words, to be engaged.

The walls separating several classrooms had been torn down, turning the room into a huge art studio with one section for drawing and painting, one for sculpting and one with desks and chairs for lectures. That's where Chloe was sitting, too wrapped up in her blanket of misery to notice me either.

I cleared my throat. My throat clearing must have been louder than I thought, probably more like choking, and Parnell looked over at me. Chloe glanced up briefly, then her head went right back down as if she couldn't look me in the eye.

"Well, hello, my missing-in-action student," Parnell said dryly, staring straight at me with that gaze of hers that made you feel like her eyes were a digital camera, capturing every single element of you for storage in her memory.

"Hey, Ms. Parnell," I said. "How are you doing?" We went through this same rigmarole each time we met in the hallways. I had taken one of her art classes a year ago. I had to admit it had been extremely interesting, though I also had to admit I stunk at art creation. I couldn't draw. I had no colour sense. I had the hand control and creativity of your below-average kindergarten student. And my sculptures . . . every material I worked in always ended up looking like a lumpy bowling ball. But I was engaged. Parnell was a walking, talking art encyclopaedia, and could spiel the life, the work, the techniques and dishy gossip about artists through the ages in a way that kept you, if you were engaged, listening with fascination to her every word.

The lazy types who'd selected her class were soon sorry. The workload in the class could be as brutal as that of calculus, algebra or chemistry. The difference was, and this was the difference that had made me not choose it as one of my electives this past year, that Parnell built plenty of time in class for sitting there and thinking. At the beginning of my grade eleven year, my mother had taken a turn for the worse, and I couldn't handle any course that gave me free moments for my mind to wander.

Chloe glanced up, and we went silent.

Just then, the perfect icebreaker sniffed into view. Emma, Ms. Parnell's elderly, overweight, arthritic, malodorous beagle sped towards me as if I was Meals on Wheels. In the year I'd been in Parnell's class, I'd never seen Emma lift her head from the ground. She had a one-track nose, sniffing every centimetre of the floor, and anything on it. Parnell's focus was nothing on Emma's. Emma put any cadaver dog to shame.

Even when I patted Emma, which I would do occasionally, she would never raise her head to look at me. She would merely sniff right past me as if my scent was hardly worthy of her consideration.

Not today. Reaching me, Emma jumped up (I didn't know the old girl had it in her) and started sniffing and barking, her tail going like a metronome. I suppose I was a field day of rank odours – sweat, earth and flowers from the cemetery, and dust, dirt and mouse droppings from the bookstore. Her nose was all over me, her head bobbing so rapidly I couldn't catch it to pat it.

"Emma, that's enough!" Parnell boomed.

Emma didn't think so and continued to sniff frantically and press her forepaws onto my thighs, her nails so sharp and long they went right through my cargo pants.

Parnell strode over, grabbed Emma by the collar and dragged her off me. Then we burst out laughing, and Emma joined in, baying and barking, which made us laugh harder.

When we stopped, I looked over at Chloe. In a second, she stopped laughing and looked as if she was going to cry. "Chloe, what happened?"

She shifted in the chair with such screeching force that even Emma turned her head away from me, the jackpot of smells, to give Chloe an appraising stare. Chloe's face reddened until it was the shade of her hair, then her head once again dropped so low her chin was almost on her chest. She was clearly too humiliated to tell me what had taken place.

"Chloe, do you want to tell Alice, or should I?" Parnell said.

"I took Kevin's shirt when he went outside to smoke during break time," she whispered.

Not a good sign. Kevin must be getting ready to dump her. What a dog (and please, no offence meant, Emma) Kevin was.

When one of her boyfriends was lighting out on her, Chloe had a habit of taking something of his as a keepsake, as a way of holding on to the person, which I could understand. Too well. It was generally small stuff, like empty cigarette packs, pens, pencils, notebooks, paperbacks, combs, lighters, shoelaces, matches. Okay, so a shirt was bigger than that. Kevin must be in a real pissy mood to make something out of that.

"A shirt," I said, shrugging. My shrugging said it all – what's the big frigging deal over one of Kevin's shirts, probably stained with paint from class anyhow.

"Kevin's shirt had his wallet in the front pocket – a wallet with over three hundred dollars in it, and two of his father's credit cards," Parnell said gruffly.

Now I got it. "Chloe's not a thief," I said louder than I intended.

"I didn't know there was a wallet in it," Chloe said in a whisper. "I wouldn't have taken his dumb shirt if I'd known there was a wallet in it."

I knew that. Kevin no doubt knew that too. But he must be more than ready to shake Chloe loose, and Chloe had presented him with the ideal circumstance to do so in a big splash of a way.

I strode over to Chloe, Emma following me, her cold wet nose practically glued to the back of my left calf. I leaned over and gave Chloe a big hug and she hugged me back, then I straightened and turned to face Parnell. Just as I was about to go into a big speech defending Chloe, Parnell hushed me.

"I understand," Parnell said, sighing. "Otherwise Chloe would be sitting in a police precinct and not here." She came over and stood on the other side of Chloe, resting a hand on Chloe's shoulder. "Chloe, I realize you took Kevin's shirt as a memento. In the same way when I travel and leave Emma with friends, in order to sleep Emma has to have two of my old sweaters nearby to sniff now and then to remind her of me."

Emma must have liked hearing that because she was licking my calf. Of course being compared to Emma wasn't the most flattering of comparisons, but it sure beat being thought a thief.

"I'm not excusing it, Chloe," Parnell continued in her familiar I'm-not-going-to-take-any-nonsense-from-anyone voice. "It's got to stop, Chloe, for your sake."

Chloe nodded, looking completely miserable. Then it hit me, duh, what a horror of a scene there must have been in class. I pictured Kevin, putting on the show of shows, freaking out and yelling accusations; his friends egging him on, and the rest of the class watching like it was some teen flick for their amusement, shouting out catcalls.

How would Chloe get through until the end of the summer session?

Chloe chose that very moment to start sobbing. "I can't come back to class. I can't. I can't. I don't care if I lose the credit or not." Heaving for breath, she bent over and I knelt down and wrapped an arm around her. I looked pleadingly at Parnell.

Chloe needed the credit if she wanted to graduate with me next spring. Though Chloe was a year and a half older than me, since I'd accelerated a grade in primary school, we were in the same grade.

"Lift up your head, Chloe," Parnell ordered. And no one dared disobey Parnell except Emma.

Chloe did, wiping her runny nose on her forearm. Her face was a splotchy patchwork of red and white spots. Her mascara had run and so had her eyeliner, making her look as if she'd been punched in the eyes.

"I'm going to make alternate arrangements," Parnell said. "I will speak to Principal Rydell to see if he will give me the go-ahead to allow you to get the credit as a work study project. I can't see why he won't. An old friend of mine, Caleb Hamilton, needs an assistant for the summer. To help him with his filing and the cataloguing of his archives."

Chloe and I both gave her blank looks.

In return, Parnell gave us a twisted, amused smile. "Not to worry. I'm not sending you on an exodus to a collector with more money than taste. Caleb has quite the reputation in the art world. He's famous all over the world for his shadow boxes and collages. I'm proud to say I recognized his talent right from the start. We met at an Art League meeting nearly thirty years ago, and have been getting together twice a month ever since. Besides helping Caleb out, I expect you to write a paper on his work as your summer project."

"Thanks so much, Ms. Parnell," Chloe said, then began to sob weakly, this time, I suspected, with relief. I rubbed her back while Parnell went off to get a box of Kleenex.

"It was so horrible!" Chloe cried out.

"Imagine, Chloe, you'll be the assistant of an artist famous around the world. It will be great."

"You think so, really?" Chloe said, taking a deep breath.

"Absolutely!" And hoped like heck I was right, for Chloe's sake. She needed to catch a break. And breaks were hard to catch, especially when you needed them most.

chapter**six**

I t was Saturday night, and in my locked fortress of solitude, there was just me and my stash of crime series tapes and DVDs. There were few things that I found as weirdly soothing as watching crime shows. And it didn't take the expertise of Dr. Freud to analyse why. Things didn't always pan out, especially in the *Law & Order* series, where the variety of conniving criminals, the same kind my father had gotten so wealthy from defending, sometimes got off. At least the cops and lawyers did their damnedest to get justice for the dead. As Parnell would say, they were engaged. And that's what counted.

I lightly touched my forearms, which were stinging now. I needed distraction. I got up from my bed and walked over to my armoire, where my TV and DVD/VCR player were, and rifled through the tapes lying around, though none interested me at the moment. Maybe I'd read instead. John had lent me P.D. James's latest mystery, *The Murder Room*.

I snatched it and made a flying leap for my bed. Big mistake. I landed full weight on my forearms, which now didn't just sting but pulsed with pain. I flipped over onto my back and began to read.

The book got to me right away. You could tell just from the first few chapters that P.D. James really understood how messed up, mixed up, miserable and lonely people could get, and what that could drive them to do, to themselves, and to others. However, as good as the book was, I put it aside, too restless to continue reading.

I should have gone with Chloe and her friends to see a movie. I hoped Lindsay and Kate had the sense, though I wasn't too optimistic on that account, not to prod Chloe to spill every single humiliating detail of what had gone down in Parnell's class. By this time everyone Chloe hung with had probably heard about it.

"I vant to be alone," I had said to Chloe in a bad Greta Garbo imitation. Of course, now that I was alone, I didn't "vant to be alone."

My bedroom had been decorated long ago by my mother. My canopied bed, dresser, night tables and armoire were French country-style – the wood delicately curved and yellowed-toned. The wallpaper had a Victorian pale yellow and rose floral pattern, as did the chintz bed coverings and drapery.

I loved the room. Most of all I loved that it was my mother's vision of what a girl's bedroom should be. My mother was everywhere in this room.

Once my father's career had taken off and he was flush with money, and still flush with love for my mother, he'd given my mother the go-ahead to decorate the house exactly the way she wanted. And so she had, in a style just like my bedroom, but not as girly. The house was furnished with antiques, country-style furniture, big, comfortable flowery couches and loveseats, velvet-covered wing chairs, lamps made of old Chinese vases with translucent silk lampshades, Chinese silk rugs and collectibles – my mother had loved to collect.

On the dining room and kitchen walls hung decorative china plates. My mother's collectibles – her valuable Steuben and Lalique glass sculptures and Royal Doulton china figurines, as well as her flea market collection of depression glass, assorted bells, glass animals, perfume bottles and straw dolls – were displayed in curios.

All this cosy warmth was no longer to my father's liking. He'd been muttering about redecorating the house, no doubt in the cold, metallic minimalist style (really, it looked just like a hospital morgue) in which he'd decorated his office. He hadn't yet. But give him time. He'd wipe my mother's presence clean from the house.

A month after my mother had died, he'd instructed the latest team of Molly Maid cleaning ladies to pack up my mother's clothing and cheaper knick-knacks to give away to charity.

I'd completely freaked out, so much so that my father had to call Chloe over to calm me down. You could totally rely on Chloe in a crisis . . . as long as it was a crisis she wasn't involved in. No wonder Leslea had so gladly handed over all the responsibility for the finances and the household to Chloe.

My voice had been so hoarse from crying that it had been easy to let Chloe do all the talking with my father, who'd justified his actions using what he considered his irresistible combination of charisma and logic. That may work wonders with jurors who don't know him, but we do.

He'd oozed on and on about how this had been done for my benefit. All of the analysts he'd conferred with had said the same things (all, indubitably, on his payroll as consultants to get his guilty-as-hell clients off).

I needed to move on with my life, and I wouldn't be able to do so with constant reminders of my mother all about.

I was brooding too much on the past.

Blah, blah, and more blah, blah.

The whole time my father had presented his case for the disposal of the "triggers" of my unhappiness – he, the main trigger, was right across from me in an armchair – I hadn't been able to look up. While Chloe had pretended to agree with him, sitting beside her on the couch I had just clutched her thigh so tightly that I'd left bruises from my fingers.

The next day we'd both skipped school and gone to a store selling storage containers and boxes and cabbed home with them. We'd spent the day packing up all of the rest of my mother's clothing – half of which now hung in my closet, the other half in Chloe's – and had cleared the curios of all her collectibles. The majority were put in boxes in my room, and some choice favourites on my dresser. Chloe had called a locksmith, and he'd put a lock on my door.

My father had been too afraid of what I would do . . . to myself, or him, if he pressed me on it. It was easier for him to assume, act as if or maybe even believe, that we had followed his counsel and given the rest of my mother's possessions to Goodwill. He hadn't seen the inside of my room since.

Remembering that, I became so agitated I could have done laps around the room; however, there was barely enough floor space left between the storage containers and boxes for me to squeeze through.

I paced around the boxes until I reached the wall beside my desk where I'd hung some pictures of my mother. She was stunning when she was young. So stunning that Eric Levitt, super-ambitious, rising young attorney, had broken the social barriers at his law firm and had asked out the new secretary, my mother. That was in the old days – before PC sexual harassment charges and IBM PCs – when secretaries made coffee, took dictation in shorthand and typed on Olympia electric typewriters, making copies with carbon paper inserted between the sheets.

I could only surmise that Eric had been less of a pompous snob in the days when my mother had been a typist/secretary. He must have had some redeeming qualities besides his charm and good looks to reel my mother in – I hoped, for my mother's sake.

Then I came along, and along with me the difficult pregnancy that set off my mother's illnesses. The diabetes. The hypertension. The circulatory problems and the peripheral artery disease from the diabetes, and from her enlarged heart (now there's a sad metaphor if there ever was one) caused by the damage to her heart muscles from the rheumatic fever she'd had as a child. And in the last few years, those spiralling illnesses had gradually debilitated my mother, restricting more and more what she was able to do.

I stood staring at an old photo of my mother. She must have been around twenty then. This was one of those moments I yearned to share Chloe's powers of description. She could describe people, things, everything so precisely I swear her words built an exact replica right before your eyes. The best description I could come with up was that my mother looked beautiful with her long, thick honey-coloured hair, turned-up nose, wide blue-grey eyes and heart-shaped face. I touched the picture with a fingertip and whispered the same thing I always said when I looked at photos of my mother. "How can you not be here?"

The rest of the pictures were of my mom, Chloe and me. Where was my father? In the same places he always was – in court, in his office, in bed with his latest mistress, girlfriend, whatever, it was the same old, same old for Mr. Unfaithful.

In April he'd started dating this woman Suzette Andrews whom he claimed to have recently met through friends. Yeah, right. That was why the name S. Andrews kept appearing on the call display of our home phone months before my mother died. And why S. Andrews hung up whenever I answered the phone.

Suzette Andrews, a class act. Calling Eric frequently at home when his wife lay dying in the house. Super-dumb bunny and/or didn't-give-a-damn bitch who couldn't even cover up her tracks by getting an unlisted number or calling from a cell phone with a private number.

He'd had the gall last week to ask me to meet Suzette.

Fume about the devil, and here he was, outside my door, knocking.

It would be so, so nice just to ignore him until he got the hint and left me alone, but he would just keep knocking until I opened the door.

"Alice, please come to the door!" he said, starting with his fake-reasonable, fake-caring voice. How long would it take me this time to get him to drop the dulcet tones?

"I'm coming," I muttered.

"Alice, I have something for you," he said.

I'd managed to steer clear of him most of the week. With a loud grunt, I opened the door only a crack, in case I needed to slam it in his face.

There he was, the Tin Man, dressed in his casual-looking, but pricey Prada shirt and pants, and likely going out for dinner with Suzette. Since he'd gone grey – distinguished grey, which meant he had a full head of grey hair – as opposed to the gone grey pathetic comb-over with strands of remaining hair, I swear he dressed to match his "distinguished head of hair," wearing only indigo blue, silver grey and slate black.

Given that we both tried our best to avoid talking about anything personal, that left his work and mine as our sole topic of conversation. He filled me in on the latest scumbag he was defending. He was handling the high-profile appeal for Ben Kajowski who had been in prison for the last twelve years for murdering his girlfriend.

Kajowski, a highly efficient killer, had murdered and disposed of his girlfriend Tina Keene without a trace. The Toronto police still hadn't found Tina's body. The circumstantial evidence, however, pointed big time to Kajowski. Still, I very grudgingly had to grant my father this much; if anyone could get that arrow pointed elsewhere, he could.

My father continued his yammering about the case despite several humungous yawns on my part. As he yammered, I remembered the news clip I'd seen yesterday of Tina's parents weeping when reporters asked what they thought about the prospect that their daughter's convicted killer could be freed.

Then I had to stop myself because I was already filled with enough rage at my father, without topping it off with my rage for what my father was putting Tina's parents through.

"I hardly see you," my father said, trying to see more of me, but most of me was hidden by the door. "Little early in the evening for pyjamas, isn't it?"

"I see you all the time on TV," I said, bypassing the pyjamas comment. "In front of the court building, at some press conference, defending another of your *innocent* clients."

Subtle I was not. My father decided that I had said enough.

"How is it working at Atticus Antiquarian Books?" he asked. "Several of my friends frequent the store. It had quite a favourable write-up in *Toronto Life* magazine last month."

"I like it there," I said softly, not wanting to reveal what I liked and who I liked – John – to my father.

"So what's your shift involve?" he asked, his fake smile showcasing his unnaturally white teeth.

This asking of questions as if he was sincerely interested was one of his prime techniques. He had to charm people – it was compulsive. Waitresses, wine stewards, carhops, grocery cashiers, store clerks, paralegals and, unfortunately for my mother, secretaries: he had to win them over. Once he had, he promptly moved on.

"The typical bookstore stuff, selling, reshelving, cataloguing, dusting, cleaning," I mumbled, attempting to bore him away from asking more questions.

"And John Atticus, I hear he's quite a character," he said, staring intently at my face like he would at a prosecution witness on the witness stand.

Character: translation – nonconformist, eccentric, oddball.

I stared back at him like a hostile witness.

He wasn't about to break the silence before I did. He'd never let me or anyone else best him in a contest for control, so glancing at the box at his feet, I reminded him, "You have something for me. From Amazon."

He picked it up, and waited as I opened the door slightly wider. Then he handed it to me. "You'll like this."

"Thanks," I mumbled.

Well, the package was too big for a gift card. He must have bought me something for a change. I tore open the box and pulled out DVDs featuring the first two seasons of *Law & Order.* An actual gift, and one he knew I would like.

Pleasantly surprised for once, I looked up at him. As I did, the long sleeves of my pyjama top slipped down to my elbows, and my father gripped me so fiercely by the shoulders that I dropped everything on the floor.

"I thought this was going to stop," he said angrily, taking one hand from my shoulder to point at my forearms. "This is your final warning. Do you understand me, Alice? Let me see those arms."

"Don't you dare touch me!" I spoke with such force that he let go of my shoulder, and I staggered back, almost falling. This caught him off guard, providing me with just enough time to squeeze myself through the half-open door, and slam and lock it in his face.

I stood on the other side of the door panting.

"What kind of girl does a thing like cutting herself?" Eric shouted. "Answer me!"

Like I would.

So why did I? I got real mad at myself, at everybody, and at everything. And another explanation: it distracted me, just like everything else I did to distract myself. And in a strange way, it somehow always calmed me. At least at first, before the pain set in.

Mr. Cool and Collected finally completely lost his cool with me. He pounded on my door.

"You'll have to open that damn door when I start showing the house to prospective buyers," he bellowed.

"That's what you think!" I bellowed back. "Just tell them you've got Bertha Rochester locked up behind the door."

"What the hell are you going on about?"

"Bertha Rochester," I yelled back. "Crazy madwoman wife of Mr. Rochester in *Jane Eyre,* duh! What, did you forget to skim the CliffsNotes summary in your freshman English lit course?"

"Well, *Bertha,* you'd better show up for the appointment I've made for you with Dr. Clennam at 10 a.m. Monday morning, or else," he said, followed by a bang on my door.

"Is he or she another of the 'psycho' analysts on your payroll as consultants? Haven't I run through them all yet?"

I'd stopped counting the number of "professionals" my father had farmed me out to. In my version of speed dating, I saw them for one session, and then refused to return for an abundance of reasons, which the "psychos" effortlessly supplied. Thanks guys and gals!

Like the psychiatrist who had fallen asleep for ten minutes, and denied it when I'd said he had, then finally admitted he'd had a bad night's sleep and had nodded off. And I was supposed to open up to a sleeping-on-the-job liar? I didn't think so. Case closed. I wasn't the daughter of a lawyer for nothing.

He banged ferociously on the door. "Don't push me any further, Alice! Be there, that's all I can say."

I squeezed around the boxes, reached my CD player, shoved in a CD and blasted the volume. I was over-the-top angry, so angry at him, and so angry there was absolutely nothing I could do about him putting the house up for sale that when I caught sight of a pair of scissors lying on my desk, I grabbed them and began hacking at my hair. I was so out of it that I kept missing my hair and nicking myself. When I finally stopped, and looked into the mirror above my dresser, I was startled – actually, shocked – to see all the trickles of blood on my forehead and neck. I hadn't felt a thing.

chapter**seven**

When I asked Chloe how Saturday night at the movies had been, she mumbled okay, turned redder than her hair, which was pretty red considering it was now dyed Crayola scarlet, then changed the subject, giving me a beseeching look to go along.

Her response told me all I needed to know. Chloe and her friends had probably run into either Kevin or some of his friends who had made some choice put-downs, crushing her.

"So what do you think of this 'distressed' look?" Chloe asked, her voice quivery as she gestured at the new furniture in her bedroom.

I went along. Why wouldn't I? I didn't want to hurt or embarrass Chloe by continuing.

I glanced around the room. Leslea was a compulsive redecorator, redoing her condo almost as often as she changed the spelling of her first name. She could select furnishings – with Chloe close at hand. However, it was Chloe's flair that made any room look homey rather than merely a stylish re-creation of some deluxe spread in a home decorating magazine.

The look was Swedish Country which, according to Chloe, was country-style furniture with modern geometrical lines, finished in a white paint treated with a glaze, "distressed," to make it look antique.

There was a big fluffy red gingham throw with matching pillow shams on Chloe's new four-poster bed, and matching gingham balloon drapes hanging off the valance. What made the room especially homey for me though were my mother's things. Chloe had flung some of my mom's scarves over the lampshades. Her costume jewellery hanging on a jewellery tree was mixed in with Chloe's, and an assortment of her collectibles was on the dresser top.

"You know me, I'd like to make a bad pun and say the room looks distressing, but it's not. It's like so beautiful, as if you don't know already," I said.

"It is, isn't it," Chloe said, sighing with satisfaction as she affectionately bumped me as I lay next to her stretched out on the gingham throw. I grimaced.

"Hey, maybe this shrink won't be such a super-moron," she said, assuming that was why I'd grimaced.

I shrugged. I just hoped I could get through the session without throwing something at him, or throwing myself out the window.

"I'm getting made over too," Chloe teased, wiggling her toes, then her chipped fingernails at me.

Though Chloe did make fun of her and Leslea's "beauty bonding" routine of going for bimonthly manicures and pedicures, facials, hair maintenance – arranged on head and removed everywhere else – even the torturous Brazilian bikini waxing, the truth was she half bought into the whole deal.

I caught the look she gave my hair and, before she could say a word, I started yapping away as if that would fool her. It wouldn't. However, it might put off the inevitable questions about number whatever in my encyclopaedic compilation of subjects I wanted to avoid like the bubonic plague.

Especially the cutting. I talked about it with no one, not even Chloe.

My mom's best friend Merle had learned *that* the hard way. Considering how she and Eric weren't exactly on speaking terms anymore, yet they'd spoken about me. Or had a couple months ago when he'd called Merle and told her about my cutting. She'd phoned and I'd hung up on her when she'd started in about it.

"How could I forget?" I said, smacking my forehead, grimacing again. That was genius. I didn't seem to have many pain-free spots this morning. However, there was no one to blame for that except myself. "It's beauty bonding day," I said, working to sound jolly when actually I wanted to moan like Jacob Marley's ghost when he materialized to warn Ebenezer Scrooge about the arrival of the Ghost of Christmas Past.

Chloe gave me another long look, then decided I needed her to play along. "And today it is multinational beautification. Starting with a French manicure and pedicure, followed by a Brazilian bikini wax and a Swedish facial and massage. Then it's off to Alex, the English hairstylist, and we're done from top to toe," she giggled.

If all this had made Chloe feel better about herself, I would have said, more power to her, go in good health and spend Uncle Samuel's money. I knew, though, that she would be comparing herself to her mother, and that she usually ended up feeling worse about her own appearance. How would Leslea have coped with a daughter who had inherited her looks instead of Uncle Samuel's? Not well, and that's an understatement.

"You should come with us some time," Chloe suggested. "It will be fun except for the waxing. Today might be a good day to start, huh?"

Start on my hair she meant, but was too kind to say. I was in too dark a mood – and getting darker by the second – to make my standard bad jokes about being insulted by the hint that I needed improvement. Instead I flipped onto my side.

"Alice, you promised!" Chloe yelped, grabbing hold of my arm.

My three-quarter length sleeves had bunched, and my arms in all their gory glory were on display. Damn sleeves that roll up! We both looked down at them. The latest cuts from Saturday afternoon were raw and red, and they were surrounded by darkened, roughened stripes healing slowly.

"You can't keep doing this, Alice," Chloe said, really upset. "Forget about the fact that if you keep doing it your arms will be scarred forever, but you could get a bad infection. Do you want that?"

With a big sigh, Chloe rolled out of bed, headed for her bathroom and came back with a medical kit. I was nothing if not predictable.

"Raise your sleeves and sit up," she ordered. Then she took out antiseptic, dabbed it on two cotton balls and swabbed my arms. It stung like hell, and I had to hang on to the bedpost. Then she applied a thin layer of Polysporin ointment and gently taped some gauze pads over the fresh cuts.

"I might as well fix up your hair while I'm at it," she said, taking the scissors she'd used to trim the adhesive tape. "Hairstyling is not a career choice I'd recommend for you," she said, wrinkling her nose as she studied my hair "cut."

I closed my eyes, waiting to hear Chloe groan when she saw the nicks and cuts.

She didn't though. I peeked over; she was swiping at her eyes where tears had formed. "Oh, Alice," she said. "What did you and your father fight over?"

I couldn't talk about it. I couldn't say the words "he's selling the house" because to say them was to make them horribly real. I bit my lip and looked away.

The reason why I was so attached to the house I was too ashamed to reveal to Chloe. Crazy, delusional, irrational, never going to happen; I had this weird belief that if the house was kept exactly as my mother had kept it, it would be there for her to come back to.

"Good thing the antiseptic is close at hand," Chloe said, sighing. She clipped my hair off my face, swallowing a gasp when she saw the nicks. "You need to sit straighter for me to even out your hair," she said, after dabbing the cuts.

"Is there time before I have to go to be probed by another inhuman?"

She nodded. "Hardly, but you've got to do it now anyway. I'll give you a long-sleeved shirt with buttoned cuffs to wear. Remember, you're seeing an inhuman on your father's payroll who will be reporting back to him about you. And you don't want to supply ammunition, do you?"

Chloe knew something. Maybe it was about the sale of my house, or something else she'd overheard Leslea and Eric scheming about. I let it pass for now as she went to the closet and tossed me a shirt. I needed all my resources to face the inhuman.

Leslea breezed into the room. Her skin appeared flawless under the skilful application of makeup, and her extremely expensive flowered Lilly Pulitzer dress showcased her amazing body. She seemed to my eyes as near as she could get to the perfection she was forever seeking. No wonder Chloe often felt so shitty after these makeover sessions. I would have too.

"Chloe, are you ready to go?" Leslea asked. "Oh, Alice, nice to see you," she trilled and walked over to the bedside. "There's no need for Chloe to do a quick fix on your hair before your appointment. We're due at Alex's in the late afternoon. Meet us there. He will work wonders, you'll see."

Eric and Leslea had discussed my "appointment." I hated that. "No thank you," I mumbled. "I'm satisfied with Chloe. She's very talented. Besides, I trust her."

"My Chloe, she's a treasure," Leslea said, slipping an arm around Chloe, who stiffened so pronouncedly that even, duh, Leslea got it, and dropped her arm. She then eyeballed the medical kit open on the bed. "Is anything wrong?"

"No, Mother," Chloe said softly.

"Are you sure?" she persisted, more out of curiosity than concern.

"Yes, Mother. You're invading my privacy," Chloe said sharply.

"By merely coming into your room and asking a few questions?" Leslea said, playing innocent.

"Why don't I just come into your bedroom and ask you a few questions the next time you're entertaining your next Tomas, Ricardo or Hernando?" Chloe said with a sourness I seldom heard in her voice. "I'm waiting for the opportunity to 'invade your privacy' again."

The quiet was agonizingly awkward.

"I will be done touching up Alice's hair soon. In more than enough time for our first appointment," Chloe eventually said, glaring at Leslea, who nodded and left the room.

Chloe then leaned over and whispered, "Don't do this anymore, Alice. Try, please, for me!"

That was a promise I couldn't be sure I could keep, even for Chloe.

chapter**eight**

I couldn't keep track, or maybe I didn't want to keep track, of just how many psychiatrists, psychologists, grief counsellors and psychiatric social workers I'd seen in the last year. I went in hostile and seething, and came out even more so after answering their rote questions with my rote monosyllables.

Here I was back on St. Clair Avenue West near Spadina Avenue, staring with dread at yet another late nineteenth-century mansion converted to house a hive of buzzing analysts. I turned at the sound of a dog barking. It was a golden retriever out for a run in the park fronting Casa Loma across the street.

Casa Loma. I closed my eyes, struggling to retrieve some of the good memories I had of visiting that fairy-tale castle, built by Sir Henry Pellatt for his adored wife Mary. But Mary had died of heart failure. And, after keeping the castle in high style put him in debt big-time, Sir Henry owed such a huge amount of property tax on it that he had no choice but to turn it over to the city of Toronto. Recalling *that* only fuelled my gloom.

I tried again. Finally, I remembered that my father's contacts had gotten Chloe, my mother and me onto the set of the first *The X-Men* movie, filmed at Casa Loma. I'd thought I'd faint when we got to be extras in a scene and I was two people away from Hugh Jackman. Wolverine, within touching distance! Chloe and my mother had fed off that story for months, teasing me about how I stared at him like I was hypnotized. Unfortunately, or maybe fortunately, considering, that scene didn't make it into the finished movie, but it made for a good memory.

Then I remembered going to the castle roof. It was the last time my mother had been able to come with Chloe and me, the circulation in her legs already so bad that it was extremely painful for her to walk for more than a few minutes at a time. Somehow, we made it and had a picnic up there. The sky had been so clear we could see right to Lake Ontario.

Well, at least today's visit wouldn't be a total write-off, since it had resurrected two good memories.

I climbed the stone steps slowly. Why rush? It was not like the inhuman I was about to see would see me on time. They never did.

Clennam was on the third floor. I went up two narrow staircases and joined the crew of people sitting on the folding chairs lining the hallways.

I headed straight for the magazine rack and grabbed all *The New Yorker* magazines, then chose a chair in the nook under the stairwell, partially hidden from view. Really, an introduction to *The New Yorker* was the only good thing I had gotten from my speed dating of therapists. Gearing up for these sessions didn't make for the best concentration for reading, but I had come to love the magazine's cartoons, especially those drawn by Roz Chast. I loved the bewildered, unhappy teen and middle-aged schlumps and sad sacks appearing in her cartoons. They reminded me of Charlie Brown and his friends.

Looking around to see if anyone was watching me – nah, that was the good thing about being in a hallway filled with egotists focussed on whatever new pickle they were going to moan over for fifty minutes – I took out my handy box-cutter from my knapsack. I'd destroyed several prize Chast cartoons with my furtive ripping of pages. Now I brought a box-cutter with me so that I could neatly slice them without being noticed, and without demolishing the entire magazine.

I read the table of contents to see if Chast had contributed a cartoon to this issue. She had, and I began flipping through the magazine until I found it. Priceless. It pictured a middle-aged woman standing on a curb beside a traffic sign that flashed "Walk," then "Why Bother!"

Exactly. I quickly excised it from the magazine to add to my collectionI peeked down at my watch. Ten minutes late already. That was fine with me. Nothing would make me happier than spending the entire fifty minutes slicing cartoons from old *New Yorker* magazines.

I heard a half-shriek coming from a woman sitting nearby. She was staring at my hand. My hand clutching the box-cutter. I tried to come up with an explanation to calm her down. I'd put it in my knapsack by mistake and thought I was gripping a pen. Same shape and colour, sort of. Before I could get an explanation out of my mouth, she scrambled away and took a chair as far as possible from me. Good, that gave me the freedom to slice cartoons at my leisure.

Well, I'd added four more choice cartoons to my collection, and still no sight of my inhuman. I was tempted to leave, but then there would be Eric to deal with. No, I'd better stay. I could then use the excuse that I had to get to my job to keep Clennam from giving me the entire fifty minutes. I always kept to my schedule, even if he didn't. Ha!

Having cleaned the cartoons from three magazines, I took a brief survey. Three women and two men were sitting in chairs in this claustrophobic hallway. What issues did they have?

Since this colony of analysts was surrounded on either side by Forest Hill, one of the most exclusive and expensive Toronto neighbourhoods (where your garden variety house cost a million and a half at the minimum), it tended to attract rich malcontents rather than those truly, desperately miserable. Of course, I was here, but I guess I had a foot in both those camps, given my father's bank account.

How did I know?

Reason number one: from listening in on countless cell phone and hallway conversations that I would have preferred not to overhear. Spend as much time as I have in waiting rooms, and you'll be wishing too for the old days when people kept a stiff upper lip.

Reason number two: forced participation in a couple of group therapy sessions. My father and some therapist had claimed it would be good for me to learn that other people had problems too.

All I heard about was how so and so didn't love them enough, how so and so wanted too much or too little sex, how their boss didn't appreciate them, how their kids didn't appreciate them, how nobody appreciated all their efforts, sacrifices, whatever. When it came my turn to participate, I felt like shouting, you don't know what real problems are. Actually, I did shout that, and got kicked out.

There was, however, one group where the people did have real problems – a bereavement group. I had to leave that group for another reason.

After hearing one guy talk about his boyfriend who had just died of AIDS, a wife whose husband had died of Alzheimer's, a father whose son had died in a drowning accident, I'd felt completely wrecked. Wrecked by not being able to mumble anything more than "I'm so sorry, that's so horrible," or to come up with anything to say that could ease their grief a little.

When I had to speak, I could barely put together more than a few strangled sentences. And I'd been so depressed afterwards that the social worker leading the group had advised my father that "one-on-one" therapy might be more useful to me at "this stage of my bereavement."

So here I was waiting for my next "one on one," hoping that the twenty minutes I'd been here would be taken off my appointment.

The door to Dr. Clennam's office opened and his patient, an expensively suited middle-aged businessman, jogged past him like he couldn't make his departure fast enough. Either he had a very full bladder, or it was a foreshadowing of how I would be feeling soon.

"Alice," he said. "This way, please."

No hello, no handshake. This guy was all business, except I guess he forgot that the business he was in was the human business. He signalled for me to sit on the couch nearest the door. I assumed he would sit down on the settee at a right angle to it, but he didn't. Instead he scurried across his huge office to the far end next to the bay windows, and over to a black leather Eames lounge chair with an ottoman.

The guy had to be at least fifteen metres away from me and the rest of his patients. I practically needed binoculars to see him. He was nerdy-looking, short, thin, his brown floppy bangs covering the frames of his tortoise-framed glasses. When he sat down he propped his feet immediately onto the ottoman as if otherwise his feet would be dangling in the air, his legs too teeny to touch the hardwood floor. I almost burst out laughing. Though if I had, he probably couldn't have seen my expression, or heard my laughter.

Fine with me. This room would have been ideal for the sleeping psychiatrist.

I glanced about. Groan. The room was decorated in the antiseptic, stainless steel morgue fashion favoured by my father. The avocado green leather couch was hard as a bus bench, and the tables were made of glass and metal, as was the shelving.

This was making me almost nostalgic for what's-his-name's office on Avenue Road, who must have set up his place clutching a picture of Dr. Sigmund Freud's office Berggasse 19 in Vienna. The dark room (the shutters were closed) was crammed with African statues, masks and primitive art knick-knacks. There was macramé hanging on the walls and handwoven rugs on the floor. There, the fifty minutes had whizzed by.

While he'd lectured me on his methodology and beliefs, I'd nodded abstractedly as I checked out his stuff, which was as fascinating as any display in the Royal Ontario Museum.

There was no stuff to stare at here, no fingerprints even on the glass-topped coffee table. Maybe he sprayed it with Windex between patients. And everything else with disinfectant. The room did have the lingering, sharp odour of too many toxic cleaning products.

In an emotionless voice as flat, tinny and mechanical as those recorded voice-mail messages on answering machines, he went down a clipboard list of questions.

The first bunch was of the stat-gathering variety; the next grouping, more personal. I replied to those with as few words and details as possible while sneaking glimpses at my watch, timing my escape.

"So when did your mother die?"

"In January."

"How did that make you feel?"

What do you think, you insensitive pinhead? I made a face.

"How do you think it made me feel? Like shit."

"I hear you."

How the hell could he hear me? He was sitting a continent away. I super-loathed that phrase "I hear you." The most loathsome and lacking in empathy of the analysts always used that phrase, to reassure their poor patients they understood, they felt your pain. Yeah, right. If you had to say "I hear you" to someone, it was clear you didn't. Any person who was in pain, and was talking about it, knew by looking at the therapist's face whether he or she had "heard" him or her or not, and by literally "hearing" the therapist's understanding in the follow-up questions and comments.

"How do you cope with feeling so poorly?"

"Not well," I muttered.

"How does 'not well' manifest itself?" he said, giving me the once-over, like a claims agent doing a damage assessment.

Automatically I tugged at my sleeves. Could he see the gauze pads through them? The white cotton was pretty transparent, so I collapsed my arms against my sides just in case.

"You know, the usual," I said with a shrug, deciding to throw him a few generalities to get him onto the next line of stupid questions. "Depressed. Moody."

He nodded. "Thank you for sharing."

Another phoney phrase of concern that made me clench my teeth.

"No self-infliction of injuries?" he continued with his checklist questions.

Eric must have given him a rundown. I had to say something. "On occasion."

"On what occasions?"

"On the occasions I really miss my mother and I know there's nothing I can do about it," I said between clenched teeth.

That dynamic duo, pain and anger, were marshalling forces for . . . well it wasn't for "serenity now" as George's father, Mr. Costanza, had bellowed in one of my favourite *Seinfeld* episodes.

My mother had loved the *Seinfeld* series. We used to watch the reruns, which were on practically every channel – the show had been that popular in the nineties (the series had started when my prime-time viewing was *Sesame Street* and the Saturday morning cartoon shows).

"I'm sorry for your loss," he said in the monotone of someone who has said it repeatedly and has yet to mean it.

Now, along with clenching my teeth, I clenched my fists. I hated that phrase as much as I hated "I hear you," "thank you for sharing" and what was inevitably coming next, the speech about the work of mourning. The inhumans were nothing if not predictable cuckoo clocks.

"You cannot begin the work of mourning until you begin sharing," he droned flatly, now sounding like an iPod whose batteries were nearly drained out.

And like that was just the kind of opening that would get me or any one else to "begin sharing."

"I don't think I'm ready to 'share' with you."

"Talking will help you with processing your pain. It is part of the work of mourning."

I shook my head. "Talking will help *you*. It won't help *me*. So I think I'll pass."

How the hell could talking help?

Like talking was going to change anything. Like it was going to bring my mother back to life. Like it was going to prevent her from having died alone. Like it was going to stop me from hating the way she died, so humiliated and miserable by being so weak and in such pain and so dependent? Like it was going to stop me from missing her so much?

"I can see you are upset. I know how you are feeling."

I leapt up from the couch and stood behind it, resting my hands on the top. "You don't know me. You don't know what I'm feeling, and you might have a better chance if you weren't sitting across the Atlantic Ocean from me."

With a strength that surprised me, I then shoved the couch across the room. Okay, I didn't need that much strength. Did I know the couch was on coaster wheels? I watched it fly across the room and Clennam jump out of his chair to avoid being creamed. Then I made my exit. Running.

chapter**nine**

By the time I arrived at Atticus Antiquarian Books I was about as far from "serenity now" as Mr. Costanza in his worst spitting-mad moments. I'd kept repeating "serenity now, serenity now" on the subway. Still, no amount of reciting it could wash away that I had almost (and I did sincerely hope *almost* even though Clennam was a pinhead) creamed a psychiatrist with his own couch. Did his insurance cover any possible damage I'd done? Did my father's? My father. I could just picture how not serene he would be after Clennam gave him an update.

I entered Atticus's all agitated and sweaty for the second time in two weeks.

John was cool with it. And to make me cool with it, he told me to stay downstairs to cool off before going to the steamy "moon" upstairs. He went into his office and came out with a Thermos and two plastic cups.

"Eileen's lemonade. She makes it extra tart, she says, to keep my syllables crisp. A glass or two of lemonade and any dude, even one from Trenton, sounds more like a Shakespearean actor and less like a Mafioso, don't you agree, Alaace!"

I gave a listless nod of agreement.

John then stretched out on the couch, clasping his hands behind his head and stretching his feet out in front of him.

The air-conditioning was so cool I was getting goosebumps, goosebumps I was grateful for since they were ungluing my clothing from my skin. And the lemonade, it was tart. I could count all the taste buds on my tongue after gulping down half a glass. Nonetheless, I got all flushed again when I caught John taking one quick-but-getting-it-all glance; and clearly getting that I wasn't in the best shape.

The gauze pads on my forearms were evident through the sleeves, and my bangs were clumped together by sweat, likely revealing the nicks on my forehead.

"Did I ever tell you about my job disasters prior to falling into my calling, selling antiquarian books?" he asked, seeming to sense that I wanted out from thinking about how I hated myself, and how horribly ashamed of my behaviour I was right now.

I shook my head.

"Eileen and I met at the New School in New York City studying English lit. Married two months after we met," he said. "Eileen had already gotten her teaching degree. Thank God one of us was practical at the beginning and earned a living for us to scrape by on. Now the first thing you have to know about English majors with minors in philosophy, like yours truly, is that earning a living is something they don't think or worry about. They should. But they don't. So there I was, living off poor Eileen as I searched for a job, and discovered I had zero marketable job skills. I could read and I could pontificate on the meaning of life, and to no one's amazement but my own, there weren't a lot of employers demanding those skills."

"But those skills turned out be useful," I said, forcing my

mouth to say the words clearly enough for him to realize I was talking and not just making jumbled sounds. When I got really depressed, as I was now, every part of me felt weighed down, even my tongue, making it difficult to form words.

"Not until years down the pike. First, I had to inflict my ineffectual self on many unsuspecting employers. You want incompetence and irresponsibility, Alaace, here it comes," he said, taking one hand from behind his head, and waving like a hammy master of ceremonies introducing the performer next on the bill. "The food industry jobs. I started off working in a hamburger joint. The type you youngsters weaned on McDonald's don't even know exists. The ones only slighter bigger than your average dining and living room with an open kitchen, consisting of a grill, several fryers, a fridge and a short-order cook and a waitress. For a short time, and I do mean short, I was a short-order cook.

"What could be hard about cooking up fries, onion rings and hamburgers, I thought? All you had to do was dunk baskets filled with fries and rings in vats of boiling oil, flip hamburgers on a grill and toast buns. Any dimwit could do it. Alas, not this dimwit. Two hours into the job and I was a bundle of nerves. And this from a late afternoon shift with the place half empty. It was too much pressure, remembering which hamburgers had to be flipped, which were ready to serve, which fries were fried and which onion rings weren't fried yet. On my break, I went out to have a smoke. I saw a bus coming in the distance. It beckoned irresistibly. Like a zombie wearing a food-splattered chef's apron and hat, I got on that bus."

"You mean you just left the place in the lurch?" I said, startled to find myself smiling a bit at the picture of John in a chef's apron heading for the bus, and being a jerk by leaving the place with no cook.

"When I got home and told Eileen, she made me go straight back and apologize. I got an earful, let me tell you, not that I didn't deserve it."

I was beginning to feel a tad better. Not enough to break into song and dance, but less like jumping in front of a subway train.

Mr. Marcus, a regular customer of John's, strolled in. Since there were still no customers upstairs in the attic, John let me help with the sale. He'd been doing that whenever he got the chance.

At first, I thought he was doing it just to be nice. Lately it seemed as if he was apprenticing me on the ins and outs of antiquarian bookselling to see if I had the taste and knack for it. The taste I had because of my fascination with all things old and my love of books. Whether I had the knack for it, I wasn't too sure. In my better moments, I thought I might.

Mr. Marcus was looking for a gift for his grandson. A first edition, naturally. I hoped his grandson didn't eat cheesies when he was reading (that's what I used to do; the pages of my Nancy Drew mysteries were bookmarked with cheesie fingerprints).

As John had taught me, I asked Mr. Marcus some questions to try and figure out what his grandson would like. The first editions of kids' books that John currently had in stock were mostly books girls would like – *The Secret Garden* and *Charlotte's Web.* Maybe his grandson would like a book of Charlie Brown cartoons, *You Don't Look 35, Charlie Brown!.* I suggested it. Mr. Marcus said if his grandson didn't, he would, and bought it for $1,500. Yes!

My improved mood lasted almost through a very busy afternoon in the attic. People kept coming in non-stop and buying. I didn't have time to take a sip of water, it was that crazy busy. Finally, there was a lull, and I was gulping down a bottle, water spilling out the sides of my mouth, when John came upstairs.

"You had a call from your father," he said.

"Had?"

"He just told me to pass on this message: Dr. Clennam has

informed me of your conduct, and we will discuss it later."

Leaving that message with John was my father's way of sticking it to me. I was mortified and furious.

"Fathers," he said, with a sigh and a shake of his head. "Finish drinking your water. I hear the tread of customer footsteps."

As he went back downstairs, two people came upstairs, then another, and though my mood had sunk back to jumping-in-front-of-a-subway-train level, I sold up a storm. Counting the Charlie Brown book, I made more in sales than I ever had. It was like a contest for me, though there was no kick today for topping my previous high. My father had taken care of that. And I had too, by shoving that damn couch.

chapter**ten**

I just wasn't up to going home and having it out with Eric so I called Chloe, asking her to meet me at Harbourfront.

There was this little alcove near the marina that I came to regularly in the summer. I was sitting there, staring out at the lake, watching the rays of the sun glint off the water, relaxing a little as I listened to the rhythmic lapping of the waves and felt the heat of the sun beating down on me – my form of a Swedish massage.

Straight ahead of me in the distance was Centre Island, and to the right of it the Island Airport. For someone who wasn't the calmest of passengers, I did love to watch those small propeller planes soar and land.

Now if I could talk to my mother, this would be the place. It was the same deal here, though, as at her gravesite.

If only some analyst could tell me why I had to do battle with my brain to remember good memories – when there were so many of them. If only one could tell me why every single moment of the months she was dying rZemained as inescapably solid and real to me as the piece of concrete I was sitting on, I would stop my speed-dating with them and settle in for the "work of mourning."

A month after the doctor had told us that my mother was dying, when not groggy from the painkillers, she still had the interest and energy to chat, watch TV and DVDs and read a little.

For a change of scenery from the bedroom, I would help her into her wheelchair and wheel her into the den, her exclusive movie screening room, I teased. One of her very favourites was *Roman Holiday*, starring Audrey Hepburn and Gregory Peck. We made it halfway through it again when my mother said she didn't have the concentration anymore. And she never watched anything again after that day, just lay in bed, talking a little sometimes, eating a little, mostly just silent and almost gone already.

I was remembering another time she was her old self again, though this memory was yet another I wished I didn't remember. To show my mother I had learned how to cook her recipe for oven-roasted lemon chicken with vegetables and baby potatoes, I took her into the kitchen in her wheelchair and wheeled her to the table where Chloe was sitting waiting for us.

I took the roasting pan out of the oven and got ready to section the chicken with an electric knife as my mother did. She could carve roasts into just the right size slices, not too thin or thick. Mine came out either as thick clumps of meat or pieces so paper-thin you could barely spear them with a fork. She chopped through chicken bones with none of the exertion I went through. From the way I panted and heaved you'd think I was sawing through planks of wood instead of small chicken bones.

Although she couldn't stand for longer than a minute, she insisted I wheel her over to the counter so that she could rise to section the chicken. I refused, insisting I would show her I could do it. I didn't understand why she was making such a big fuss about it.

She kept insisting. I kept refusing, and went ahead and did it. She started to weep, and ate hardly any of the chicken. There were tears in Chloe's eyes too.

Afterwards I asked Chloe why my mother had gotten so upset. I was just trying to show how much I had learned from her. Chloe explained that not being able to section the chicken was just more proof to my mother of what bad shape she was in; how she couldn't do any of the things she used to; and how dependent she was on everyone for everything, when it used to be everyone was dependent on her. I felt like a total idiot.

My eyes shut to hold back my tears, I sat there rocking for a few minutes, opening my eyes when I smelled the familiar scent of Chloe's perfume – Pleasures by Estée Lauder.

She leaned over, her face inches from mine. "This one a bigger goof than usual?" she asked.

"I couldn't tell. He was sitting too far away for me to see. He was like a football field away from me," I said, and then told Chloe about my "touchdown" with the couch.

She was shaking so much from laughing that her head landed on my shoulder. I joined in, knowing I shouldn't be laughing, all things considered – number one being my father – but I couldn't stop myself.

She plopped down beside me. "I suppose the goof has already called your father."

That sobered me up quick. "Eric called the store and told John to give me a message."

I didn't have to say more. After all, Chloe did know my father.

Suddenly Chloe whirled up. "Forget him! What do you think of the almost new me?"

She held out her hands and slipped her feet out of her sandals so I could admire her white-tipped French manicure and pedicure. Then she came closer so I could see her expertly waxed eyebrows and expertly dyed eyelashes and hair, which she had dyed back to a brownish red closer to her natural colour. I touched her hair. "Cool! This is the best colour yet."

"You mean the most natural. I thought I would take your advice . . . for once," she said, then elbowed me.

"I see you went shopping too! Looking good," I said. She was wearing a silky-looking aqua empire waist camisole with a paisley print sateen pleated skirt.

I was glad that at least this beautification outing had left Chloe not just looking good, but feeling good about herself.

Suddenly I felt like a total car wreck. Which I was. Which mostly I didn't care about, or at least I told myself I didn't care about, but then this wave of self-loathing hit like a tsunami.

I guess that was obvious from my really down-in-the-dumps expression because out of the blue Chloe said, "Let's play the take-off game."

We'd been playing this game since we were little kids. I don't know which one of us came up with the idea that if you wished upon a plane taking off, it would take your wishes to heaven to be answered by God.

While I didn't believe in God and heaven anymore, I couldn't totally give up on wishing, so I continued to play along whenever Chloe and I came here.

One propeller plane after another landed, but none took off. We stared out, shielding our eyes from the brightness of the sunbeams hitting the lake, waiting for a takeoff.

Finally, we saw a tiny plane taxi down the runway.

"You go first," Chloe insisted, as if I was more in need of wish fulfillment than she was.

Wishing took a lot more energy and hope than I could muster up, especially right now. "I already did," I said. "I wished for a plane to take off and it is just about to, so get wishing, girl."

As the plane took off, not soaring really, but more sputtering and groaning as it pushed upward into the sky, Chloe said, "I wish we could take off to Sausalito. Settle down in a little house with a view of the bay. We could get a couple of dogs, and some bunnies and birds."

"And we can call our house Noah's Ark," I kidded, and Chloe elbowed me again.

I glanced over at her. Things must be really getting to Chloe for her to make a wish like that. Usually she would wish for her current boyfriend to love her, or to lose weight. Here and now sort of stuff. But here and now stuff must be piling up on her. Like with Kevin in Parnell's class. Like with Leslea's new loud and messy boyfriend, who was over there all the time.

The plane finally sputtered out of view, and as we waited for another to take off, Chloe searched through her bag and grabbed hold of pointy scissors. "For you," she said. "I asked Alex if I could borrow them after he cut my hair. He said I could have them."

"That's generous," I said.

Chloe shrugged. "It's shrewd. My mother gives him a ton of business. This morning was a trim. This is going to be a styling. Sit forward and close your eyes for your personal stylist with professional scissors."

As Chloe evened my bangs, and shaped the hair at the sides of my head, I felt, dare I say, almost mellow from the feel of the sun on my head, the breeze on my face and the sound of the lap, lap, lap of the waves.

Then I heard male voices nearby.

"These Canadians are a strange species with their outdoor haircuts, don't you think, Luke?"

"I don't know about that, Eddie. It does save the labour of having to sweep the hair off the floor when you've got the wind to do your dirty work."

I opened my eyes.

These guys were hotties, though not in an intimidating way. Both were tall and lanky. And both radiated this laid-back quality.

I blurted out, flirtatiously (for me!), "Don't you think it's dangerous to identify yourselves as Americans?" I pointed at the tiny American flag decals pinned on their knapsacks.

"Tell me about it! Man, how many times have we heard it – Iraq's a major mess, Bush is a moron, and the only good thing your prime minister has done in years was not to join 'the coalition of the willing' in the Iraq war, the next Vietnam. Did I get the drill down right, Miss?" he said.

I had to laugh. "Yup. Ready for prime time on CNN."

"Jesus H. Murphy, it should be. Eddie and I have heard it enough times. What can I say? You're fortunate he's not your moron."

Chloe gave me a startled but amused look at the emergence of my long dormant (I would have guessed flown the coop until this second) flirting impulse, then smiled widely at them.

If there were two guys who were going to bring it out of hibernation, these were the guys. They were clearly checking us out too.

Luke introduced himself, and then Eddie. As their accents revealed, Luke and Eddie were from the Boston area. Toronto was the last destination on their tour of eastern Canada, starting in the Maritimes. Now they were hanging around waiting to take a GO bus from Union Station to the airport later in the evening.

Luke had thick, wavy brown hair to his shirt collar, deep blue eyes with long lashes and beard stubble that only accented his dimples when he smiled. But what hooked me was his open, friendly smile, along with his self-consciousness when he caught me staring at his chipped front teeth.

"These . . . I stumbled getting into a canoe and clipped my teeth on the side," Luke said with a frown. "And that's how I got the vampire fangs."

"If only you could keep your mouth shut, man, for longer than a minute. But Luke loves to talk and talk," Eddie said with an exaggerated moan, turning to face Chloe. "Think you could give me a trim to buy me some good will from my old man? He sees me with long hair, he freaks out," he said, flipping his hair, which grazed his shoulders.

"Absolutely," Chloe said, and then pointed to the concrete abutment we were sitting on. "Welcome to my salon."

That was how Chloe got paired up with Eddie, and me with Luke, not that I had any complaints. I was already attracted to him, my deep-sixed lust out for an airing. It felt so great to feel that rush again . . . and even the jumpiness.

"So . . ." Luke coughed out, self-consciously covering his mouth.

"So . . ." I swallowed hard, self-consciously tugging down my sleeves.

Suddenly we both burst out laughing, laughing out of nerves, and laughing at our nervousness. The proverbial icebreaker, our laughter, and I remembered my previous encounter with another icebreaker, Emma, and told him the story about being a hallowed ground of delectable scents for old Emma.

"You should have seen Emma go, whoa momma!" I giggled. "Her tail wagging, her nostrils sniffing away, she was in doggy heaven. She was determined to identify every single stinky smell on my body."

In the middle of telling him, I suddenly became self-conscious and nervous all over again, realizing what I was saying wasn't exactly flattering and enticing . . . unless you were trying to attract a beagle.

I peered over at Luke, worried I was turning him off. I caught him staring at me, then looking away as I met his gaze. I did that too – when I liked a guy, when I liked to look at him, and when I didn't want that to be horribly obvious.

Luke actually seemed to be attracted to me, staring at me like I was some hottie, which I was far from, except literally – I was baking hot in my heavy cotton black skirt and Chloe's long-sleeved shirt. Good thing that Chloe had just fixed up my hair.

He sniffed hard and smiled. "You smell fine to me. Of course my sense of smell isn't as sharp as Emma's," he teased. "I only smell perfume, and it's got a sweet, flowery scent."

Some of Chloe's Pleasure perfume must have rubbed off on me.

"Thank you," I said, his teasing making me relaxed enough to tease him back. "Kind of you not to ask if I use it to mask all the other not so nice scents."

He hooted, and automatically his hand went up over his mouth again, then he dropped it. "Doesn't take long for a bad habit to become a bad habit. Every time I look in the mirror, I get a shock when I see those choppers staring out at me."

"I hardly notice them." And I didn't. "Next time your hand goes up I'm going to grab it and hold on tight and not let go," I joked.

"Then I'd better cover my mouth fast," he joked back, and when he did, I grabbed his hand, and from then on we sat side by side holding hands.

Soon I was completely at ease (well as completely as I ever got) talking to Luke about his trip and then about American politics. Lucky for me I'd already been primed on the basics by John, who, when he wasn't raving about books and ancient TV series, was ranting about the cutthroat politics of the Bush White House and the ineffectual bellyachers that made up the Democratic Party.

When they returned home, he and Eddie were going to start working for the campaign of Senator John Kerry, the de facto winner of the Democratic presidential primaries, who was already slugging it out with Bush.

It was getting harder and harder to concentrate and come up with something somewhat intelligent to say as I fell into this very pleasant (how pleasant I had forgotten and was so glad to remember) dazed-with-lust state. With his free hand, Luke would occasionally stroke my leg as he talked, and I would touch his forearm.

I half-listened to Chloe and Eddie. Usually Chloe got tense and anxious around guys she liked, but she wasn't with Eddie. While giving him a good trim (to my eyes) she was sparring with him in a fun, flirty, romantic comedy way.

So maybe I was not my standard "tied-up-in-a-knot" and sweating self and Chloe was not her standard "desperate for attention" and "fearfully waiting for rejection" self with these guys because they were leaving for the airport in four hours.

That was probably a part of it. Mostly it was due to Luke and Eddie.

They were comfortable with themselves, so we were too.

For the rest of the afternoon and into the early evening I lost myself in enjoyment.

In enjoying Luke's company, and the prospect of keeping in touch after we exchanged email addresses and phone numbers. In enjoying seeing how happy Chloe was with Eddie. In enjoying being with Luke, Chloe and Eddie on a cruise of the Toronto Islands. In enjoying what I had wished for on the plane taking off, even though I didn't even know I was wishing for it.

chapter**eleven**

"You don't look so great," Chloe whispered, slumping against me.

"You don't look so great either," I hissed, inching away from Chloe, the light pressure of her side on mine painful. Inching away was labour-intensive on Leslea's sinkhole of a couch – probably why she'd bought it. Once any male sat down beside Leslea on the oversized sofa, he'd need the flexibility of Spiderman to squirm away from her clutches, if he was so inclined . . . which few were.

"What's your problem?" Chloe snapped.

"What's your problem?" I snapped back like some crabby myna bird. So I wasn't at the top of my game tonight on making sparkling repartee. Who could be sparkling when my forearms were a chorus of ouch, eech, aah, oooh every time I shifted on this super-soft couch filled with the feathers of countless dead geese. I couldn't blame my body; what else could it say to its abusive owner.

I was in one of those foul, foul moods where everything and everybody drives you nuts. You know you're being a rude, mean pig, but you can't stop, which makes you even more disgusted with yourself.

Even Chloe was pissing me off. Dressing to look hot, she looked awful. Her low-rise jeans were sizes too small and her cropped peasant blouse exposed thick rolls of baby fat at her midriff. Her blouse was so sheer I could see almost all of her breasts pushed up by her lace demi-bra. The lipstick on her swollen lips was smeared and there were a couple of hickeys on her neck. *Obviously,* she hadn't gone over to Caleb Hamilton's. Again.

"So how was it *filing* this afternoon at Caleb's?" I sneered.

"Why don't you try working in a filthy unfinished basement reeking of glue and paint, and with no air-conditioning?"

"Who cares if you need the credit? Who cares that Parnell put herself on the line getting you out of that class? Who cares that it got you out of a class where everyone thinks you're a thief?"

Chloe didn't defend herself; she just curled forward as if she was trying to protect herself in this sad, defensive posture. On an attack roll, I couldn't shut up though.

"And those," I shouted, pointing at her hickeys. "Kevin actually touched you. I'm astonished."

"He wanted to make up for what happened in class," she mumbled, briefly looking over at me, then away, her eyes squeezed tight like she didn't want to see my reaction.

"Make up with you, right! He wanted to have sex. You were around. Everyone else is on vacation."

I sunk deeper into the couch. Kevin wanting to have sex, I had wormed out of Chloe, usually meant her going down on him.

I realized I shouldn't say any more, but I was out of control, smarting from shifting around on the couch, and smarting from how thick Chloe could be when it came to Kevin.

What I was about to say would crush her, but I plunged ahead anyway. "Kevin hardly ever touches you, for God's sake. I get more physical contact from the customers at Atticus's Attic."

Of course, there was the physical fact of the hickeys. Suddenly I got a very sick feeling in my stomach, anticipating what Chloe was going to say next.

Her eyes still closed, her arms wrapped around herself, she cried out, "What do you know? We did it. Three times."

Jeez, just the response I didn't want to hear. Chloe looked so terrible, tears leaking out of her squeezed-shut eyes, her nose dripping, I reached over and embraced her, which was good for Chloe, and not too good for my arms. It took a couple of seconds to catch my breath.

"He did use condoms, didn't he?" I asked. Chloe was on the pill, had been for the last three years. Leslea had taken her to her gynie, another of their bonding rituals I supposed.

"Twice," she said, and I made a face.

"Chloe, you know the drill. AIDS, STDs, babies."

"You're not my mother," she muttered. "I'm sorry. You're right. It was dumb. Worse than dumb."

She gazed straight into my eyes, and I saw in her face that she got that he'd called her because everyone else was out of the city. Yet, she'd gone with him anyway, travelling on that stream of stupid, faint hopes that we all travelled on, hers being that somehow she could make Kevin care about her, as if the self-centered prick was capable of caring for anyone, other than the love of his life, himself. "No more, promise," I pleaded.

"No more, I promise," she said, then clutched my forearm, and I bit my lip. My reflexes weren't as quick as usual at hiding the evidence, given how woozy I was feeling, and shivery, so Chloe was able to grab my forearms before I could shift away.

"Alice, your left arm is burning hot. Let me see," she said.

The pain, and the effort it had taken to argue with Chloe over Kevin, had taken away most of my limited energy, yet I made a feeble attempt at deflection. "I'll show you later. It's nothing. Your mother . . . and my father might come in any moment."

Chloe and I were awaiting another "joyous" family dinner. Generally, these torture chamber occasions with the high-priced delicacies for the child prisoners occurred only on some alleged family celebration or holiday, "helliday," as Chloe and I referred to them.

Both Chloe and I knew that Leslea's decision to hold a late Thursday evening dinner at her condo meant that tonight's "helliday" would truly be one. These attempts at quality family time mainly took place in restaurants. That we were going to eat off Leslea's dining room table, used more often for table sex than meal settings, meant that Leslea and Eric, marshalling forces, were about to lace into us about something.

I could guess what were the top five items on my rap sheet, but what had Chloe done? It wasn't being with Kevin. Leslea was all for Chloe having boyfriends and being popular, whatever it took.

"Mother, how are you doing in the kitchen?" Chloe abruptly called out. "Need some help with the food?" She turned to me and said softly, "Let me ask how long she's going to be out there."

"I'm fine, thank you. I'll call you when I need your help," Leslea sang back.

You could bet five dollars on that one. What didn't Chloe help with? It was more Chloe's household than Leslea's. Chloe had bought the food for dinner at Delano's, a high-priced gourmet food shop. Chilled gazpacho soup. Pasta salad. Baby spinach and arugula with dried figs and pecans in a black fig vinaigrette. Jumbo shrimp with a seafood sauce. An assortment of cheeses served with dried fruits, nuts and crackers. Platters of assorted veggies, fruit and bakehouse breads.

The cold food was because of Eric's arrival times for dinners. Late. Later. Even later.

"Show me your arm right now," Chloe whispered.

It hurt even to lift my sleeve. A couple of cuts on my forearm had become an inflamed, puffy, oozy mess. Chloe sighed, and then touched my forehead. "You're burning up. Your cuts are infected. You have to see a doctor. Like tonight."

Before I could halt her, she slid off the couch, got onto the carpet, pushed up my pant legs and saw several more cuts on my calves.

"Alice," she said, resting her forehead against my kneecap. "You caught the real estate agent in the house with Eric, didn't you?"

"You knew?"

She sighed louder. "I overheard my mother on the phone. I should have told you. I was hoping, I guess, that Eric wouldn't go through with it."

That damn stream of stupid, faint hopes.

"Have a change of heartlessness, right?" I said bitterly.

She gave me an embarrassed shrug as she carefully tugged down my pant leg. "After dinner, we'll say we're going to the movies, double date or something, and head off to Mount Sinai emergency. I'll get a sweater for you. It'll help with the shivering."

A testament to how woozy and rotten I was feeling: I actually agreed to go to see a doctor.

She went to her bedroom and I rested my head against the couch, praying I could keep it together. This was one time both Chloe and I had wanted Len, Leslea's latest Lothario, to join our family foursome as a buffer. Leslea must have told him what was in store as the evening's entertainment as he'd fled to the closest bar to wait it out. I would have too, if I'd been him.

The real estate agent was the last nail in the coffin between my father and me. Strangers in elevators had longer conversations than we did since we had had a top-of-the-lungs slugfest over what he called my "escapade" with Dr. Clennam. Not either of our battling styles, really. My style was seething, sullen, passive-aggression. His style was pseudo-reasonable pseudo-calm, which he'd perfected palming off his guilty-as-sin clients on jurors.

He started in that mode, eventually completely losing it after I erupted with "Go to hell!" when he threatened me, "One day you're going to push me too far."

After fulfilling our verbal quota for months in that slugfest, we'd scarcely spoken at all till I'd come home early from work to find my father charming a real estate agent dressed to the nines, likely wanting to hook not only the listing, but also the so-called grieving widower.

We three got off to a swell start. The first words out of my mouth were to the real estate agent: "You wasted your time getting dolled up. He's already taken. You've got to move fast with these 'grieving' widowers. Just a tip for when the next one comes available."

Being used to a wide variety of outrageous behaviour from the wide variety of criminals he represented, my father took that with his standard sang-froid. Not even a flicker of emotion in his face appeared as he prepared to drop one of his stored face-saving lines. Which one would he say this time? "Alice is not herself these days." "It's the grief speaking." "It's especially difficult to lose a mother at this stage of life." "They were very close."

It had been lines one and three that day. What could the real estate agent say or do anyhow? She wanted to get the listing at least.

Next Eric attempted to placate me before I said or did anything further to spoil the image of him as sorrowful widower and loving papa. "I'm not selling the house. I'm only getting an estimate of its market value."

"Liar!" I slung out. "You're selling this house over my dead body!" With that cliffhanger, I bolted right up the stairs and into my bedroom.

Chloe came back into the living room carrying a heavy cotton sweater. "You'll stop, promise me!" she said, her voice rising as if she was going to cry.

"I'll try." I just couldn't make a promise I wasn't sure I could keep . . . especially to Chloe. She handed me the sweater. I put it on; however, my shivering didn't stop. She got up again, went to the kitchen and returned with a mug of herbal tea and two Tylenol. I gulped them down. I had to get through the next hour or so somehow, and they had better do the trick.

Eric was in even-later mode tonight. Leslea had been breezing in for the past hour, placing the food on the dining room table in slow motion, and still no sign of Eric. Eventually she was left with nothing to do but rearrange the platters.

I was shivering, even with the herbal tea and honey that Chloe had been pouring down my throat. The thought of eating food, especially cold food, made me want to gag.

Standing up, Chloe went over to the table, grabbed a plate, and started filling it with food.

"What are you doing?" Leslea asked. "Uncle Eric isn't here yet."

Chloe just gave her a dismissive look, continuing to pile cold pasta, shrimp, nuts and sour bread onto her plate.

"It's rude to eat before Eric arrives," Leslea said, trying to get in food police position between Chloe and the platters, but failing.

"It's *rude* for Uncle Eric always to show up hours late. 'Hello folks! I'm *so* sorry. What can I do? The client pays the bills.'"

If I had the strength to snigger I would have. Chloe had my father down pat, from hand gestures to high-voltage smile.

"See, Alice has enough respect to wait," Leslea said, giving me a small smile of approval.

That smile of approval was enough to get me off a deathbed. I stood up, hobbled over to the table and started filling a plate with food. Leslea gave us both an outraged glare, and flounced out, her full skirt making an especially effective flounce statement.

Chloe gulped down both plates of food while we channel-surfed.

"The second the lecture is over we're out of here," she said, looking anxiously at the door, then at her watch.

I was already half out of here; I was that zoned out.

Finally, at nine-thirty, my father breezed in. "Hello folks! I'm *so* sorry. What can I do? The client pays the bills."

Chloe's hysterical giggling drowned out the rest. I could just manage a few snorts. Chloe, though, made up for my lack of volume.

"Girls, stop it this moment!" Leslea said. "You're being bad mannered!

"Not as bad mannered as showing up hours late with that lame excuse. Try a new one next time, Uncle Eric. We all know there will be a next time, next time!" Chloe went back to giggling so much that she was soon hiccupping.

It was satisfying to see my father nonplussed by Chloe's behaviour. He looked over at me as if it was my fault that Chloe was being defiant.

Leslea then murmured something in Eric's ear, probably begging him to hold the gunfire until lecture time. She ushered him over to an oversized arm chair – large enough for a giant – and brought him a glass of wine and a plate of food. She sat perched on the arm, softly chatting away to him.

Meanwhile, it was only having Chloe's solid body next to me that was keeping me upright. Chloe kept glancing at them, her watch, and me. Neither of them seemed to notice that I looked as if I was mere minutes away from needing to be carried out of the room on a stretcher.

"Can you two just spit it out already?" Chloe asked, the unease in her voice seemingly audible only to me. "I have a date with Kevin. We're meeting him at the Varsity Theatre. He's bringing someone for Alice. He lost his cell, so I can't call him."

Eric and Leslea passed knowing looks. Leslea got up from her perch, and came over to us. "Chloe, Mrs. Parnell called. She said that you're not going to Caleb Hamilton's as expected. She did you a favour. Now what do you do? You don't go. You need the credit."

"It's *Ms.* Parnell," Chloe muttered.

What could Chloe say in defence? Zip. Leslea was right. Parnell had done Chloe a big favour.

"I promise, I will go every day. I'll call Ms. Parnell tomorrow to apologize, and I'll apologize to Mr. Hamilton too."

Leslea smiled at Chloe, then over at Eric, her smile saying "see how easily and well that went?" Well, Eric was living in fantasyland if he thought his turn at the parental lectern would go equally smoothly.

He took the plate off his lap and arranged himself in a staged posture of relaxation in the chair.

I fazed out soon after my father's familiar opening line, "This is all for your own good, Alice." I heard snatches of phrases like "self-destructive behaviour," "excessive grieving," "automatic hostility and resistance to any advice or help offered," "make a commitment to getting help, getting well," "not every psychiatrist and psychologist in Toronto . . ."

" . . . can be a useless screwball. I don't know about that."

"Keep that up Alice, and I'll . . ."

I leapt up and yelled hoarsely, " . . . sell the house, dump all the furnishings Mom picked out at Goodwill and then dump me into some boarding school out of the city or in some nuthouse."

From the twitch in my father's right eye and Leslea's intense contemplation of her French-manicured nails, I saw I'd scored a bull's eye.

Like some damsel in distress in a gothic romance, I would have fallen to the ground had Chloe not jumped to her feet, wrapped an arm around my waist and towed me out of the living room.

"We have to go. See you later." Chloe had to work to keep my dead weight upright.

"Girls," Leslea meowed. "We . . ."

Eric cut her short. "Let them go!"

I was about to turn and spit out, "You crummy bastard!" when Chloe shushed my name in warning, and I shut up. What I had to do now was to get to the hospital and not to continue what would inevitably be a losing battle with my father.

In the cab, Chloe had me lie down in the back seat. At Mount Sinai, the driver helped Chloe get me to the triage desk in the emergency ward.

Chloe did all the talking while I just leaned against her, dazed and shivering. One of the nurses led us to an examining room, and she and Chloe helped me onto a bed.

Before I passed out, I wondered briefly what Chloe had told them about my cuts. At that point though, all I cared about was sleep and extra blankets.

chapter**twelve**

Pumped up on IV fluid and antibiotics, and with a prescription for a two-week supply of antibiotics, medicated salve and gauze bandages for the cuts, I was raring to go – where else but to work?

I was meandering around the main lobby of the hospital waiting for Chloe to drive me to Atticus's when I saw a notice on the bulletin board between the elevators advertising short-term work for data entry clerks.

Chloe already thought I was loco for working twenty-five hours a week at ten dollars an hour at Atticus's Attic. I worked there not just to keep busy, but for the just-in-case-I-need-it money. Clearly, the need for a slush fund had grown since last night's flash. And making twenty-one dollars an hour would be a big boost.

I wiggled my fingers. They were slender, long and flexible like my mother's. I was a speed typist, my mother having taught me to type on her old IBM Selectric typewriter.

I saw Chloe hurrying towards me. She gave me a fierce embrace, as if I had returned from the dead.

"You must be better," she said. "I can smell coffee on your breath and there are muffin crumbs all over your top. I told my mom that Kevin dropped us off at Renee's and, because it was so late, we ended up sleeping over."

I nodded, "Look at this!" gesturing to the ad for data entry clerks. "Great pay, huh?"

"Another job?" Chloe said, in a voice that said she thought I was out of my mind. Chloe had no qualms, and why should she, about taking as much money as she could squeeze out of Leslea. Blood money, she called it, demanding more the more her mother hurt her.

Curiously, the money she received from her father she didn't spend, but put in the bank. And she would never ask her dad for extra. Then again she didn't have to. Uncle Samuel never forgot any of Chloe's hints about what she wanted. No gift cards ever came as ersatz presents from Uncle Samuel, even to me. Santa Claus had nothing on Uncle Samuel for gift giving. I never received a present from him that I didn't love. My mother must have filled him in on my likes and dislikes, and he always remembered.

"The money will help," I said, shrugging, my shrug saying it all, and Chloe let it go. I wrote down the information. Then I borrowed Chloe's cell phone and called, making an appointment for an interview the next morning.

I know going to work right after getting out of the emergency ward may seem seriously deranged but really, it wasn't. What else was I going to do? Chloe was off to Caleb's, and that would have left me lying in bed in my bedroom, thinking. I'd done more than my share after Chloe had gone home in the early morning. Alone, with nothing to do . . . fatal, fatal . . . but think and think, I'd promised myself to do more than just try to stop cutting.

Forget the scarring, the certain infections and worse, if I kept this up. If I kept this up, it was a prima facie evidence for Eric to ship me off to a penitentiary-style boarding school, or to commit me to a fancy nuthouse.

At work, John kept popping upstairs to help me out, and to keep an eye on me, I suspected. Chloe had told him something. Whatever, it was reassuring to have him checking up on me and helping me out when it got busy. I felt weak and tired the entire day.

I went straight to bed after downing my dinner of two strawberry organic yogurts and a glass of milk. As if we were two warships passing in the night, I slipped by my father in the upstairs hallway, picked up my stride and sped into my bedroom. I locked the door, got into bed and fell asleep instantly, sleeping dreamlessly right till morning.

On the quick, I dressed and grabbed some fruit and cereal bars to eat for breakfast as I hurried down Avenue Road to my interview. As I approached the Ontario Hydro Building, I swear the sun was glinting off every pane of the revolting aquamarine-coloured glass that coated that most hideous of buildings.

With all those alien-spaceship-style death rays beaming off it, I could hardly see the buildings I admired – the pink sandstone, turreted Ontario College of Art adjacent to it, and the beautiful Romanesque revival parliament buildings of Queen's Park across the street.

I was so, so familiar with the architecture of this particular stretch of University Avenue. It was the northern outpost of a row of hospitals, all of which I had been in and out of visiting my mother – Princess Margaret, Toronto General and Mount Sinai.

I had stood at a window with my mother last November when she'd been recovering from surgery at Mount Sinai, and she'd commented on how pretty the Christmas lights decorating SickKids Hospital were. It was a good day for her, she walked the hallways and ate, and we were feeling optimistic about how improved she was. Wrong, wrong, wrong.

I pummelled through the revolving doors of the Hydro Building. Fortunately, no one else was in with me, or the force of my whirl would have had him or her splat on the tiled floor. Third floor, that's where I was headed.

It was a rabbit warren maze of low wall dividers and cubicles. There looked to be hundreds of gynaecologists and infertility specialists with offices on this floor. And everywhere I glanced, even at this hour of the morning, there were women, some with husbands and boyfriends, some with their mothers, a few others by themselves.

I found the cubicle of Elizabeth Rainey, the nurse-manager doing the hiring. She told me to take a seat at one of the banks of computers. Ms. Rainey, who seemed briskly efficient, and brusque period, gave me a couple of tests to check out my typing speed and ability to correctly and speedily enter patient information on specialized medical data forms. I aced them, which flabbergasted her.

She hired me on the spot. As she assigned me to the first shift from seven to eleven, she gave me a shifty-eyed look as if she expected I'd protest. That shift, though, was perfect for me. I could go right to Atticus's afterwards.

Then she launched into what seemed to be her standard introduction for new employees. So all these women had tried and tried to get pregnant with no luck. Their next step was in vitro fertilization. Ms. Rainey recited a capsule summary of the main reasons why women of all ages, but mostly age thirty-five and above whose fertility was a downward slide toward the nada of menopause, had difficulty getting pregnant. It was damn depressing. I never knew. I'd always assumed from how a chorus line of parents, teachers and school nurses went on and on about pregnancy, that it was too easy to get pregnant.

Ms. Rainey continued to scrutinize me as she handed me the package of pamphlets and articles describing every aspect in copious detail because she said I would make fewer errors if I understood what I was inputting.

I thanked her, and waited for her to say something about me wearing a long-sleeved shirt in the midst of a heat wave because her gaze was as fixed as a flashlight beam as she stared at my sleeves. "You haven't got a rash . . . or anything else contagious or communicable, have you?"

"No, I just like long sleeves," I said, shielding myself with the package. That was true; I had to like long sleeves, just as a bank bandit had to like a ski mask.

"Then I'll see you at seven sharp!" she said, and swivelled so rapidly the rubber soles of her shoes squealed like a hot rod doing a U-turn.

I nodded to her retreating back, pleased that my dance card work schedule was all filled up. Busy, busy, busy, that was my motto; that along with filling the coffers of my slush fund to evade, escape, whatever, the future Eric thought he had in store for me.

chapter**thirteen**

Just after five o'clock, I made it over to Caleb Hamilton's house in the Upper Annex. Chloe was anticipating my arrival like a prisoner eager for her weekly visitation of friends and family. I was here not just to keep Chloe company, but to make her see that helping out Caleb Hamilton was something she should consider herself lucky to be doing.

It had been too busy at Atticus's Attic to google Caleb Hamilton. The English department at the University of Toronto must have done a mass mailing of their course readings because the attic was swarming with students waving sheets at me. I'd done so much bending, stretching, squeezing and leaping to find and reach books that I felt like I was in a callisthenics class.

I would just have to improvise a list that would make Chloe thrilled to be working for such a world-famous artist. So, thrilled was pushing it, but I'd settle for interested, and maybe eventually, in Parnell parlance, "engaged."

Chloe had trouble facing new things. The trouble was she wouldn't face them. Even as an infant. My mom used to tease Chloe about how she would only eat one type of Gerber's baby food, spitting out any new variety at my mother. Trying to get

Chloe to try applesauce instead of pears all the time, carrots instead of peas all the time, had taken brainpower, imagination and a big load of wash. Of course, then Chloe would get stuck on that new fruit or vegetable.

She was still like that. When we revisited any restaurant, she would have continually ordered the same dish if I'd let her. But I didn't. I would let her, and then would make all this commotion about how tasty whatever I was eating was until I could get Chloe to take a bite. After she had, she'd like it because she was more open than she allowed herself to be. Then we'd share, and the next time she'd order whatever I had ordered the last time.

From grade school on, I'd been Chloe's "interest-opener." Whenever Chloe was resisting something new in class, her teacher would call my mom. It never took long for any of Chloe's teachers to clue into the fact that it was a waste of time to call her mother. Leslea would just sigh dramatically and say "that's just Chloe."

My mom would arrange for me to go to Chloe's class to get her interested in whatever she was resisting this time.

When Chloe hadn't wanted to do gymnastics in gym glass, I'd sparked her interest in the balance beam, and managed to survive, given that my hand and eye coordination was non-existent. Chloe had gone on to become good at gymnastics, winning several school competitions.

Weirdly, almost everything interested me . . . even at my most depressed. A therapist a couple of months back had labelled me "a high-functioning depressive." Unlike most depressives, who slept twenty hours a day, who didn't talk, bathe, eat, didn't do anything but be depressed, I functioned, like the machine girl I am. Or should I say, functioned in my malfunctioning way.

Reaching Caleb Hamilton's house on Albany Avenue, I stood by the fence for a moment, taking it in. From Chloe's grumblings

I'd half-expected his home to look like the Bates Motel in the movie *Psycho,* with dirt-encrusted windows, grass and weeds waist high, peeling paint, missing shingles, but it didn't. Not at all. Not only was beauty in the eye of the beholder, but ugliness too. Chloe hated being there, so the place was ugly to her.

Like a lot of the houses above Davenport in the Upper Annex, the place was a narrow, tiny two-storey. It was extremely well maintained. Its lacework trim and picket fence had been freshly painted the colour of eggshells; the lawn was a lush green and lilac bushes just past their bloom surrounded the porch. All over the front yard were bird feeders, though calling them feeders scarcely did them justice; they were more like bird mansions . . . intricately carved little houses in different styles and colours.

Apparently Caleb was not a cat person . . . a definite minority in the Annex where cats ruled due to the neighbourhood's ever-thriving rodent population.

I knocked on the front door. I barely made out Chloe's "We're downstairs in the basement" through the hammering in the distance. "Make sure you close the doors, front and basement, when you come in, so Frederick can't get out!" she then called out mechanically as if she'd been coached.

I entered. There were brightly coloured Mexican woven rugs scattered all over the dark brown hardwood floors. Near the window was a burgundy leather couch and a matching recliner, and next to it Tiffany table lamps standing on honey-coloured pine end tables. Dominating the room was an oversized abstract painting, all streaks and strokes of colour.

I stepped deeper into the room onto one of the woven rugs, and my sneaker toe went into something squishy. I looked down. This unmistakably was Frederick, his tricolour coat blending too well for his safety with the rug. Frederick, a pretty fat and very long basset hound lay there on the rug panting and dribbling drool. I supposed I'd be panting and drooling too if I ever reached Frederick's age. The lack of air conditioning didn't help. There were two fans going, but really all they did was distribute Frederick's drool like tiny raindrops over my calves.

Frederick slowly raised himself, his poor little skinny legs quivering from the effort of getting his huge torso up off the rug. With a hurricane-strength pant, he placed his front paws on my knees and started sniffling. I was evidently a babe in the eyes, or should I say in the nostrils, of elderly dogs.

I sniffed myself. I was a little sweaty, though definitely not as ripe as I'd been when I'd become the object of Emma's intense attraction. Frederick's head moved to the left, and sniffed. Aha! It was not just my mildly sweaty odour that was enticing Frederick, but also my uneaten lunch.

"Frederick," I said, grasping his front paws and putting them back on the rug. "One minute please!" His head stretched upward as if he was a tourist in front of the Empire State Building, he watched as I shifted my knapsack loose off my shoulders and placed it on the floor. I had a granola bar and fresh roasted turkey sandwich on whole wheat bread. Either or probably both were just what Frederick had in mind. I guessed his teeth and tummy were likely way past digesting granola bars, even if he thought otherwise, so I broke up my sandwich, slowly feeding him pieces of turkey, then bread.

"Where are you?" Chloe shouted as I was turning out to be one hell of a slowpoke Lone Ranger coming to her rescue.

"I'll be down in a second. I'm with Frederick."

Sandwich finished, Frederick was now licking my hands in appreciation. "I know you're grateful," I said, scratching his head.

I started to walk away, but Frederick, rather than flopping back onto the rug in chameleon position, followed close at my heels.

"We're in the basement," Chloe called out, as if I'd forgotten. And I kind of had, distracted by Frederick. A love of art wasn't the only thing Parnell and Caleb Hamilton had in common. "I'm coming!"

Right before the door to the basement was a room. I knew I shouldn't go in. It wasn't my house, yet I couldn't resist.

The room had wall-to-wall bookshelves, except instead of books on the shelves there were things. A collector's paradise was what it was. The siren call of collectibles . . . my mother certainly couldn't resist it. Neither evidently could Caleb, who made my mother look like a small fry collector in comparison.

What wasn't in here? There were crystal wine goblets of various shapes and colours, seashells, paperweights, bells made of crystal and silver, assorted china cups and saucers, Depression glass, pipes, globes, marbles, leather-bound books, maps of the constellations, postcards, stuffed birds, feathers, age-old toys. It would take forever to list everything. In the far corner was a dresser with its drawers half ajar, each drawer bursting with costume jewellery – necklaces, rings, beads, lockets.

My mother would have loved all this. And all the things she'd collected with such passion, and displayed with such pride, were now packed away in boxes like coffins.

"Alliccce!"

"I'm at the door," I shouted to Chloe. Frederick was there waiting for me at the door to the basement.

Before I could ask if Frederick could come downstairs with me, I heard Chloe say, "Remember, close the door behind you. Frederick can't come downstairs."

I saw why when I opened it. The steps were just wide planks of wood a foot apart with no backing. Frederick would never make it down them alive. Those little legs couldn't leap from one step to the next.

Frederick was quivering and panting as he stood next to my leg. So close to his master and another place to explore, maybe even another sandwich, yet soon the door would be shut in his face again. I knew the feeling. I swear I could feel his little heart beating with desperate desire.

"Your wish is my command," I said, and lifted Frederick in my arms. He was ecstatic, licking me all over my face. Two seconds later, with way too many pounds of squirming dog flesh in my arms, I knew why Frederick remained earthbound.

I adjusted him, resting his head over one shoulder, and carefully walked down the steps. Frederick was like a first-time airplane passenger, overjoyed by the view, his head moving about as much as it could without crashing into the side of my neck. My arms. I'd forgotten about the infected cuts on my arms, now throbbing from the pressure of Frederick's body.

I lowered Frederick to the ground and he toddled over to Caleb Hamilton.

"Yes, yes, it's been a time, yes it has, my boy, since you've been down here!" he said, kneeling to pat Frederick as he studied me, the kind of studied look I imagined an anthropologist would give some member of a newly discovered tribe he'd come upon in the jungle. Inquisitive, but detached.

Unlike the look of dismay on Chloe's face as she wagged her head at me as if to say, take a look at yourself, and fast. Yet again my traitorous sleeves, this time belonging to my grey T-shirt, had slipped past my elbows exposing the bandaging and the dull red slashes of several healing cuts.

I tried to look casual as I yanked the sleeves down. Chloe and I stood still, both barely breathing. However, as Caleb went on patting and murmuring to Frederick, I realized I had nothing to worry about, at least on that front. But I still had to come up with some way to get to Caleb for Chloe's sake, since I was here in the role of "interest-opener."

What did John always say about how to reach a customer? You had to find the thing that got their heart pumping.

Frederick was clearly one, but how much could you say about Frederick? He was a sweetie, but not an endless topic of conversation. Caleb's artwork. Duh, double duh!

I did a fast sweep of the room. It resembled your prototypical Santa's Workshop. There were two long rectangular tables with benches on either side. The table nearest to Caleb was covered with carpentry and woodworking tools, saws, hammers, pliers, nails and wood polishers and varnishes. The table where Chloe was working was covered with files, new file folders and labels, pictures, postcards, antique glass bottles, maps, greeting cards, newspapers, magazines. Adjacent to the table were five rusted file cabinets.

What was wrong with this picture? Chloe was most definitively not a happy whistle-while-she-worked elf; she looked steamed and resentful, glancing between Caleb and me.

And Caleb was most definitively not a jolly, warm and tubby Santa Claus senior citizen type. He was tall, well over six feet, and so skinny that he looked like a cadaver, and this was more than just my aptitude for seeing death everywhere like some warped medium. His head was bald except for a tiny little fringe of white hair cut down practically to the roots. His oval-shaped face was all bones – cheekbones, bony long nose, sharply defined square jaw – and his skin, speckled with age spots, was as tight as a bad facelift. His arms, though thin, seemed muscular and strong, as did his hands, even with his finger joints swollen with arthritis, I speculated, from all that elaborate woodworking.

I stepped towards him, debating whether to shake his hand, but he didn't seem like a hand shaker, so instead I called out, "I'm

Chloe's cousin, Alice Levitt, and I know who you are, Caleb Hamilton, and I really know who Frederick is."

Frederick squirmed away from Caleb and over to me, gazing at me with what I could only describe as adoration. Less for me though, and more for my delivery of that turkey sandwich, which must have really hit the spot.

Now most people would have said something like "I can see Frederick likes you," or made some kind of joke, but not Caleb.

There was a collage on an easel behind him. I sidestepped Frederick and went over to look. And in a second, it got to me; I felt this odd surge.

Unfinished, it resembled a bristol board scrapbook collection of things collected by some boy years ago . . . wrappers from two-cent Nestlé milk chocolate bars and Hershey's Kisses, Double Bubble gum and chocolate Popsicles, ancient postcards picturing Montreal and Quebec City, baseball cards, Crayola wrappers, birthday cards, torn covers of Superman and Spiderman comic books and part of the cardboard packaging from a Clue game. They were the sort of bits and pieces that most people would have thrown away, but Caleb had reclaimed them, like some Piped Piper of lost possessions, or possessions from lost people.

"It's like a lost and found, the collage," I blurted out, then instantly felt like an idiot. If there was one thing I'd already figured out about Caleb Hamilton, it was he didn't react like most people, and I was unsure whether what I'd said would put the kibosh on it for Chloe.

He looked at me with those watery green eyes of his, as if he was seeing me clearly for the first time.

"It is, isn't it?" he said matter-of-factly, then said nothing more.

Was everything he did like the collage?

I started asking him questions. Sentence fragments and the occasional full sentence began replacing his former monosyllabic replies. Chloe inched over and I could see her interest was growing. Just as mine was.

chapter**fourteen**

By my third visit to Caleb's, it was unmistakable – Chloe was engaged.

Instead of feeling like a secretary doing plain old boring filing, she felt like a curator's assistant at a gallery or museum, doing archiving and cataloguing. I helped her with her work.

Caleb scarcely noticed me, working away in a state of immersion that put anyone else's I'd ever seen to shame.

Actually, it kind of creeped me out. He was so immersed standing before his easel working on a collage or building a shadow box that I bet you could fall at his feet in an epileptic fit, and even if he did notice you, he'd still keep on working.

I didn't mention that to Chloe. I wanted her to stay, not have her flee screaming out of the house. Caleb was like a ghost materializing when he wanted to, then disappearing.

On my return visit, I explained that I'd come to help Chloe out; recreational filing, I joked. He smiled; I didn't know if at the joke or the prospect of the work finally getting done.

I was completely fascinated by all the stuff Caleb had collected for possible future use in one of his collages or shadow boxes. There were old greeting cards, letters and postcards, even some from the turn of the twentieth century. I'd trace the curves of the people's handwriting. And as Hallmark card sappy as it sounds, it was almost like I could reach out and touch the person, feel their presence just by touching their writing and reading their words.

While I was feeding Frederick roast beef on whole wheat bread, Caleb came over. I stretched it out, wanting to find out how and where Caleb had collected this stuff. All he said was, "It's amazing what people throw out."

I was about to see some of Caleb's completed work. It was on exhibit at a gallery a few blocks away from Atticus's. I was leaning in the doorway of the bookstore, and not in the most agreeable frame of mind.

Chloe pulled up in her mother's Lexus and I got in. She was all happy, happy, happy, and no surprise why. Yesterday, John had sent me to deliver a book to one of the residents who lived in the condos above the Hazelton Lanes shopping mall. There in the mall, I'd caught sight of Chloe and Kevin practically doing it on a bench, in sight of anyone with a pair of eyes.

I vowed to bite my tongue . . . for now.

That turned out to be easier than I'd assumed. The minute I walked into the gallery exhibition of Caleb's art, his artwork was the only thing I could think about. The shadow boxes really got to me, more than the collages, though they were good too.

Entranced, I stood in front of each of the boxes, ever so slowly taking them in from every angle. These wooden shadow boxes resembled miniaturized stage sets with a pane of glass in front, museum display case style. Or maybe an even better description might be dollhouses with the front section missing to expose the interior.

It was as if each shadow box was a home and a stage setting for a bunch of objects that wouldn't normally be placed together.

The different objects played off each other, much like in a dream, where the comings and goings of people, images and events from the past and present made the dream world seem new, and yet familiar, all at once.

And to figure out what it meant, you had to put the pieces together, except, unlike a puzzle where there was only one picture when assembled, with a shadow box, the objects suggested various things, rather than saying, "I mean this," "I am this."

I kept circling back to stare at this one particular shadow box. On the back wall of the shadow box, Caleb had glued an ancient constellation map of the stars. There were narrow shelves like a row of bedrooms on either side of the box; in them Caleb had placed a cranberry wine goblet filled with coloured marbles, old British and French coins, a nineteenth-century child's china piggy bank, an antique compass, a paperweight, a doll's head, a toy soldier and a tiny bird. The open centre area looked like a living room, with a floor to ceiling window with a clear view of the night sky, and there was tattered lace draped on each side of the map like curtains drawn back.

The box was a haunted house, haunted by the people these things had once belonged to, and haunted by the dreams, fantasies and emotions the objects had set off in the children and adults who'd once owned them. His artwork was so full of feeling . . . intensely emotional, but in a secretive, elusive way.

The owner of the gallery told me that the box had sold for $160,000 to a couple who were donating it to the Art Gallery of Ontario. Every single one of Caleb's exhibited pieces were sold already. She said she couldn't keep up with the demand.

At long last I had gotten around to researching Caleb Hamilton. While there was a ton of information about his artwork in the Toronto Reference Library's online databases, I'd only found a few biographical profiles.

He'd been born and raised in Toronto, in the same house he still lived in. His father had died when he was teenager, and Caleb had worked as a sales rep for one of the many textile factories that used to be on Spadina Avenue. The various textures, colours and patterns of the materials must have interested him, but the selling – I couldn't imagine how he'd handled it. But I guess we all do what have to do to get by, and he had done it until he reached his forties, when his mother died.

From then on, he'd lived on the small inheritance she'd left him and off his work, which was beginning to sell. Never married, he'd taken care of his younger brother Artie, who had cerebral palsy. Artie had died ten years ago.

I thought about the collage I'd seen Caleb working on, the one with the candy wrappers and old baseball cards from the fifties and sixties, and wondered if those things had once been Artie's.

I went over to the collages. If the shadow boxes were like dollhouses, the collages were like memorials for abandoned keepsakes. These fragments of things neglected and forgotten, things ready to blow off in the wind or be tossed into the garbage, had been lovingly rescued and reassembled by Caleb.

Like the Christmas collage in front of me, constructed of fragments of decades-old Eaton's department store Christmas ads, somebody's gift list, scraps of wrapping paper and ribbon, some torn Christmas cards, a piece of a doll's dress, a broken charm bracelet, a crayoned sketch of a train, lines from Christmas carols and much more.

I half-listened as Chloe gabbed away with the owner, gone way past interest to full-blown enthusiasm.

I suppose I could have joined in the conversation, but Chloe was annoying me like crazy. Her voice squeaked when she got excited, and now she sounded like Daffy Duck, hyperventilating with excitement.

Before we left, I asked the owner for a list of the items on exhibit and the gallery's hours, as I was going to come back as soon as I could.

Trapped as she was with surly me in the car as we drove to the cemetery, Chloe cottoned on to my crappy mood. When she made it out of downtown and into the suburbs where the traffic was lighter and the roads less congested, she turned her head towards me and said, "Why don't you just say what's bothering you already?"

"I saw you yesterday in Hazelton Lanes making out with Kevin. Didn't you say you were finished with him? You promised, didn't you?"

"I did," Chloe mumbled, a flush creeping over her face.

"What's the deal then? You do have other choices, you know. What about Eddie? Isn't he emailing you?"

I knew he was because Luke had told me that in a recent email. Just yesterday he'd emailed me a photo of himself to show me that his front teeth had been capped. It really got to me that he wanted me to see that he looked better. The picture, and the stuff I was learning about him in our emails and talks, fed these little fantasy scenarios I made up about Luke and me before I fell asleep, and sometimes even during the day. He was definitely boyfriend material, long distance or not. And maybe Eddie could be too, for Chloe. Or if not, at least even as friends, she could be with the kind of guy she should be with. Deserved to be with.

Chloe didn't look at me, just stared straight ahead, her fingers tightening on the steering wheel. "I like Eddie," she finally squeezed out after a few minutes. "But Eddie's not here, and I need to have a boyfriend here. Kevin says he likes me."

I lost it. "That's choice. He likes you. He likes being sucked off, that's what he likes about you. You call that having a boyfriend!"

"That's enough Alice!"

We both shut up after that. I passed the occasional glance over at Chloe; her face had an expression of concentration and unhappiness. Though, to be honest, I may have been the cause of that, as much as any regrets about Kevin. She had to have regrets. How could she not?

The uncomfortable, awkward silence continued until we reached the outskirts, then Chloe broke it when she started making the usual comments about the ugliness of Vaughan Township. I went along, the strain of the silence getting to me too. Besides, I didn't want her to be hurt by me. I was frustrated with her, yes, and she probably was wishing I would mind my own business. Both of us, though, didn't want Kevin, of all people, to come between us, so we trotted out the same old lines as if they were brand new ones.

"You couldn't pay me to live here," I said.

"You would have to pay me to live here," Chloe said.

"Houses for garages, that's what they are," I said, pointing out houses that had three-car garages larger than the houses themselves.

"Car dealer township, that's what they should call it," Chloe said, gesturing at a strip mall with ten stores and what looked to be at least a hundred parking spaces.

Soon Chloe was back to chatty mode, which I was glad of because it was hard enough to visit my mother's gravesite without there being tension between us.

chapter**fifteen**

Chloe was digging up the flower bed in front of my mother's gravestone, replacing the dead and withering flowers with fresh ones. As she yanked out several geraniums, she started off by telling my mother about Caleb Hamilton, and her work as his assistant.

"Remember the sixties-style jewellery you bought for us at the street fair on Spadina Road from that hippy lady with the long braid?" Chloe flicked her dangling earrings. "I'm wearing the earrings today. See? I still wear the mood ring too."

I stared at the earrings. I hadn't recognized them, or remembered any of that. The envy I felt at how effortlessly those happy memories flowed out of Chloe was as stinging as a slap.

I read in a self-help book that mourners had to accept that their old relationship to the person who had died was over, and that they had to build a new one.

I hadn't figured out yet what that meant for me.

While I went through my drill of polishing the gravestone with a chamois, placing a stone on the top, reciting the *Eil Malei Rachamim* prayer for my mother, I silently recited the lines I always said. "I love you. I miss you so much. I'm so sorry you had to die alone."

"Here, help me with the digging," Chloe said, tossing me a gardening spade.

Glad to go to work, I dug.

Chloe went on with her replanting while continuing to fill my mother in on everything new in her life. She kept pausing while talking, hoping that this time I would say something, but I didn't.

Putting down the spade, Chloe suddenly reached out and grasped my hand and held on to it as if she was going over the edge of something and I was grounding her.

"We have to talk," she said.

Grasping my hand tightly, she pulled me up along with her as she stood and we went over to the blanket we'd spread out next to the flower bed, and sat down.

Every time I'd heard "we have to talk" in the past two years, it wasn't about something good.

"Hey, you're cutting off the circulation in my hand," I said, trying to joke away my concern. "I need that blood for the healing process."

Chloe gave me a forced smile as she continued to wring the guts out of my fingers. "Your suspicions are right . . ."

I had so many suspicions. "About what?"

"I overheard my mother and Eric. He's bought a place in our building."

That was no shocker, really. What with the real estate agent casing our house, how could it be?

The sinking feeling in the stomach shocker was that Chloe didn't add how wonderful it would be to live together in the same building.

Clearly, I wasn't going to be living there. "He really is going to ship me off somewhere, isn't he?" And I guess where depended on how back to normal I was by the end of the summer. That would determine where I was going to end up . . . boarding school or nuthouse.

Chloe nodded. "He says he can't handle you anymore."

"When did he ever?" I said bitterly.

"We won't let him!" Chloe cried out.

"We won't let him. It won't happen," I said, trying to sound more reassuring than I felt. "Let me just digest this!"

I got up and went for a walk, not that there was anywhere to walk other than the gravel roadway. I paced, kicking up gravel, still kind of stunned even with what I had already known.

Not that I wasn't a pessimist, realist, whatever you want to call it. You can be both and still not see what's happening right in front of your eyes. Or maybe admit was the better word.

I remembered the day the doctor had told my mother, father and I that the artificial grafts bringing blood flow to her legs had blocked up, and no more grafts could be put in. The only option was amputation of her legs, and even that was risky.

My mother said she didn't want to lose her legs. And duh, I took biology and anatomy, and did I get what that meant? No. I just thought – or did I just want to think – that she would just be confined to a wheelchair, and in pain, controlled by drugs. Stupid, stupid, stupid.

I couldn't stop wishing I'd understood before it had been too late: no one can live for long with a limb that has no blood going to it. The limb eventually gets gangrene, and the toxins released from the gangrene kill you.

Had my parents known that keeping my mother's legs was a death sentence? Not exactly a subject I wanted to discuss with my father. And maybe I was afraid to know too. I did know one thing for sure – most doctors couldn't explain how to cross the street safely in plain, comprehensible English.

Three weeks later, my mother was in terrible shape. She'd always taken such care and pride in her appearance, and she was a mess that day. There were food stains on her blouse, her lips were really chapped and bloody and she was weak from the pain in her legs. By then she wanted to have her legs amputated. It was too late though.

Only then did the doctor say, at least in front of me, that there had been only a short window of opportunity for my mother to survive amputation surgery (which at best had a 40 percent survival rate) and it had passed. Now he believed she would die on the operating table. She took the doctor's news quietly. If only I had known earlier, I wouldn't have stopped begging her to have the surgery. It was 40 percent versus inevitable death.

Why hadn't she first agreed to amputation? Did she fear total dependence? Had she given up? Had she not fully understood what the doctor had said?

I should have understood.

When I returned to the gravesite, Chloe got up and came over to my side. "We'll come up with something. We will."

Suddenly exhausted, too exhausted to say a word, I just leaned against her.

chapter**sixteen**

opened the door to my walk-in closet. My clothes hung untidily on the left side of the closet; my mother's on the right, neatly sorted and arranged by category, as they'd been in her closet. The shirts and blouses first, then the blazers and jackets, dresses, skirts and pants.

I could smell the faint scent of the Oscar de la Renta perfume that she'd worn lingering on some of her clothes. There was the pink and black wool suit that she'd often worn to the Sabbath services at the synagogue. I stroked the sleeve of her blue patchwork quilted housecoat.

Some of her shoes were lined up on my shoe rack, starting with the gold metallic flats she'd loved, but they were mostly SAS shoes, orthopaedic shoes with rubber soles donned mostly by nurses and little old ladies for support. She'd hated them, but had no choice.

I closed the closet door, and went over to the dresser. There I touched the few collectibles I had out. The Royal Doulton figurine of two nineteenth-century women in big flouncy dresses having late afternoon tea. The tiny sterling silver bells. A mother and child figurine made of straw. The refrigerator magnet in the shape of a two-storey house. Two of the Post-it Note instructions she was forever leaving for me.

Chloe and I had been making phone calls to storage companies. If I wasn't moving into my father's new condo, neither were my mother's possessions. We had to find a place fast to store all those "sad reminders" as Eric called them.

They weren't sad reminders. They were triggers, like a genie in a bottle, all I had to bring back good memories of my mother.

My father had always been a looking-ahead kind of guy. When he lost a case, he'd breeze it off as if it had never happened, already on to the next case.

Even when he was there, he wasn't really there. I was stupid and needy enough as a kid to long for his whole attention, the way kids do. I would start telling him a story about some kid, or something at school. After a few minutes I would sense that he wanted me to spit it out, speed along, wrap it up. Then I'd lose track of where I was in the story, start to stutter, feeling as if what I was saying was too boring, and too dumb for words. I'd watch him do the same thing to my mother, and I couldn't get why. I loved listening to her. She was so funny, and she could transform whatever had happened to her into a funny story . . . the bad stuff too . . . for almost all of her life.

But you can give me this much: I'm a fast learner. By the time I was a miserable pain-in-the-ass teen, to get back at my father, when he'd ask me "What's new?" I'd torture him by telling him a story going nowhere slowly, and with endless detail. I'd watch as his eyes darted, he bit down yawns, and struggled to find some way to shut me up politely so he could escape.

I heard voices in the hallway. I put my ear against the door. Eric was schmoozing it up with Heidi Mullens, the real estate agent. There were more voices. A couple.

I'd been eating my breakfast this morning when Eric had

passed through the kitchen, duded up in a navy blue suit, crisp white shirt and royal blue tie. In the past, I would have made some comment about his going to set loose yet another criminal on the unsuspecting citizenry, but we weren't exactly on speaking terms.

So I'd presumed. He'd paused beside the table, then announced, "I'm selling the house. Get used to it!"

I swallowed down a big spoonful of cereal; otherwise, I knew I'd be yelling out "How much rehearsal did that line take?"

Well, he'd be selling the house without showing my room. Any couple buying it would just have to take it on faith that behind the locked door was a reasonably sized, nicely decorated bedroom with an excess of boxes, and not something out of a horror movie.

He could sell the house all right; I wasn't about to make it easy.

He knocked on my door, and called out, "Alice, please open the door. We won't step inside your room. We only want a glimpse."

Did he really believe that I was going to open the door? Was this for show? Or maybe he thought that his will could conquer mine. Never.

"No!"

He knocked again, harder. "Alice!"

"We will respect your privacy," I heard a girly sounding voice call out. The wife. "I hated it when my parents snooped through my room," she said, with a tremor in her voice.

Suddenly I felt badly for the couple. If they had just been there alone without Eric and Heidi, I would have opened the door.

"Alice, open this door. Right now!" my father ordered, banging on the door. "Teenagers," he said in a softer voice, to the couple. "Alice, open it now or else!"

"I'll open it when hell freezes over with you in it," I called out, in a mock sweet voice. Then I bumped my way through the boxes, and stood with my back against the wall. So I had won this skirmish, but I was going to lose the war over the house. And then what?

chapter**seventeen**

I had an even earlier shift at the fertility clinic today. Since the subway didn't start running until after six, I walked down University Avenue to the clinic. The streets were still empty of people and traffic, unlike the clinic where it was rush-hour busy. That was when all the women undergoing in vitro fertilization and fertility treatments arrived to have their tests done.

Usually I just inputted the patients' new data into their computer file. This week though, since the clinic was short-staffed because of the summer vacations, I first assisted the nurses by checking the women's health cards, registering them and creating name tag labels to wrap around the vials to identify their blood work.

This was the closest I had gotten to the patients; previously I'd just watched them through the glass partition surrounding the computer station area. The majority looked to be in their thirties and forties; a few, unexpectedly, in their twenties.

Whatever their ages, all were restless. I didn't know whether that was a side effect of all the fertility drugs they were taking or nerves. Or both.

At the start I was a bit jumpy. Didn't know what to say, didn't want to say the wrong thing, or a false thing. All that pamphlet and article rereading had paid off, so I was able to talk with the women without embarrassing them or myself.

And most of them needed to talk – to pass the time in the long lines, to share their experiences and to boost each other up. After a couple of cycles when various things went wrong and the women didn't get or remain pregnant, which was the norm statistically, these women needed all the encouragement they could get.

This one patient really stood out because she was so young, appearing not much older than Chloe. She was plump with straight long blond hair, a little acne and braces on her upper teeth.

She stood out too because she was so much more pleasant and easy to deal with than some of the older women. Several had tried pushing their way to the front of the line saying they were ready to ovulate and they had to be first in line at the ultrasound. Try a better excuse, ladies. No procedures were scheduled until everyone had been tested.

Some others had carped on and on about having to show their health insurance card. Didn't I know who they were? No, and clearly we were all interchangeable. Didn't they realize they'd never seen me before?

This morning, as the young patient I'd been watching handed me her health card, I dropped it. We both bent down at the same time to get it, and bumped heads.

"I'm so sorry," she said. "Are you all right?"

"Nothing to be sorry about," I said, as I scrambled back into my seat. "It's my fault. I dropped it."

"You dropped it because I missed your hand," she said.

"No, I missed your hand," I said.

She smiled. "We both missed."

"Listen, girls, this isn't the time for a chit-chat," a middle-aged woman dressed in a pantsuit said rudely.

The young patient turned her head. "I'm sorry. I didn't mean to hold up the line. You go ahead. I'm in no rush. I'm only going to be sitting around in the waiting room anyhow."

Like that mouthy woman wasn't going to be too!

I registered her and a few other women, then the young patient.

"Here's my card," she said.

"I promise not to drop it this time," I said, smiling at her.

"I'm Lindy McConnell," she said. "Of course you know that from my health card."

"I'm Alice Levitt," I said. "If I'd remembered to wear my hospital ID you probably would have known that."

Since for now there were no more women lining up, Lindy stood by the side of my desk and we talked.

Even though Lindy was only twenty-six years old, this was her third go at in vitro fertilization. Her fallopian tubes were blocked so it was impossible for her eggs to be fertilized through plain old sex. She and her husband Don had put a second mortgage on their house to pay for the treatments and the fertility drugs. which were very expensive (and not covered by provincial health insurance). This third attempt had used up the last of their mortgage money, so if it didn't work, it was going to be their last.

Lindy drove in every morning from Oakville, an hour's drive from Toronto. She had two older sisters, with three kids each and no problem having them. She'd married Don after graduating from high school and worked part-time at a neighbourhood Dominion supermarket. The pay was good, she said, as if she had to justify herself. She was just working until she had a family.

After that we talked every morning. From the way she treated people she seemed as if she would be a good mum. She was kind and respectful. When she talked to me, she was really listening, not just waiting for her moment to take centre stage. She paid attention, cared.

As much as I looked forward to chatting with Lindy, on Friday morning I wasn't up to it, even with someone I liked as much as I did Lindy. I hadn't had the best of nights, tossed, turned . . . cut. I'd promised Chloe I wouldn't, but I had. I had gone all self-righteous and ragged Chloe for being all over Kevin in Hazelton Lanes, going on and on, the big implication underneath being that she had never intended to keep the promise. But last night, duh, I'd realized you could intend never to break a promise, and then break it all the same, aware that what you were doing was wrong, bad, self-destructive, and yet not be able to stop yourself from doing it.

The sleep killers – self-loathing and shame – had kept me up all night. I was sleepy, grumpy and sweating from wearing a fleece hoodie though it was already twenty-three degrees Celsius and heading towards over thirty.

"You don't feel well, do you?" she said softly as she leaned over to hand me her health card.

I couldn't meet her eyes.

"You need this more than me," she said, offering me the Tim Horton's coffee she'd been about to drink. "Besides, with any luck, I'll be given sedation soon so I won't need the coffee buzz."

Likely, Lindy's eggs had matured, and if so, she'd have the retrieval surgery in the afternoon. Her gynie, Dr. Hollister, would take the eggs out of Lindy's ovary with a catheter needle, and combine them with her husband Don's sperm in a petri dish. When the eggs fertilized, the embryos would be placed back in Lindy's uterus where one or two might implant.

"Are you sure?"

She nodded.

"Thanks," I said, and took it gratefully. It picked me up fast and got me through the rest of the registrations. Before I started inputting, I searched out Lindy in the waiting room, wanting to hear the news, and to wish her good luck. It wasn't easy to find anyone in this rabbit warren, once they'd left the area where the labs and ultrasound equipment were. Finally, I sighted Lindy. Getting lost had given me the time to prepare something to say.

I knew what I wasn't going to say. "This time it will work, for sure." I'd actually heard those words from some of the nurses, who knew better, medically and statistically. Gutless prevaricators of false hope, there was a plague of them in the medical profession.

Lindy was sitting in a corner with a magazine in her lap. She saw me and waved. "It is today!" she said, sounding both happy and anxious.

"I just came to wish you lots and lots of good luck," I said, flopping down into the chair beside her.

"Thanks," she said, then twisted her wedding band.

"You'd be a great mother. I just know it," I said.

"Thank you for saying that." Her voice cracked with emotion.

"Don't thank me. It's the truth." I stood up. "I've got to go. Inputting data beckons. I'll see you in two weeks or so."

She nodded. "See you then. And get someone to look at your right arm. It looks like it's bothering you."

No surprise, as tuned in as she was to the feelings of others, that Lindy had noticed.

"I will," I said quietly and did that at a walk-in clinic on Dundas Avenue before I went to Atticus's.

chapter**eighteen**

was waiting in the Colonnade for the jewellery shop owner who had bought a first edition of Hemingway's *Death in the Afternoon* to show up so I could deliver his book. A sign on the door said "I'll be back in five minutes." In the universe I lived in those five minutes had passed twenty-seven minutes ago.

Since this plaza targeted a pretty ritzy crowd there wasn't much for me to window-shop in the stores in eyeshot of the jewellery store. I stared at the shoes in the women's shoe store. Every single pair appeared to be excruciatingly impossible to walk in. The mules showcased at the front of the window were so flimsy that my guess was that it would take only a few steps before your heel headed for the pavement, and you along with it.

Next I stared at the window of the store selling cigars. Their stench, even unlit, drove me back to the bench where I'd been sitting before. I sat down, checking my watch to see how many more five minutes had passed.

Beside the bench was a garbage container. I looked in to see if there were any newspapers in readable condition. *The Globe & Mail* was too soggy from wet garbage to read, but the *People* magazine next to it was touchable so I got up and bent over to take it out.

"Hello stranger!"

I didn't need to turn around to know who was speaking. "Hi Merle," I said. I knew I sounded like a sulky six-year-old trotted out by her parents to greet their friends.

"Long time no see," she said, giving me these measuring looks as if she could see right through my long sleeves. Figures that was where her gaze went immediately.

"For a playwright, you sure like clichés," I said in greeting, then flushed.

As if I didn't. My excuse was I liked to say them because they brought back this fun game my mom and I played where we spoke to each other using only clichés and catchphrases. Come to think of it, it was Merle who had come up with that – it was a playwriting exercise that she employed in workshops to make her theatre arts students more aware of how they overused them in the dialogue of their plays.

"You've been reading reviews of my plays, haven't you?" she joked, taking my crankiness in stride. "Too busy to call me back or email me?"

I shrugged. "You know, school, and then I have two jobs."

"Another job besides working at the bookstore?" she asked.

"Yeah," I said.

Since I'd hung up on her in big bang style in April, at first she'd left messages (I never answered the phone without checking to make sure her name wasn't showing on the call display). When I hadn't phoned back, she'd started emailing me. Friendly updates, like nothing had happened between us, telling me where she was, where she was going, where she could be reached, assuming I was going to reach out to her eventually.

I hadn't.

I hadn't for a bunch of reasons way beyond the hideousness of our last conversation.

I just wasn't up to having another reminiscing session about my mom with Merle. I recognized she thought it would comfort me, as it comforted her. But it didn't. It made me miss my mother unbearably. After each of those sessions, I was so revved up, so agitated I could only calm myself down by cutting.

She couldn't see the gauze bandages through my sleeves. That didn't stop me, however, from touching my arms, and she caught me. She didn't say anything though.

Merle had been my mom's best friend since childhood. They'd grown up in the same neighbourhood in Montreal, Côte St-Luc. Their families had moved to Toronto, the Adlers moving a year after my mom's family, and had settled in the same neighbourhood again, this time in Bathurst Manor.

After high school my mom had gone straight to work while Merle had gone to university, studying drama and English literature at York University. They'd gotten together practically every weekend, and had both dated like crazy. "Wild girls" was how Merle had described them before my mother, laughing and slightly embarrassed, silenced her.

They'd stayed close as their lives changed, my mom marrying and having me, and Merle, who didn't marry though she had several long relationships, moving around from place to place, from job to job as she tried to make it as a playwright.

She had, sort of. Four of her plays had been produced at small theatres around the country, which brought in some money, though not enough to live on. So she'd worked as a freelance editor and writer and part-time teacher.

My mother had admired Merle, admired her independence and take-no-prisoners style, so different from her own. And Merle had admired my mom too, for who she was and, maybe at times, even envied her life. Though why, for a woman who prided herself on being a keen observer of human nature, she had been staggered by Eric's unfaithfulness remained a mystery.

There were other reasons I found it gruelling to be around her. Her constant harping at my mom to do something about Eric's cheating burned me. It was hard enough for my mom to live with it, but she had chosen to, for whatever reasons.

A few months before my mom died, I'd caught Eric and Merle furiously going at each other in the kitchen. "How could you? How could you?" she repeated. Out on a dinner date, she'd seen Eric and Suzette, all cosy together. Undeniably it was satisfying to see her lay into him; however, their arguing was loud enough for my mother, who was lying on the couch, to overhear.

"Mom's in the next room, so can it!" I hissed.

When I hurried back to the living room, my mother was lying with her face against the couch. She'd heard.

What could I do though? Merle was devoted to my mom. She kept visiting several times a week, bringing books, magazines and flowers, and telling her funny stories. Nonetheless, the final straw for me had been the movie she'd brought my mom to see: *The House of Mirth.*

I'd come into the den as Merle and my mom were watching the tail end of it.

It was really sad. I hadn't even seen the whole movie, and I got teary. However, my mom and Merle were basket cases. My mother was weeping so fiercely she couldn't catch her breath. And Merle, after she'd gotten back some control, made some feeble jokes about seeing herself on the Lily Bart career path.

In other words, Merle had identified way too much with the nineteenth century heroine of the movie, Lily Bart. Lily, who thought she had all the time and freedom to marry who she wished, when she wished. Lily who thought she knew what she was doing;

who trusted the wrong people and made the wrong choices; and who ended up up shit's creek, abandoned by her society friends, poor as a church mouse, and with nowhere to go but downhill. So she killed herself.

What the heck had Merle been thinking to choose that DVD to bring over when my mother was dying, and no doubt going over and over her choices, even though she hadn't said a word.

I just wasn't up to any of Merle's well-meaning efforts, and put her at the top of the list of people I wanted to avoid.

"So how are things?" Merle asked, now fiddling with the strap of her purse after having transferred it from one shoulder to the other.

I guess I was making her uncomfortable. Good. Maybe then she'd leave me alone. This was instantly followed by a surge of guilt. Merle was my mother's best friend. She'd been there for my mom her whole life. She loved my mother and my mother loved her. My mom wouldn't like me to be rude and worse, and to cut her short.

But how could I answer Merle's loaded question without being any of the above? So I shrugged again.

"How are things with you?" I asked.

"The Jewish trick, answering a question with a question," Merle said dryly. "Great! Where's a piece of wood to knock on?" She knocked on the bench.

"I was having lunch at the Chinese restaurant here with a production manager at the Tarragon Theatre and it looks like they're going to stage my new play next season."

"That's fantastic news!" I said. My mother never missed a play of Merle's, going back repeatedly. Merle said that my mom could play every role because she knew them all by heart.

"It'll be next spring, I think," Merle said. "I'm living in Montreal now. I'm teaching playwriting full-time at a community college."

"Beats freelancing?" I said

"You bet," she said.

Out of the corner of my eye, I saw a short, balding Armani-suited man unlocking the door to the jewellery store. Mister Five Minutes had returned. I glanced at my watch. Fifty-nine minutes after those five minutes had elapsed.

"I have to deliver a book to that store owner and then go back to work at the bookstore," I said, pointing to the jewellery store.

"We'll keep in touch?" she asked. "I promise just to talk about myself. You know us playwrights – we're always looking for an audience, and you know how wordy we can be. Promise not to let you get a word in edgewise. Promise to give your ears a workout. You'll have a front row centre seat at a one woman show starring the incompetent, no I meant incomparable, Merle Adler. See, ego always trumps id. Take that Dr. Freud and your dratted Freudian slips."

I laughed in spite of myself. Still, I hesitated.

"Hey, wothehell, Alice, wothehell, it's cheerio my deario that pulls a lady through," she said softly.

That was a line that my mom and Merle always said to each other. It was from a poem titled *Cheerio my Deario,* which was part of a series of very funny satirical poems, written by this American newspaper columnist, Don Marquis, in the twenties.

They said it to buck each other up when things got rough in their lives. For Merle that meant when her plays were being rejected or reviews were bad, when a romance went sour, when money was really tight and prospects looked grim. For my mom that meant when she was facing more treatments and surgeries, and the one-two punch of her parents' deaths one after another.

When I was old enough to appreciate Marquis's humour, my mom and I would read his poems out loud together. Marquis claimed that they were written in the deserted newsroom at night by Archy the cockroach on Marquis's old manual typewriter. Archy tapped them out by leaping from key to key. Mostly Archy wrote about his friendship with Mehitabel the cat.

I would take the role of the cynical, wise guy Archy who held he'd been a poet in a former life, while my mom took the part of the indomitable, adventurous Mehitabel, an alley cat who believed she'd been Cleopatra in her former life.

Another line popped into my head, and though the last thing I wanted was to tear up in front of Merle, I did, recollecting what Archy said about Mehitabel – "always a lady in spite of hell and transmigration . . . I admire her spirit."

"Well . . ." Merle said, stretching it out for comic effect, but I could hear the nervousness.

"Sure," I said.

"Good," she said, and kissed me on the cheek. "Give Chloe my best and . . . tell Leslea I'm disappointed that she didn't take my last piece of advice and go jump in Lake Ontario. She hasn't, has she?"

Laughing again, I shook my head no.

"One can only hope," she said. "Remember, don't be a stranger anymore, okay?"

"I won't."

And I wouldn't be.

chapter**nineteen**

You're eating your second roast beef sandwich. Not wrapping it up for later as usual, you carnivore you!" John teased, as he leaned against the cash register desk.

John and Eileen were vegans, so that was the explanation for the running carnivore joke between us. And for the running stevedore joke, too. He said I had the appetite of a longshoreman. Anyone with two paying jobs and a recreational filing job would have.

"I'm hungry," I said, shovelling the second half of the second sandwich into my mouth.

"I thought you were saving it to share with someone special," he said, still teasing me.

"I was," I said, through a mouthful of roast beef on multi-grain bread. "For Frederick."

"A boyfriend?"

"A basset hound."

He hooted. We heard the tinkle alarm that signalled someone opening the door. "It's time to go make money." And he straightened his jacket and left.

There was no time today for even brief interludes in Luke fantasyland, I was so busy searching and ringing up sales. I didn't even hear Randy come upstairs. It was the end of my shift. He flirted with two women in the corner while I was trying to help this guy decide between two historical novels featuring killers – *The Alienist* by Caleb Carr and *Alias Grace* by Margaret Atwood. I must have been on a roll because I got him to buy both.

"I'm here. Pack up and depart. Your cousin's waiting for you downstairs with this super old dude," he said. As usual, Randy was groomed to the nth. His dark brown hair was slicked back, and his white T-shirt was immaculate, as were his boot-cut black jeans.

It hit me then and there that Randy and Chloe would be, if not perfect, a lot better together than Kevin and Chloe. And unlike Eddie, he was here in person, and looking for a girlfriend. His last one, Julia, had dumped him two weeks ago because he was getting too serious, she'd said. That would a pleasant problem for Chloe to face for once, if they clicked.

"Did you speak to Chloe?" I asked.

"Yeah. She's all excited about working for that old dude," he said.

"She's looking good, huh," I said. So what if tact wasn't part of my matchmaking repertoire. Okay, so it wasn't part of my repertoire, period. "Chloe and I are going to see a movie at the Cumberland on the weekend. Can you come with us on Sunday?"

Just in case he was having a fright thinking that Alice, the Pigpen book clerk, had a thing for him, I said quickly, "Chloe and her boyfriend just broke up." Technically, not completely a lie.

"Yeah?"

Good, his yeah sounded interested as opposed to who cares. "Sure." He took one of the bookmarks advertising the store and wrote down his home phone number.

Mission accomplished, I went down the stairs with a bounce in my step, a song in my heart. Not really, but an improvement over my standard depressive clop, clop, clop, knowing I was headed back to Battlefield Levitt on Tranby Avenue. And even that soon to become only another memory fragment.

Caleb was leafing through some books on the display table.

"So this is who you are doing the recreational filing for," John said, turning his head to look over at me. "The book dismemberer. Not my babies, my first editions, just old textbooks and encyclopaedias," he added in a whisper.

He didn't need to have bothered. Caleb's gaze didn't waver from the pages he was flipping through. John crinkled his lips in amusement at Caleb's obliviousness, as if he too had grown accustomed to it. I guess anyone who had regular dealings with Caleb had to.

I knew I had seen Caleb before. Here. Buying old books to use as wallpaper on the back walls of his shadow boxes

Chloe came over to my side, and started flicking at the dust on my skirt.

"Hey, stop it!" I joked. "I'm only going to get all dusty again." John looked bewildered.

"Chloe and I are going with Caleb on a shopping spree to some second-hand stores selling clothing, collectibles, records, knick-knacks. My latest job is as recreational inventory list-maker."

"A treasure hunt for the great master," John said, winking at me.

"For me, too," Chloe said eagerly.

I hadn't lied about how good Chloe was looking these days. Her hair was pulled back in a ponytail tied with a ribbon and she had hardly any makeup on, only eyeliner and lipgloss; she was wearing a flattering peachy striped stretch shirt with three-quarter sleeves and an olive cargo miniskirt.

"I'm looking for material for my collage," she said. "Ms. Parnell said I could do a collage or two for my credit instead of writing an essay on Caleb."

"That's great!" I said. "Recreational inventory list-making for two, coming up, Miss."

"I'll take these," Caleb said, materializing out of his daze. "Oh, Alice," he said, finally seeing that I was there.

I said hi to Caleb, goodbye to John, and as we followed behind Caleb on Queen Street East, I told Chloe about Randy.

"He likes me?" she said.

"Why not? You're a total sweetie . . . and a budding artist to boot. What's not to like?"

She playfully smacked me. Caleb, focused on finding a store that might beckon him to enter, ignored our giggling, or didn't hear us, or both.

The first store that drew Caleb was a rundown antique store, not really filled with antiques, just with old things, two steps above the things you'd find in a Goodwill store. However, for Caleb and Chloe, the store turned out to be a treasure trove. I stood a metre away as they picked up various objects and discussed them.

Caleb really seemed to want Chloe's opinion of things. and praised her when she discovered something for him to use.

I was glad for Chloe. Caleb now trusted Chloe, so not only did he benefit from her help and company, but she would benefit too. I hoped.

Chloe called me over, and I started writing in my reporter's notebook all the things she'd bought. Old store catalogues, paperbacks, greeting cards, costume jewellery, old magazines, a diary.

What kind of so-and-so pawned off their loved one's diary to a second-hand store? The store was depressing me. All this stuff was like ghosts haunting me. I knew I was going woo-woo yet again, but I swore I could feel the sorrowful spirits of the former owners murmuring, "Look, all those things I cherished, all chucked like so much trash, abandoned, forgotten. And me too?"

Get a grip girl, I told myself. I still had to write down Caleb's list. The stuff he bought was not light, like Chloe's, to paste on a collage, but things to place inside a shadow box. A miniature toy truck, pineapple candlesticks, two chipped cups and saucers, books, playing cards, marbles, a whistle, a unicorn ornament, a snow globe with a couple dressed in nineteenth-century clothing skating together, cufflinks and a bronze bird perched on a pedestal.

The owner packed up everything Caleb had bought and placed it in two heavy-duty plastic bags. Caleb glanced at me, as if I was a Sherpa. The things I did for Chloe. With a mental groan, I picked them up.

Then I groaned out loud. It wasn't that they were especially weighty to carry. It was just that my arm was sore.

"Give me those," Chloe whispered, and grabbed them out of my hands. "You promised me."

That I had.

As we walked out the door and trailed behind Caleb, Chloe whispered, "The ER doctor told you your arms are a bad infection waiting to happen. You have to stop. If you can't stop for you, stop for me. What would I do without you? Got it?"

Maybe this time I would.

chapter**twenty**

I came home to the sound of voices.

I heard a woman's breathy voice, then my father's. As I clambered up the stairs, the woman's voice began to sound familiar. It was the woman who'd come with her husband to look at the house.

I had resigned myself to the fact that Eric was going to sell the house, and there was nothing I could do about it. I reached the landing and saw Eric in my room, with the couple hovering uneasily at the doorway. He must have jimmied the lock.

I wedged between the couple, nearly knocking over the husband. "What are you doing in here?"

Eric seemed genuinely shocked by my arrival, and by the sight of just how many of my mother's things were here in my room labelled and boxed, and not given away to Goodwill.

"I guess you're already packing for the move," the wife said timidly.

"No," I snapped and was instantly sorry. The couple seemed decent, and who could blame them for wanting to see the room? Eric was asking over a million for the house. For that amount of cash, who wouldn't want to see all the rooms, especially the locked one?

"These are boxes filled with my mother's things. After my mother died, my father wanted to give away everything to Goodwill. That's why the door is locked. To stop him!"

For once, for a hideous, glorious moment, I witnessed Eric being shown up. The wife and the husband gazed at each other, then at him with barely veiled distaste. He shifted from foot to foot.

"We're sorry to hear about your mother's death," the wife said, a catch in her voice.

I nodded, willing myself not to get even more upset in front of them.

"We're also sorry," the husband added, waving towards the door, then at Eric, "about this." He sighed.

I nodded again. "Thanks. I know you couldn't fork out that amount without seeing everything you're paying for."

"We've seen enough," the wife said. "We're very sorry."

The couple turned and went down the stairs without another word to Eric. He and I just stared at each other for a minute, then I muttered, "Leave!"

He did, and I heard him hurrying down the stairs after the couple. I shut the door, and sagged against it. I had to get the boxes out of here, and fast.

I called Chloe at Caleb's and told her, babbling through my story so incoherently that Chloe had to ask me several times to repeat myself.

"Hold on!" she said.

I heard some murmuring in the background. I'd gotten through the scene on adrenaline, all which suddenly whooshed out like air from a punctured tire. My legs started to shake like crazy, barely carrying me over to my bed, where I fell flat on my face.

"Alice, Alice, are you still there?" Chloe shouted so loudly I heard her even though the handset had fallen between my pillows.

I stretched and grabbed hold of it. "Yeah, yeah, I'm here."

"Caleb said we can store the boxes in one of his spare bedrooms. Pack up everything that isn't already. How much time do you need? Caleb has a pickup truck. He said I can borrow it, and we'll take everything to his place."

"Thanks," I mumbled. I knew I should say more, express my gratitude and thanks to Caleb. I would later. At this point I just needed the blessed escape of sleep.

chapter**twenty-one**

My room didn't feel like my room any more, stripped clean of my mother's things. While my room was empty of boxes, the rest of the house was filling up with them. That couple had made an offer on the house. Though it was lower than the price my father had listed the house at, he'd grabbed it. He was unmistakably raring to be done with the house, and to be done with the drama of trying to sell the house with his very own homegrown Bertha Rochester to greet prospective buyers.

The latest team of Molly Maids was handling the organizing and packing with the aid of professional packers. The closing date for the house, and me too, was the end of August.

My father was moving to the Prince Arthur, 38 Avenue Road. Where was I headed? Had my father made up his mind? When he and I had the misfortune to run into each other, we more or less just made sounds at each other. Sounds like me slurping down my cereal or soup, then him slamming shut the kitchen door. Sounds like me flipping up a magazine to cover my face as he went past me in the living room.

I had to do something. The end of August wasn't that far away, but I had returned to that zombie state I was in for the first few weeks after my mother died.

Had I not had the two jobs to go to, I would have spent the whole day holed up in my room sleeping. Worker drone me, though, kept working; not at top form, but the jobs did get done. It took all of what little energy and concentration I had. All – which left me less inclined than usual to chat or socialize.

That worked out fine in the mornings when I was inputting medical data, the nurse doing the patient registration back from vacation. Since the temperature had been over thirty-five degrees Celsius for a week, entering Atticus's Attic felt like walking into a baker's oven, reducing customer browsing and chatting time to a sweaty minimum.

As for John and me, I tried my best to keep up my end in our conversations, but he got how down I was. So he brought me more tapes of *The Honeymooners,* and made the serving of Eileen's lemonade a daily ritual, nicknaming it "the lemonade hour." Proof, as if I needed it, of how fuzzed up my brain was – the first time John said that, I didn't get the wordplay on "the cocktail hour." Then John had explained the joke while, feeling like an idiot, I nodded along.

Not that I could watch *The Honeymooners* or any of my taped crime TV shows or DVDs. Or even respond to Luke's long emails with more than a short summary of my daily activities. The last thing I could handle was for him to hear how slurred and slow my speech had become. I wrote to tell him I wasn't feeling well, wasn't up to talking and would give him a call when I was. I was brain-dead by the time I got home. I would gulp down a bowl of soup, yogurt and some fruit, shower and collapse on my bed, falling asleep instantly.

Disturbing my attempt to sink into deep coma sleep was that damn ringing phone. Chloe again, I bet. I opened one bleary eye and gazed at my digital alarm clock. It was 8:03 p.m. I was so tempted to let it just ring. If I let the phone kick into voice mail, she'd be banging at the front door soon. With a moan I reached for the phone.

"What are you doing?" Chloe asked, her energized voice a jolt to my ear.

"What do you think I'm doing," I muttered, so groggy all I wanted to do was drop the handset and snore off. "I'm sleeping."

"It's early," Chloe said, some of the enthusiasm in her voice leaking out after hearing my slurred monotone. "You've got all those tapes and DVDs. Put something on."

"Can't concentrate," I said, with a big yawn.

You know how sometimes when you get a cold, you can't think, you can't even focus your eyes to watch something, even the stupidest something on TV? That's what I felt like. And my tongue felt like it weighed a ton.

"If you just lie there, you'll feel worse," Chloe said.

"If I just lie here, I'll soon be asleep. Which is the game plan."

"You want me to come over, I can be there in ten minutes," Chloe said.

"Please don't. I feel like a slug. Do you want to watch me lie here and sleep? That's what you're going to see."

"Alice! Don't fall asleep yet. I've got something to tell you."

Good. Listening was all I was barely up to. Chloe told me all about the collage she was working on. I'd never heard her so into anything before. Thank Caleb for that.

"You'll come see it soon . . ."

"Yeah, I promise."

There was a long silence then. I guess the word promise was a loaded word for both of us. I knew what she was gearing up to ask me so I beat her to it.

"I kept the other promise, you know."

I heard her breathe heavily into the phone, as if she'd expected that I hadn't.

"I kept my promise too. You know what? Randy asked me out. We're meeting for dinner."

"That's great." And it was. Good news as that was though, I swear I was still about to fall asleep.

"You know how much you matter to me," she reminded me, as if she had to quickly come up with reasons why I shouldn't off myself. No energy for that either, though I wouldn't have minded not waking up tomorrow morning – permanently.

"Same for me," I said, forcing my lips to enunciate the words clearly.

"I talked to my father," Chloe said. "I asked him if he would pay for boarding school . . . if you get sent to one. He said he would. He said it was a good idea for me . . ."

" . . . to get the hell away from Leslea. The farther the better. Does he know of boarding schools in Tasmania we could attend?"

Chloe giggled.

As washed out as I felt, that safety net gave me a tiny boost.

chapter**twenty-two**

Alexandro's was just the kind of showy restaurant my father adored, with its potted palm trees, bamboo furniture, Royal Wedgwood china, crystal stemware and cloth napkins wrapped around enough cutlery for a day's worth of meals.

I wasn't planning to do much eating here. Neither was my father, by the looks of it. Late, as usual. If he came much later, the kitchen would be closed, and the restaurant would be serving only drinks and desserts.

He had chosen Alexandro's as the setting for "our talk" about my future, presuming that I wouldn't make a scene, or maybe not such a big scene, in a public place.

As a kid, I'd seen my mother lay into Eric more than a few times. Those were the days when she had the will, vigour and hopefulness to fight back. Because fighting back meant you believed you could make things better. And because fighting back also meant you believed you had power and strength equal not just to the situation, but also to the other person. But the illnesses that sapped my mother's physical strength sapped her spark too.

I knew I had to restrain myself, for my own advantage. He wasn't the only one about to do a sales pitch tonight. I hadn't worn a short-sleeved top and a miniskirt in ages. This evening, though, I was wearing a lemon scoop-necked T-shirt with three-quarter sleeves, a dark green trouser skirt and flip-flops.

Okay, I had darkened marks and several healing cuts on my forearms, but the good thing about having young skin (this according to Chloe, my beauty consultant) was that it had resilience and healed fast. Chloe was right, as she was on so many things, that the sight of the healed skin would make me less inclined to crap it all up again.

Another motivation was those kissing and more fantasies with Luke I played out in my hopeful moments. And they didn't feature me wearing long-sleeved shirts with cuffs buttoned as tight as handcuffs.

Luke had called, despite my email plea not to call. I had started off slurred and slow on the uptake, but he'd persisted. Just when I thought he hadn't noticed, he'd said out of the blue, "You don't have to hide feeling bad from me, you know, Alice. Give me a little credit, will you?"

I didn't say anything for a moment, first feeling a flush of shame, then such warmth (hardly the word), my liking for him skyrocketing.

So I'd told him about my father wanting to ship me off. And Luke had helped me come up with a way to present my case. By the time I'd put down the phone, I'd felt so much better I was even surprised myself. Luke hadn't run for the hills after encountering me feeling so crummy.

I went over the pitch we'd prepared. My bottom line was that I was improving, so I didn't need to be sent away for my "own good."

Forty minutes late, my father strolled in, greeting, handshaking, back-slapping, murmuring in the ears of the maître d,' several of the wait staff and even some people at tables, as if he was George Clooney arriving at a premiere.

I was seated at a table next to a potted palm and close to an exit. Close to an exit was always my favourite spot.

After glad-handing half of the restaurant, my father made it over to me, and I could see the hesitation in his expression. Did he dare, in front of an audience, to attempt a pseudo-affectionate grab of my shoulder blades? Wisely, he thought not, and just sat down in the bamboo throne chair opposite me.

"Hello Alice! I'm *so* sorry. What could I do? The client pays the bills."

I shrugged. I thought I'd throw him off by being agreeable. "So how's work going?" I asked.

"Crazy busy," he said. "Just preparing for some cases pending for fall trials." Then he leaned over and picked up his briefcase, and rifled through it.

For a second I thought he was searching for notes, to share the details about some new low-life he was defending. Instead he took out a hefty brochure titled "Regent's Academy, Kingston, Ontario." He was about to hand it to me, but instantly thought better of it, and slid it next to my plate.

I was getting ready to start my argument about how much better I was when cagey Eric launched into defence lawyer speechifying mode. Definition – a non-stop marathon of twisted arguments, excuses, half-truths, half-lies, out-and-out whoppers all thrown together until they were blended into a stew where you couldn't tell what from what, spieled out with all the bluster, muster and faked passion at the lawyer's disposal.

As I was still planning to launch my own counterattack spiel, I mostly tuned out his advertising pitch for Regent's Academy. Did I care if its graduates excelled academically, and were accepted with scholarships by the *crème de la crème* of Canadian and American universities? Duh, Eric. My grade average was already 96%, good enough to get into Harvard or Yale, I supposed, if I so desired. Which I didn't.

Did I care if its graduates went on to become the crème de la crème of Canadian professional life? Not my ambition.

Did he not know me at all? Was he that oblivious? I mean, anyone who knew me even a little would know that those reasons were precisely the ones that would never appeal to me, that would turn me off big time.

Aha, then I got it! He had to make himself actually believe all this bullshit, like the excellent liar of a defence attorney he was, so caught up in the fictions he created that he convinced himself along with the jury.

His hook, line and sinker persuasion was aimed at proving he was a caring father doing the best for his daughter to set her up for the kind of life he thought was the good life. The kind of "good" life he had made for himself.

Kill me first, please!

Would this man ever take a breath so I could start my defence? I silently thanked the waiter for the arrival of Eric's vodka tonic. When he took a sip to lubricate and fortify, I launched into my defence.

Evidence number one being arms and legs, exposed in mixed company for the first time in a while.

I was, despite everything, highly productive (great grades, two jobs), independent, and even had a boyfriend (so what if he lived far away in Brookline, outside of Boston – that was a mere technicality).

He stared impassively at me as I talked. He didn't nod; he didn't interrupt, just sustained his performance of listening. My heart sank.

Not an encouraging sign. Nothing I was saying was moving him a fraction from his position, altering his plans for my future or his thoughts about me.

It was fortunate for me and for Eric that our dishes arrived soon afterwards because what I was itching to use the cutlery for had nothing to do with food and lots to do with giving Eric a stab of his own medicine. The salad fork looked up to the job.

Eric attacked his Dover sole like a mighty hunter. He was that charged with the thrill of his opening argument to me.

I picked away at my salmon, partly to keep the fork safely on my plate, and partly because the tiny piece of salmon, the tiny vegetables, the tiny relish of parsley and who knew what other food groups lounging artfully, made grabbing a forkful of anything impossible. You sure didn't have worry about getting fat at this restaurant.

I had to keep my mind on that, because I felt a "scenes r us" moment coming on, and had to swallow it down with the salmon tidbits. A scene would prove Eric's point about me needing to be socialized and civilized at Regent's Academy.

Another vodka tonic for lubrication, and Eric was ready for round two.

"A new environment will invigorate you," he said.

Invigorate you is what you really mean, I thought, but kept my focus on getting any food group onto my fork. He had his parlour tricks. I had mine. He wanted me to argue back, plead. Therefore, I didn't.

"A fresh new start with new people will provide you with new friendships so that you can be released from your morbid attachment to your mother and her possessions."

Ever hear of being sentimental, you big creep? I thought. That phraseology was straight from the larynx of one of his analyst consultants, who had clearly supplied Eric with talking points.

Had not a single one of them ever mentioned to him that my mourning behaviour was more the norm than Iceberg Eric's dead-and-gone style?

Admittedly, I was on the far end of the mourning spectrum. My "style" might even be considered excessive, if you consider missing someone you loved, and wanting keepsakes of that some-one around, not to torture you but to console you, excessive. For god's sake, how could I not be attached to my mother's keepsakes? They were all I had left.

"You will be better able to continue your healing work away from reminders of the past," he said, spearing a tiny roasted potato and swallowing it down whole like a snake swallowing a rodent delicacy in one gulp. He glanced briefly at my arms and then away, as if my arms embarrassed him.

I *was* an embarrassment to him, just as my dying mother had been. We spoiled the perfect pretty picture he wanted his life to be.

I fingered the brochure, preparing myself for my closing argu-ment. I liked Emerson, I liked Toronto, I liked working at John's, and even at the fertility clinic, and most of all I loved Chloe. I sup-posed I could do without what I liked, but I couldn't do without Chloe.

"Chloe spoke to Uncle Samuel. He's agreeable to having her go to boarding school with me. Leslea doesn't have to worry about the expense; Uncle Samuel is going to pay for everything."

"Leslea and I have already discussed this. We think it's best if Chloe does not join you," he said, his lips twisting. Could it be with guilt?

I really expected no argument on this. But even Ms. Smarty Pants was floored by the unexpectedness of Eric's sucker punch.

Seething with rage, I struggled to keep composed. How could I have overlooked Leslea's self-centredness? After all, how could she function without Chloe as accountant, chef, valet, confidante, personal companion and maid?

Eric's reasoning, though, was more complicated to figure out. Was it his way of twisting the knife in me, now that he had the grip on it, to get back at me? Or was it just easier to go along with what dear little sis wanted as a payback favour?

I stabbed away at my chocolate layer cake.

chapter**twenty-three**

You would think that after having been given my marching papers by Eric, I would have had trouble sleeping that night. The minute I lay down on my bed, with not one moment devoted to my usual Luke nighttime fantasies, I was dead asleep. I stayed dead asleep in my clothes until I was awoken the next morning by my father's footsteps on the stairs.

That meant only one thing – I was massively late for the extra shift I'd taken on at the last-minute request of Ms. Rainey, doing the registration for the women getting their blood work done. It was six-thirty, and I was supposed to have been at work an hour ago. The good thing about falling asleep in my clothes was that at least it saved me time getting dressed. I just brushed my teeth and hair, and then ran out, wrinkled clothes and all.

When I arrived, Mrs. Erlich, the nurse doing the blood work laced into me right in front of the patients. She went on and on about the irresponsibility of today's youth and how critical it was for the women's blood work to be done first thing, and how she'd had to do both jobs, registration and drawing of the blood. And so there were many patients still lined up, and they could blame me for the long wait.

Mrs. Erlich was notorious for not wanting to do one duty more than her shift required, sighing like a martyr if asked and then taking her bloody sweet time to do it.

All the same, she was right about the domino effect caused by my lateness. I pitied the women having their blood drawn by her; likely their arms were going to be bruised and sore tomorrow. That was my fault though too.

I apologized, took a seat at the registration desk and got through the rest of the women quickly.

As a parting shot, she said, "Is that the style? Looking like you slept in your clothes?"

"Is that the style? Drawing blood like you are Countess Dracula?" I snapped.

Some of the women pressing on their veins to staunch the blood and prevent bruising laughed, and one whistled, "You go, girl! My butcher is gentler handling his cuts of meat than this one!"

I would pay for this later, but at least I'd proved to be of some entertainment value.

On the way to the computer room I spotted Lindy in the waiting room. Crying.

Damn. Damn. Damn. That could mean only one thing. She wasn't pregnant. I hurried over, feeling sick.

Tears were streaming down her face as she tried to stop herself from crying even harder.

"Hey, Lindy," I said softly, placing my hand on her shoulder. I waited for her to catch her breath to speak.

"It didn't work . . . again," she whispered, weeping softly.

I sat in the chair next to her and wrapped an arm around her. "I'm so sorry. I'm so sorry," I repeated, not knowing what else to say. I just couldn't for the life of me trot out one of those grue-somely cheerful platitudes like "You have to have faith," and "There's always a miracle."

She shifted towards me in her seat, and the movement caused her to seize her side in pain. Lindy's stomach was as bloated out as if she was pregnant, and her ankles and feet were swollen,

"What is it? What can I do?" I asked, alarmed.

"It's my right ovary," she gasped. "The drugs made it swell up. It's so sore and it's making me throw up. I'm here to see Dr. Hollister after I have an ultrasound. If it's still enlarged, he said, I'm going to have to stay in Mount Sinai Hospital."

Double damn. The list of possible side effects with fertility drugs was as long as a giant's leg, I'd learned from the introduction package given to me by Ms. Rainey. A common one was "ovarian hyperstimulation syndrome." Sometimes the ovary that had produced this month's egg supply got enlarged from working overtime to produce so many eggs. In severe cases, the doctors had to remove it.

The nurse called Lindy in. She could barely straighten herself up to walk. I helped her over to the ultrasound room, and stood outside. She needed somebody here right now.

She came out, all freshly teary again and even more depressed. "As big as a grapefruit," she said, her voice breaking.

I then helped her walk over to Dr. Hollister's waiting area.

"I'll come visit you in the hospital tomorrow," I said.

"I don't know where I'll be," she said.

"Don't worry. I know Mount Sinai like the back of my hand," I said with a sigh.

She looked confused.

But I couldn't get into it . . . especially now when I felt two seconds away from bursting into tears myself, so I hugged her and left.

I was about to enter the computer area when the urge to cry hit me. I sped down the hallway. Near a bank of elevators, I leaned face forward against the wall, and began bawling.

For Lindy. For myself too, just as I had in the bereavement group. I felt so sad and so angry at how unfair, unjust and cruel life could be. Soon I was howling loud enough for three miserable people. And who should find me but Ms. Rainey, likely ready to tear into me for mouthing off.

"Alice, Alice," she said, lightly patting my back. "What's wrong?"

Everything. And she'd be stuck listening until the next millennium if I got started.

I sort of made a strangled sound, not turning around to look at her.

"Alice, I hope you're not crying over work. Just express your regrets for your remark and for losing your temper to Mrs. Erlich, will you?"

She'd never struck me as the tea and sympathy type, but I was wrong. I sobbed out my thanks and said I would. "It's hormones . . . PMS," I mumbled.

Hormones, what a lame lie that was. But it was all I could come up with. On this floor, the women were always weepy, weepy because of the drugs, weepy because they didn't get pregnant, weepy because they miscarried.

She handed me some Kleenex. I wiped my face, and she accompanied me to the computer area. I began typing like a fiend, throwing myself into data inputting as if it was a lifeline. And it was.

chapter**twenty-four**

t felt like eons since I'd been at Caleb's. And I wasn't in the frame of mind to show up today really, with Lindy and everything else happening.

Promises, promises, though. I'd promised Chloe that I would come for sure. She was so eager for me to see the collage she was working on, and I didn't want to disappoint her. Plus I had to do the dirty deed of telling her that criminal co-conspirators Eric and Leslea had decided it was in their own best interests for me to be exiled to Kingston, and Chloe left behind, manacled to her worthless mother.

I was still wearing yesterday's clothes, now super-wrinkled, sweaty and dust-streaked. There hadn't been enough customers to keep me distracted at Atticus's Attic so I had gone cleaning crazy – dusting, mopping, washing the windows and the filter on the air conditioner.

I heard my first howl of happiness all day. From Frederick, clearly thrilled to see me, and my sandwich. Store-bought this time. I'd stopped to get it on the way over, not wanting to disappoint him either.

I sat on the steps leading to the second floor, and fed the ham and roll to Frederick, who repaid me in big slobbery licks all over my knees, hands and chin.

"Tell Frederick to hurry up and finish the sandwich already," Chloe shouted.

"He has, and we're coming!"

I stood up and Frederick followed, his paw nails scraping my heels, exposed by my sandals. I paused by what I now called the keepsakes room.

Caleb had saved everything here. Soon he was going to make new homes for them in his shadow boxes, where they would be displayed like the dear treasures they'd once been to somebody.

Corny, yes, but there it was. Weren't we all, in some way or other, attached to some old thing? A doll. A hockey sweater. Battered copies of Nancy Drew or The Hardy Boys. Birthday and valentine cards. Love letters. Diplomas. Sports awards. A wedding dress. A baby bootie. Weren't those all personal memory machines, artifacts of our personal history?

Weren't collections at museums like the Royal Ontario Museum basically just bigger-sized displays of once personal treasures from centuries ago to the present? Goblets. Dishes. Jewellery. Tapestries. Suits of Armour. Paintings. Sculptures. Clothing. Furniture. Those all belonged to somebody once, meant something to somebody, and had a personal history before they became cultural and historical relics, *objets d'art*.

"Where are you?" Chloe shouted, which sparked a prolonged howl from Frederick. Pepped up by the ham sandwich, he was waiting for his Air Alice flight down the stairs.

I knelt and picked up Frederick. Unlike most dogs who wiggle like crazy in your arms, Frederick just found his own comfortable seating, resting his head on my shoulder, hooking his front paws into my bra thanks to the scoop neck of my T-shirt, and squeezing his bum comfortably (for him!) in my clasped hands.

"We're ready for takeoff, huh," I whispered in his left flopping ear and headed for the stairs to the basement. His head was twisting from side to side, happily taking in the room as we went down the stairs like a tourist viewing the Sistine Chapel.

"It took you long enough!" Chloe grumbled in a mock-teasing way, coming over to help Frederick deplane.

Caleb gave me a nod hello as he crouched, then patted and scratched Frederick's ears. Then, straightening, he went back to hammering a shadow box he was assembling.

Chloe grabbed my hand and pulled me over, chattering about the collage.

I didn't catch much of what she was saying, to be honest. Seeing Caleb's and Chloe's artwork made me think again about an idea I had been rolling around in my head lately, about looking into what it took to become a museum curator. At the Attic, as I'd leafed through a remaindered handbook from the J. Paul Getty Museum, I was mesmerized by the photos showing just some of their magnificent collections of antiquities, manuscripts, paintings, decorative art and drawings. How great would it be to work in a place like that! I resolved to call Parnell and ask her to meet me for coffee to discuss it.

Caleb's intermittent hammering, along with Frederick's barking at the hammering, wasn't helping either as I struggled to hear what Chloe was saying.

Through all that, I could still see how different Chloe was. Her appearance, for starters. Her hair was tied up in two messy pigtails. No makeup and she was wearing a tangerine coloured T-shirt and tan cargo shorts. Her pockets were jammed with various-sized brushes for gluing.

She looked energized but peaceful. Happy. Happy not just with her work, but happy with who she was. She didn't have to hide, disguise or run from herself. Not here at least. Her customary anxiousness for attention, approval, affection, and the fear that she would get none of the above, was absent.

"You can't see from *over there!*" Chloe said, tugging at me to stand in front of her easel.

When I got there, I understood why she emphasized the words "over there!" That was what I would have called her collage. Maybe that would have just given it away or maybe not. The title *Heart of Darkness* gave away Conrad's novella, or maybe it just opened your mind to what was there to explore.

For as long as I could remember, Chloe was always taking photos. Some of those photos were part of the nearly completed collage, along with postcard pictures, illustrations from children's picture books, magazine pictures and glued on small objects: seashells, a key chain and a rabbit-foot charm.

To me, the images captured moments when someone had gone to some "over there" place, here on earth or in their imagination, and was waiting, wanting something out of the ordinary, something maybe even miraculous to happen. Like the photo Chloe had taken of a little boy standing at a fence staring into an empty school playground. Or the one of a shadow of a person's arm reaching for the doorknob on a half-open door.

"It's awesome, Chloe!" I said.

"You really think so?" Chloe said, her voice trembling a little.

Coming over to study the collage, Caleb announced, "Fine work." "Thank you, and thank you," Chloe said, blushing slightly, and she did a little curtsey in my direction, then in Caleb's.

I could tell from his intent expression that he did believe what he had said. He wouldn't have had the time of day for someone he didn't think had talent. His work was everything to him, for good and bad, I supposed. He lived to work; his leisure activities fed his work too, according to Chloe. He read, he went to the movies, theatre, galleries; he wandered the downtown streets collecting things, and he worked. She said the phone hardly rang and when it did, it was some artsy type. You had to be an artsy type to communicate with him.

"Last week I gave Ms. Parnell the small collages I did as my summer project," Chloe continued. "A few days later she called to tell me that she was going to write me a recommendation for admission to either York University's art program or the Ontario College of Art, once I decide where I want to go after high school."

In all the excitement, Chloe had forgotten our conversation about the boarding school deal. I guess I didn't have to worry about her being upset when I told her. That was a mean and selfish thought. She needed to be here. Working with Caleb, taking Parnell's art classes, not holed up in some snob factory academy in Kingston.

Not that I was planning to go either. Now how to get from here to my "over there," wherever that place was going to be, that was the rub, as Hamlet said.

Chloe and Caleb then started poring over some objects, pictures, newspaper and poem fragments she had spread on a table next to the easel, Chloe pointing to something and discussing it, then Caleb either nodding or pointing to something else.

I was delighted for Chloe, and envious too. Of her joy in her work. Of her Zen-like ability to be in the moment. To concentrate, not to escape, but to find yourself, be yourself. What a concept!

Though I had to admit I had my moments too, and more of them lately than I'd had in the longest while. Times when I was hanging out with Chloe. That afternoon at Harbourfront with Eddie and Luke. When I was talking to Luke and writing him emails, and gabbing away about books, politics, ancient TV series, whatever with John.

Caleb and Chloe were still discussing the pile on the table, so I went to Caleb's worktable and lifted Frederick, cradling him in my arms. He rested contentedly as we both looked over the shadow box Caleb was working on.

The setting here was a train station waiting room. The back wall of the shadow box was a travel collage made of train schedules, travel ads clipped from old newspapers, ticket stubs and pages ripped from guidebooks surrounding an arched "window" with a colour illustration of the night sky. Most of the compartments were yet to be filled. There was a crystal wine glass in one, a clay pipe in another – the kind of stuff armchair travellers use to jumpstart their daydreams about voyaging somewhere.

This unfinished shadow box radiated feelings of painful longing for some escape voyage to a faraway paradise, along with this sense of melancholy and loss, for a trip that had been, or perhaps, a trip that never would be.

I wanted to say something profound, something that would tell Caleb just how much his shadow boxes meant to me when he came back to the worktable, standing beside me, but every phrase seemed stilted or pretentious, so I just said softly, "I really, really like this!"

He gave me a little smile, pleased.

Before I had gone into major coma mode I'd been about to ask Caleb if I could help with the construction of the boxes. "Can I help you out with the making of the boxes?" I said almost shyly, hoping like anything he would agree.

"If you want to," he said, scratching Frederick's head, which was bobbing with delight.

Not a ringing endorsement, but I really, really wanted to know how he made them. Not just because I was fascinated by how he did what he did, but because suddenly I wanted very much to make a shadow box to give to Lindy. I could put in some of my mother's keepsakes; maybe they would bring Lindy luck in becoming a mom. At the least, it could cheer her up.

"Can I make one of my own?"

"Plenty of wood for that," he said. "Come, I'll show you."

I followed him, carrying Frederick up the stairs to the back-yard. What I expected to see was there . . . a small shed filled with planks of pine. What took me for a loop though were the shadow boxes sitting in the high grass like garden ornaments. Caleb was so protective of his things, so why were they out here to be rained on and faded by the sun?

I put Frederick down. I guess he knew better than to do normal dog things like sniff or paw the boxes. Instead, he stretched out on the small patio, barked with bliss at the heat radiating off the stones and promptly fell asleep.

"Suntanning?" I joked, sweeping my arm out in the direction of the boxes.

He looked at me as if I'd said my joke, feeble as it was, in Croatian.

"Aren't you worried that the boxes are going to get wrecked out here?" I persisted.

He gave me this look as if I didn't know anything, and said, "That's the point, Alice."

I flinched a bit at the put-down, but I wanted so much to learn how he did what he did that I started popping out questions one after another anyhow, even if they did make him think I was a dummy when it came to art.

Since the objects that were placed in the shadow boxes were old, it wouldn't fit to put them in shadow boxes that appeared freshly made . . . even if they were. So Caleb "antiqued" them. He applied several coats of house paint to the exterior and interior of the boxes so the surface appeared old and crusty. In the winter, he baked them in the oven so the paint peeled and cracked, and in the summer he left them outside to be weathered by the sun and rain. He stained the outside with several coats of varnish, then blotted off some of the varnish with paint remover so that the boxes appeared tarnished by time in spots.

"I'm in a rush with my box," I said after he finished explaining. "I'm making the box for a friend in the hospital. She's . . ."

He blanked out immediately when I started talking about Lindy. I was annoyed with him, and myself. I should have known better.

"Thanks for telling me all this, and for letting me make a box," I said uncomfortably, and followed several paces behind as he headed for the shed to pick up some planks of pine for Lindy's shadow box.

chapter**twenty-five**

Everyone was moving on with his or her life, except for me, stuck in limbo land. Pity party declaration, but true all the same.

Eric was moving into a brand new condo and was, I bet, calculating the socially acceptable amount of time that had to pass before he could "out" former partner-in-adultery Suzette Andrews as more than someone he'd just begun dating.

Leslea was "formally" living with Len, who'd given up his apartment and moved himself and the little he owned in. Well, to be precise, he was living with and off her (and, by proxy, Uncle Samuel). Her prop business had taken off this summer (thanks to the tons of American TV movies and features being filmed in Toronto) and she'd sold six pricey Forest Hill houses. It was *only* because the market was hot. Frederick could have sold those homes and made a killing in commissions.

Chloe was in the best shape I'd ever seen. She had finally found something she loved to do, and was turning out to be good at it. Good enough even maybe to make it her life's work. All the stuff she used to obsess about – her weight, Kevin – she didn't seem to think much about anymore.

I hadn't brought up Regent's Academy yet. I didn't want to rain on her parade – the unselfish motivation. Also, because I was being a big baby and was feeling hurt and left out. All the time I thought she couldn't cope without me, and actually, it was the reverse. Get over yourself, girl! And lastly, because I was waiting for a plan to descend on my brain to lift me out of limbo land. It hadn't arrived yet though.

Even Luke was moving on. He'd been accepted at Amherst College. He'd decided to enrol part-time in the fall semester so he could work on John Kerry's presidential campaign.

Now that I was on a major self-pity, poor-me roll, why didn't I just mention every single person I barely knew. Four-year-old Farley, who lived on the end of the street, was moving on from daycare to junior kindergarten.

Okay I was "moving on" too, technically. I was being moved out by Eric.

Stop it! I ordered myself. Right now, I needed concentration. Twice already I'd hammered my fingers instead of a nail, and earlier I'd almost sawed Caleb's worktable along with the plank of pine I'd been cutting.

I stared down again at the diagram of the box, keeping in mind which piece of wood went where. I looked up. At the far end of the table, Caleb was absorbed in reworking the wallpaper in his travel shadow box. Chloe was standing in front of her easel, sheets in one hand, glue brush in the other. Not that I could move far (how symbolic!) even if I had wanted to disturb them. Frederick was fast sleep, on my feet.

I had to get past my thing about it being perfect. It didn't need to be perfect, because my shadow box was a display box for some of my mother's keepsakes. All I cared about was making the box as sturdy and attractive as I was capable of making it. It wasn't like one of Caleb's boxes where the shelves and the spacing had to be just so because he was creating a setting for the objects to play off each other. His was art. Mine, mementoes. His, though, were mementoes, in their way. Everything he did was. You could say that his collages and shadow boxes were collections of other people's mementoes, transformed through the magic wand of art into mementoes of his experiences, musings and fantasies, as with the shadow box on travel he was working on now.

A few were, in fact, just mementoes. Hung on the wall beside the staircase leading to the second floor were collages devoted to Artie, made of Artie's drawings, baseball cards, homemade birthday cards, cardboard box pictures of train sets (Artie had loved model trains; there was a photo of Artie sitting beside one nearly the size of the whole living room) and pages torn from Artie's favourite children's books.

Were others, besides Caleb and Chloe, as attached to their loved ones' things as I was? That wasn't a question I could go around asking people.

So I had been more grateful than Caleb would ever realize when he'd given me a little lecture on mementoes after I'd revealed to him what I was putting in my box.

The Victorians were big on keepsakes, obsessed about them, said Caleb, quoting a popular nineteenth-century proverb about mementoes: "When you see this, remember me."

They'd woven brooches and rope necklaces out of the hair of their dead loved ones, and preserved strands in lockets. They'd sewn memory quilts using the clothing of the dead, stitched mourning samplers with the name, favourite saying and date of death of the ones they'd lost, embroidered mourning pictures out of silk, portraying the deceased's favourite scenes and personalized old photographs with fabric, flowers, embroidery and knick-knacks belonging to the person who had died.

He'd shown me a museum catalogue of an exhibition devoted to these embellished family photos from the late nineteenth-century to nowadays. Okay, some of these mini-shrines were undeniably a tad over the top in their display of devotion, but that sure beat people who erased their loved ones from their lives, as if they had never lived.

For me, my mother's things were like genies, bringing her back to life in my memory. In a box underneath the table were a few of my mother's keepsakes that I was going to put in the shadow box. They were pieces I could remember helping her select at flea and antique markets. I had chosen them for that reason, and also because they were all tokens of family and home that I hoped would comfort Lindy. A tiny china vase. A silver dinner bell. A straw figure of a mother standing embracing two children. A miniature china table with four chairs. A glass paperweight with a cottage and garden inside it. A glass dove.

I found it peaceful working on the box. Thinking of my mother as I arranged her collectibles, I was sad, missing her like anything, but yet peaceful . . . in that moment.

I hoped that Lindy would like this box of mementoes. That was silly. She would, just for the thought of it, even if it was less than perfect.

After leaving Caleb's, I went to visit Lindy at Mount Sinai. She was asleep. From the way her older sisters were sprawled in the chairs on either side of her bed, looking as if they'd been watching over Lindy all day, I knew the news wasn't good.

One of her sisters quietly got out of her chair and came over to me, and in a soft voice introduced herself as Elaine, Lindy's oldest sister, and then introduced me to Caitlin, the middle sister.

Elaine told me that Dr. Hollister had ended up doing surgery on Lindy and removing the swollen ovary.

"For me?" Lindy said, groggily, opening her eyes and struggling to shift into sitting position.

I had brought Lindy a blooming hot pink azalea plant. I hated cut flowers in a hospital. A plant, at least, would live.

"You mentioned once when we talked about botanical gardens that you liked azaleas," I said, with shrug.

"That's so kind of you!" she said, clearly making an effort to sound strong and as if everything was okay. "Good thing we head-butted each other, huh?"

"You bet!" I said, working to sound livelier.

"You want something to eat or drink?" Lindy asked. "Not hospital food," she giggled. "My nightstand is filled with goodies – chocolates, candies, cookies, drinks, applesauce, puddings. I guess everyone thinks I'm too skinny, huh?"

Elaine and Caitlin snickered.

"I guess they don't think I'm too skinny," she said. "They think the hospital food sucks."

My mother's hospital nightstand had been filled with goodies for the same reason. I used to bring my mom corned-beef sandwiches and chicken noodle soup from the Druxy's deli across the street from the hospital.

Seeing Lindy was making me remember the times I'd visited my mom in the hospital. No matter what surgery she'd gone through, she was like Lindy, being positive, behaving as if it was no big deal.

"I'm making you something," I said, breathing in and out to control myself.

"You'd better not be encroaching on Lindy's knitting territory," Elaine joked. "Caitlin and I gave up knitting because Lindy puts anything we knit to shame. We cower and bow before her knitting majesty."

Caitlin got up out of her chair, and she and Elaine both bowed to Lindy. "Oh ye of the mastery of the knitting needles, please no more scarves!"

Lindy laughed, then doubled over. Elaine and Caitlin rushed to her bedside.

"Just forgot that you need stomach muscles that aren't stitched and sore to laugh," she said, gasping. "Do I get a hint of what you're making?"

"No hints, please!" Caitlin said. "Lindy can sniff out what gift she is getting like Miss Marple. Surprise her. We've been trying for years. Somebody's gotta succeed!"

I tried to smile. "No hints then! Just a delivery date. A week from now."

I didn't stay much longer. Not just because I didn't want to wear Lindy out, but because I felt close to breaking down. I could see my mother everywhere in the hospital.

chapter**twenty-six**

L uke's decision to attend college part-time had inspired me with a plan of my own. I was all geared up by its excellence. I would rent an apartment, work, and go to school part-time. So what if it took me longer to finish high school?

I was just about to give the plan its first rollout with Parnell, whom I was meeting in a Second Cup coffee shop near Emerson. At the counter I was about to order a dark roast coffee, then changed my mind. I was too buzzed as it was without the extra caffeine charge; instead I ordered a chamomile tea. Two teas later, Parnell arrived. She grinned as she came towards me.

I couldn't decide which of my excellent plans to discuss first, but Parnell beat me to the punch, immediately launching into how I would go about becoming a curator.

"I knew I'd get you back in my class, my missing-in-action student," Parnell said, startling me.

"How'd you know?" I asked.

"You were truly 'engaged.'" she said, and smiled at me. My questions, answers and essays, though, we both laughingly agreed, not my artwork, exposed just how engaged I was by art.

Parnell told me that the University of Toronto had a solid

undergraduate program leading to B.A. in Fine Arts History. I would need to learn another language other than French, either German or Italian. It would help me, both to find out if this was what I wanted and to gain admission, if I interned at the Art Gallery of Ontario or the Royal Ontario Museum. Since it was so competitive to be admitted to the program, Parnell insisted that I would need more than high grades; I would need to have several recommendations from museum curators.

She was excited to have me in her class next year, and to set up an internship for me as an independent study.

One excellent plan down, I plunged into my other plan about working while attending Emerson part-time, and completing the rest of my high school credits at night a a neighbouring community college. Plunged was the right word, because my heart did exactly that as I watched Parnell's face. Her expression was sympathetic as I gave her a brief outline of my situation at home and my relationship with my father. But she was also dismayed.

"You don't know what it is like to be without money, really without money. To be constantly worrying about food money, rent money, unexpected expenses money," she said. Obviously, she did. "If you think you can work, continue to have high grades, high enough for the program and maybe even a scholarship, and then throw an internship into the mix, you are fooling yourself. Even you, Alice, workhorse that you are, won't be able to handle that. And who do you think will be hurt most by this? Your father? Wrong. It's you. Get real, Alice!"

There was nothing she said that wasn't right and wasn't true, though it wasn't easy to take in, and even harder to accept.

The truth was I didn't accept it. After leaving Parnell, I walked for a while, going over in my head the next rollout to Luke when I got home, trying to take into account what Parnell had said.

If that reality check hadn't been enough, Luke gave me another after listening to me, now nervously stuttering through my plan. It would be good for me to live without the daily conflict, he said, but I should do it in a way that worked for me. And that meant facing my father and talking things out. That meant staying in some kind of truce arrangement, or moving out with his support, at least money wise.

"Alice, my girl," Luke said.

I relaxed at the sound of affection in his voice, worried that he now considered me naïve, even stupid, and that I might have turned him off.

"Yes, Lukey," I teased, calling him by the nickname he'd told me only his gran still used.

"You will think it over carefully," he said.

"I will," I said.

"And thanks for the photo. It took you long enough to send it. My friends were beginning to think I had made you up. So now you exist. Not just in my heart," he said, assuming the voice of a bad actor laying it on thick in an attempt, and a failed one at that, to sound sincere. "But on my bulletin board too. Nice picture by the way. You're attractive, girl!"

"Yeah, yeah," I grumbled, pleased all the same. Chloe had taken a picture of me sitting on Caleb's porch, wearing shorts and a t-shirt, with Frederick resting his head on my knee, gazing up at me with adoration . . . or was that just anticipation of another sandwich? Only Frederick knew.

I'd finally felt I looked half decent, and I wasn't about to send Luke a photo of me covered up burka-style. "And thanks for the advice, again," I said. "You're wise beyond your years, you know."

"It's me years that have made me wise," he said, now assuming a broad Irish accent, and then he sighed. "Enough to drive me to the priesthood, if I was so inclined."

"As far as I can tell, it's like *so* the opposite."

That made him laugh.

"You won't get an argument on that, but you will if you don't think over what I just said, okay?"

"Right, right," I said, conscious that what Parnell and Luke said to me had staying power . . . more staying power than I was comfortable with.

"Keep me informed."

"Every excruciating detail."

"Can't wait," he said, and hung up.

All the same, the urge to move was still more gripping than either Parnell's or Luke's commonsense solutions. Right now, moving felt like the only way.

I needed a time-out from our Punch and Judy show. Who knew if it affected Eric, or whether it all rolled off him just like the ranting of his clients? It affected me; I spent way too much energy and emotion on him. And I wanted to be freed from that.

What really felt strange about all this was that I hadn't talked it through first with Chloe. I felt both guilty, disloyal somehow, and yet weirdly good that there were other people who cared about me, and whom I cared about, people I could trust and rely on. I felt like I was finally crawling out of that solitary confinement bunker I'd been holed up in during my mother's last year and since her death.

After hanging up with Luke, I called Chloe and arranged to see her to bring her up to speed. It wasn't something I wanted to blurt out to her on the phone.

Next on my agenda would be to go through the classified ads for furnished basement apartments and rooms – they were what I could barely afford.

At least I was packed to go, I thought, as I stretched in bed, ready to get up early this morning even though I could have slept in for once because I had no work to go to until later in the day.

My bedroom was as stripped down and impersonal as a motel room. My mother's keepsakes had been gone for weeks, and my stuff – clothing, books, DVDs, videos, TV, DVD-VCR player – was packed and coded, ready to come with me, wherever I was going.

The only things unpacked were my laptop computer and printer on my desk, where I was headed to check out the ads in *The Toronto Star* after showering and grabbing something for breakfast.

I'd researched the refund policy at Regent's Academy, so I could break my news to Eric without being guilt-tripped about the loss of the tuition deposit.

I knew I would hate it there. I hated everything the school stood for. And I didn't intend to waste the next year hating the school, and Eric for sending me there. I too, finally, finally wanted to move on. Move. I certainly had that word on the brain.

After scrolling through columns and columns of ads for furnished apartments way beyond my budget, I found a couple, wondering what the places looked like as I printed them out . Liveable, I hoped.

My father had said, reassuringly he assumed, that by the time I came back for the Thanksgiving break in October, my new bedroom would be ready for me. Everything would be new, newer, newest. Our furniture was to be sold in a huge contents sale arranged by Heidi, the real estate agent. If my father had done otherwise, that would have been the shocker.

My response to this "news" was that it would be a show bedroom, to show off to my father's cronies that he was, despite all the evidence to the contrary, a dedicated dad. With his cronies, it would likely work. But that wasn't my problem; finding a place was.

Having printed five ads, I took a breather by clicking through some websites recommended by Luke. Though the war-mongering policies of George W. Bush were no laughing matter, the dictionary-sized collection of his "Bushisms" – the best comically, the worst linguistically of Bush's mangling, misspeaking, mispronouncing of words and sentences – was.

I was giggling over an especially awful traffic accident of words when my father came into my bedroom, after warning me first by knocking on the door frame, drawn probably by the rare sound of me laughing.

"What's so funny?" he asked, and I pointed to two of the latest "Bushisms."

He read them out loud.

"'Our enemies are innovative and resourceful, and so are we. They never stop thinking about new ways to harm our country and neither do we.'

'I promise you I will listen to what has been said here, even though I wasn't here.'"

He grimaced. "'Moron' doesn't do him justice."

"I'm hoping Senator Kerry will win in November. A friend of mine is working on his campaign," I said. Then it hit me; I was having a conversation with my father, not a confrontation, and in my unlocked bedroom. And I had revealed something personal to him.

I thought of what Luke kept saying to me: "Just start talking to him, will you, chit-chat, small talk, whatever."

"Luke Malone, he lives in Brookline. Chloe and I, we met him at Harbourfront in July when he was visiting Toronto. We've been talking on the phone and emailing since then."

He looked pleased, a highly unusual phenomenon when it came to me. I saw his eyes quickly scan my arms and legs, which were in full view since I was wearing a tank top and shorts. There were still stripes of reddish scars, but they were getting fainter and fainter.

"I totally stopped," I said quietly.

"Terrific," he said back, then gave me another questioning look as if he wanted to know what had made me stop.

The reasons were way too complicated to say; especially to someone I didn't trust.

So I just said, "Willpower."

"Which you have in abundance," he replied dryly.

Enough said there – his willpower versus my willpower; the source of many a fight between the two of us.

He straightened up. He was dressed to go out, his casual expensive look, as opposed to his professional expensive look. Likely going off to meet Suzette for brunch.

I made a fast prayer that he wouldn't spoil this one rare decent moment between us by asking me again to meet her. My stomach knotted at the thought, and I started to get worked up.

He didn't. Instead, he glanced around, and then noticed the shadow box I'd made for Lindy on my dresser. I was going tomorrow to the hospital to give it to her. He walked over to the dresser and checked it out. "I see Chloe isn't the only one influenced by Caleb Hamilton."

"It's a shadow box, but not a real shadow box, more a display case . . ."

He squinted to read the metal nameplate I'd placed on the bottom. "Memory Genie 1."

"These are your mother's things," he said.

"I made the box for Lindy. I met her at the fertility clinic. She's been trying to get pregnant and the drugs, they wrecked one of her

167

ovaries, and the doctor had to take it out. It's a gift for her, to help cheer her up."

"That's thoughtful of you, Alice," he said, giving me another pleased look that said louder than words that I was inching closer to his vision of a "normal" teenager.

He came back over to me, and placing his hand on my head, rubbed my hair. "It'll do the trick."

I resisted the urge to shift away.

He's trying to be friendly, one part of me said. He's gloating because everything is going according to *his* plans, another part of me said. He's trying to comfort you about Lindy, yet another part of me said. What are you thinking – he's just manipulating you, playing you like he plays everyone, one more part piped in.

Was he doing that with me now? Or, giving him the benefit of the doubt big-time, was he a more complicated jumble of emotions and impulses than I had ever chosen to see or understand?

He sniffed. "Not to be insulting, Alice, but I do smell the faint odour of a dog about you."

Acknowledging all the really needling or insulting ways he could have phrased that and hadn't, I relaxed my shoulders, and gestured at the T-shirt and jean shorts lying on the chair nearby. "That's odour de Frederick. Caleb Hamilton's basset hound. I carry him around when I'm there. I noticed he needed a bath. I hosed him down in the backyard, soaped him up and hosed him down again. Now that he smells like Dove shampoo and conditioner, he won't come near me."

"He'll forget soon enough," Eric said.

At that I stiffened, and he took his hand off my head. That was Eric's mantra, his philosophy of life and death in a nutshell.

"So what are your plans for the day?" he asked after an awkward pause.

"I'm going to Atticus's. John's working on his fall catalogue, and I said I would do the proofreading."

"You're not going to take any time off before school?" he asked. I shook my head.

"If you need money, you know you can always ask me," he said.

"Thanks, but I enjoy working," I added, my voice rising. "What else is there to do? Hang out at Hazelton Lanes. Pick out a Prada purse at their Bloor Street boutique. Then go down the block and buy hundreds of dollars worth of overpriced yoga wear for when I need to stretch to reach my wallet to take out a parental credit card. After that, cruise over to HMV, buy some DVDs and CDs, then to the smoke shop, lie about my age and get a pack of smokes and sit smoking in Queen's Park. And in the evening head out to some party at someone's house whose parents are out of town."

He shook his head. "God, is that really what your friends from Emerson do?"

And what do you think my new schoolmates at Regent's Academy would be doing differently? Differently, they'd be looking for Louis Vuitton luggage for their trip to Kingston.

"The ones with rich parents . . ." I left the rest unsaid.

He had the good sense not to continue that strain of our conversation, wearing four hundred plus dollar Bruno Magli loafers.

His cell phone rang, and he answered, talking softly and rapidly. No doubt he was placating Suzette, who was probably whining about why he hadn't shown up yet.

"Have to go." He paused, his expression back to his practiced poker face. "It will be a fresh start for you, you'll see . . ."

I tensed. Here it was, the speech he'd come in to give me.

"You'll make new friends, get involved in more social activities. You'll be so busy you won't have time to . . ."

Well, at least our conversation had had some effect on him. He didn't have the guts to trot out the old standby I'd been hearing ad nauseam for months . . . like brood on the past.

I just stared at him, and then swivelled around and began furiously typing an email to no one until I heard him leave, then I pressed the backspace key, and held on until everything was deleted.

chapter**twenty-seven**

Give me that hammer!" Chloe screeched.

Before I could even pass the hammer, Chloe snatched it out of my hand. With pulverizing force she hammered in the exposed nails I'd been tapping into the sides of the shadow box I was helping Caleb construct.

I had just finished telling her how Eric and Leslea had decided it was best for me to go to Regent's Academy alone, and Chloe to remain at Emerson. It had taken Chloe all of a nanosecond to figure out that Leslea wasn't willing to give up Chloe's "services."

"That bitch!" Chloe swung the hammer so furiously that for a second I feared that she was going to send the whole shadow box flying across the room.

"She can go stick her accounting and everything else I do for her!"

Chloe was swinging the hammer back and forth like a swordsman readying to slice up an opponent.

"I'll get my dad to pay the tuition directly to the academy. He'll do it!"

"Give me the hammer back!" I said, stretching to grab it, but missing.

Chloe was too fired up with rage to listen to me. I went on anyway.

"I know your dad would. But I'm not going. I'm going to move out."

"I'll move out with you then! Screw her!" Chloe took another lumberjack swing at the shadow box. Bang! Bang!

The nails would never come loose in this box, if it survived the hammering.

"Chloe, the noise! I can't think!" Caleb said, loudly for him. He usually spoke in a raspy voice, not much above a whisper, as if he was guarding his words.

I glanced over at him. He was standing in front of an easel working on a collage not ten feet away. If he were inclined to listen, he would have heard everything.

"Sorry," Chloe muttered, and looked over at Caleb, giving me the opportunity finally to snatch that damn lethal weapon out of her hands.

"You can't move out! At least not now," I hissed. "There's going to be enough drama when I spring it on Eric. Let me settle in, see how it goes and then, if you want, you know I'd love it."

Shaking with rage, Chloe took several deep breaths to calm down.

For sure (and with too much past history as evidence) the Levitt side of our gene pool brought out the worst traits in Chloe and I. Rage, spite, defiance – all of which were more damaging to us than to Eric and Leslea.

That was why I could mutter "serenity now!" until the cows jumped over the moon, and yet stay as fuming mad as Mr. Costanza. The trick, which I had yet to learn, but was working on, was not to get sucked in.

I watched how John never lost his cool and dignity, even when dealing with the biggest horse's ass of a customer who was treating him like some lackey. He just didn't get sucked into their mael-strom of bad behaviour. Neither did Parnell, who never lost her cool and dignity with even the most piggy student.

Of course they didn't have to live with *agents provocateurs* 24/7 as Chloe and I did, though in my case not for much longer. At just the thought, I got edgy, knowing I would soon be facing the mother-lode of conflict when I faced Eric.

"I'll help you look for the apartment, and with rent money too," Chloe said. "I have money from my dad saved up."

"Thanks."

Hammer tightly in hand, I tapped in the rest of the nails, telling Chloe I was going to ask Elizabeth Rainey and John to keep me on.

I was also going to ask for John's assistance in finding an apart-ment. It seemed as if he and Eileen had moved around a lot, and would know the ins and outs. Not that I didn't want Chloe with me, but she and I knew zero about renting a place. When I had narrowed down my choices, I'd get Chloe's say on the final selection.

Chloe stayed by my side while I continued hammering away at the shadow box. She was clearly too agitated to focus on the col-lage she was working on, even after I told her about my talk with Parnell, and that we both were both going to be in the art field.

And I was as glad as ever to have her with me.

chapter**twenty-eight**

I knocked on the door-frame of John's tiny office at the back of the store. He was seated at his desk, scribbling on a yellow legal pad.

"Just writing the ad for your and Randy's replacements for the fall, now that you both are deserting me to return to school. Want to reconsider?" he asked teasingly.

"Actually I do," I said. "I was hoping you would keep me on."

He looked momentarily delighted, then his expression turned sober, as if he suspected that there was more behind my request. "You know I'm ready to dance a jig, if I knew how, but going to school and working evenings and the weekends is brutal, unless you really have to."

"I really have to," I whispered, suddenly feeling snowed under.

"Sit," he ordered, and I plopped down in the chair in front of his desk, and gave him an abbreviated account of just why I had to.

He listened intently, nodding as I spoke, his face filling with emotion. There was understanding, and something else, as if my story had hit a raw nerve.

When I finished, he got up and came over, rested his hands on my shoulders and gave me a supportive squeeze. "You've never met

Eileen. I'm meeting her for dinner at Le Bistro. Join us, please. She is a good sounding board. You should know that from my stories."

I wavered, feeling oddly timid about meeting her. Maybe I would be imposing. "Another time?"

"Nope, tonight's the night," he said. "She's been after me to meet you anyway. So, to the moon, Alaace, until eight, okay?"

"Okay!"

Just before eight, when all the customers had left, I took a Swiffer cloth and dusted myself down, removing all the dust and dirt stuck to my skirt and shirt. Then I went over the window where, in the hazy reflection, I brushed my hair and applied some lip gloss, and hoped I looked presentable, as my mother always jokingly said about herself. My mother. I sighed.

"Alaace, ready to go?" John called out.

"Be there in a minute!"

We got to Le Bistro before Eileen, and took a table at the back. I continued to feel tense about meeting her, but John ignored that, telling me about a private collection that was up for sale, rumoured to have pristine first editions of classic early twentieth-century American fiction.

"Come with me. You can be my amanuensis. Please save me from the strain of having to decipher my undecipherable handwriting!"

"I'd like that a lot," I said, so touched I couldn't meet his gaze for a second. When I looked up, Eileen had arrived.

"Johnny," she said warmly, then leaned over and kissed him. "And the other woman! We meet at last. It's Alice this, and Alice that. Johnny doesn't stop talking about you."

For a split second, I thought she might be jealous or resentful, but then she swooped over, grasped both my hands and held on tight. John must have already filled her in.

Eileen released my hands and sat in the chair next to John, resting against him. She was tall, taller than John was, even without her wedged sandals, with greying reddish hair in a loose topknot, her face freckled and clearly un-Botoxed. She was dressed casually in a sleeveless white linen shirt and cropped khaki pants.

"So Johnny's going to help you find a place to live. Well, you've come to the right pair, hasn't she?" She gave a self-mocking laugh. "We've moved so often, though, hallelujah, not in the last five years, that when I see a cardboard box I automatically assess its packing potential. Liquor boxes – sturdy cardboard, excellent for books, china and glassware. Food store boxes – flimsier cardboard, appropriate only for clothing and bedding. I could go on, but I see from Johnny's shudder that he'd like me to stop pronto."

"You bet!"

Throughout the dinner I watched them as they affectionately ragged each other. It was nice, and sad too, as inevitably I compared them to my mother and father.

I wondered why they hadn't had children. A choice, or a choice made for them? Eileen was currently a principal at a downtown middle school. Did she get her maternal fix there? Perhaps that was why she was happy that John had someone to share his interests.

"Johnny, when you go with Alice to look for a place, if you find one, don't forget you will have to guarantee it. Alice can't sign a lease. She's going to need a guarantor."

"Right, right."

I flushed. Duh, I was too young to sign a lease. A bolt of fear ran through me. I thought I had all the angles covered. Wrong again.

And what did Eileen mean by "if?" What was out there? They knew from experience. I didn't clearly, living in my privileged cocoon.

Yet I desperately wanted to move out. I felt I had no alternative. Still, how could I put the burden of guaranteeing my rent on John and Eileen? That was if I could even find a place.

Eileen stretched her arms across the table, and rested her hands on mine. "Don't worry about it, Alice. We know you won't be fleeing the country."

Pretending to twirl the ends of an imaginary super-sized moustache like some silent movie villain, John cackled, "You'll be trapped in the attic!"

Overwhelmed by their kindness, I had to clear my throat before I could thank them. Then I said, "To the moon."

"To the moon, Alaace!" John said, lifting his beer stein. Eileen raised hers, and I, my glass of Coke, and we clinked our glasses.

chapter**twenty-nine**

I could recognize only three women in the waiting room. I didn't know if that was a positive sign that the others' IVF procedures had been successful and they'd gotten pregnant or if, like Lindy, they'd stopped trying . . . for the time being or permanently.

Lindy. I was wearing three of the beaded bracelets she'd made for me. She'd given them to me several days ago when I'd visited her at Mount Sinai to deliver the shadow box. She wasn't much of a reader so as she watched TV to pass the days (I knew how the hours felt like they were passing in slow motion when you were in the hospital) she made beaded jewellery for her sisters, her nieces and her friends, now including me. Elaine had been there and said I should be thankful it was summer because otherwise I would have received something knitted. Lindy was trying her best to be upbeat, so Elaine and I had played along. They'd oohed and aahed over the shadow box as I had over the beaded bracelets, which were intricately beautiful and meticulously made.

Then Don had popped in, driving in from Oakville on his lunch hour – which he'd kidded was going to be one heck of an extended lunch hour. But he'd told his boss that he'd make up the hours in the evening.

He seemed sweet and kind of shy, awkwardly hugging Lindy like he was afraid of hurting her, then lovingly brushing her hair out of her eyes. Noticing the shadow box, he'd immediately understood that the keepsakes in it had belonged to my mother. His mother was also a collector, he'd told me.

When he'd announced he was going across the street to Druxy's to buy lunch for them all, I'd told him about the food court in the College Park office complex, assuming by this point that, as tasty as Druxy's corned beef sandwiches were, Lindy and her family must be getting tired of eating them.

On the walk over, Don had told me Lindy wasn't supposed to lift anything the least bit heavy for more than six weeks. That would keep her off work at Dominion unless the management let her work just as a cashier. I hoped they would because sitting by herself in her house, with all that free time to think, was a topnotch recipe for depression and misery.

Just look how much I brooded, and I worked all the time I could manage, I thought, recalling that conversation with Don and how much I liked him immediately, just as I had Lindy, as I went downstairs to the cafeteria on the ground floor to pick up coffees for us data entry clerks.

The patient files were piling up because there was only half the number of regulars, the rest gone on vacation. As fast as we all inputted we couldn't make headway through the huge piles. Thus it was my turn for the coffee run to keep us from falling asleep on the keyboards.

I returned with the coffees and Kristy, a nursing student working at the computer station next to mine, said, "Someone's here to see. She's in the waiting room."

Lindy must have come over to say goodbye. I looked all around and didn't see her though. As I was about to go back, I saw Chloe coming out of one of the washrooms.

Even at a distance, I could see she was in rough shape.

"Hey Chloe!" I called, waving my arm as I hurried in her direction.

Everything had seemed to be going well for Chloe this summer. Deservedly and long overdue. I hated to see her looking like this again. "You had a run-in with Kevin?" I asked.

She shrugged, and then she looked down at the beige berber carpeting.

It did have something to do with Kevin. I thought she was over him; she seemed over him, but maybe not. Perhaps she'd bumped into him on the street with his latest hookup and that had upset her.

"I've got to talk to you. In private," she said, her voice rising in pitch.

An examining room to the left was empty, though probably not for long. I gestured at it and Chloe went inside and I followed.

The second I closed the door, she said, "I'm pregnant. I took a home pregnancy test and it's positive. "

Before I could come up with some reassuring denial like that she was on the pill and Kevin used condoms, and therefore it was impossible, I flashed back on the lecture I had given her after she'd said she'd had unprotected sex with Kevin. But there was still the pill.

"I skipped days taking the pill. I forgot," she blurted out, gulping loudly. "I can't go to my mother's gynie. He'll tell her. So I came here. I can get tested here, can't I?"

This wasn't the moment to say she was going to have to tell her mother if the home test proved to be accurate. Or to say, fertility clinic was a euphemism for infertility clinic and the gynies practicing here only saw women who couldn't get pregnant.

"Wait here," I said.

I stepped out, rubbed my forehead and glanced around as if somehow a solution would pop up. Joan Lansing, one of the friendlier nurses, was bringing a woman over to the examining room Chloe was in.

"Joan, can I please speak to you . . . please!" My tone likely screamed crisis, so, without asking why, Joan asked the woman to take a seat for a minute. I huddled with Joan in a corner, coughing with nerves as I related Chloe's situation.

"She has to be tested for STDs, and HIV too. Tell her that, it's standard," Joan said, telling me to hold tight as she went towards the reception area, made a call and came back.

"Tomorrow at 4:30. I got Dr. Benedict to squeeze her in. I'm guessing Chloe is a month or more along and that doesn't leave her with much of a window of opportunity for an abortion, if that's her choice."

The last time I'd heard that phrase had been when my mother's surgeon had told her she'd missed the "window of opportunity" for amputation – her death sentence.

"There's no need to be so stressed," Joan said with a sigh. "Chloe's not the first teen and she's not going to be the last. Things have their way of working out. You'll see."

I nodded, embarrassed that I had neglected to thank her. I promptly did, though in a distracted way, too agitated to speak clearly.

What a mess. Abortion. I didn't want to think about that even before finding out for sure if Chloe was pregnant. Though she likely was, otherwise the manufacturers of those home pregnancy tests would be out of business.

I went back to the examining room to tell Chloe. What would she do? What should she do? What a grim ironic joke this was. Chloe was probably the only woman in a radius of who knew how many meters who was weeping over getting pregnant, instead of weeping because she hadn't.

chapter**thirty**

here was one *tiny* good thing about the waiting alcoves in those St. Clair Avenue mansions converted into psychiatric holding pens, and that was their magazine selection. I missed going through *The New Yorker* and slicing out its Roz Chast cartoons, and skimming *Time* and *Newsweek*.

The anxiously happy or just plain anxious boyfriends and hubbies alongside me were as uninterested as I was by the magazine selection in the gynie waiting area. *Pregnancy, Baby Talk, Parenting, Chatelaine, Flare, Family Fun.* Just like my restless male counterparts, I gave them a pass.

As I waited for Chloe, now being examined by Dr. Benedict, I had already counted up the number of the tiles in the ceiling, men in the waiting area, lighting fixtures, chairs, filing cabinets, and if I wasn't called in soon, I would be down on my hands and knees counting the fibres in the berber carpeting.

I had never been on this side of the floor. The fertility clinic was at the far right of the floor, and the gynies seeing women without fertility problems on the far left, with the labs in the middle.

What was taking so long? Though in some ways, I was almost relieved it was taking so long. That gave me time to come up with some response to Chloe's news. Unless, of course, there was a miracle occurring, and Chloe was being told she wasn't pregnant.

And if she was? She was going to ask for my advice. And what was I going to say? It wasn't going to be so easy anymore to say have an abortion, even though I was pro-choice. After meeting all those women wanting so badly to have babies, and becoming friends with Lindy, my feelings about abortion had changed.

I'd been more matter-of-fact about it before, but not anymore. Abortion should be a last resort choice. Not nonchalantly selected and approached like a form of dental floss to remove food stuck between your teeth. I knew a couple of girls at Emerson who'd had two abortions already by age seventeen.

So where did that leave me with my so-called advice for Chloe? Up shit's creek, that's where. At seventeen, it was a no-brainer that Chloe was too young to have a baby.

What would happen if Chloe decided to have the baby? How would she continue at school? The razzing would be unbearable once she started to show. And how would she be able to deal with school, her artwork and taking care of a baby?

But what if you only got one chance to have a baby, and this was it? And what about the loss of a wonderful boy or girl? Okay, realistically she could give birth to a Jeffrey Dahmer, serial killer and cannibal, as much as she could to a saintly, self-sacrificing Florence Nightingale, but what expectant mother and prospective aunt weren't rosy about the character and future of the baby about to be born?

"Alice Levitt!"

I leapt up.

It was Dr. Benedict's receptionist. "The doctor is ready to see you."

When I entered the examining room, Chloe was zipping up her skirt. Dr. Benedict stuck out her hand and introduced herself with vigorous self-confidence, "Hello, I'm Dr. Benedict."

Vigorous self-confidence from medical professionals always depressed me. It wasn't that I wanted them to be paralyzed by doubt, shaken by uncertainty (or secret drug use), but some acknowledgement of good old human fallibility would be helpful for a change. Jeez, I hoped she wasn't another one of those super-efficient garage mechanic types who treated patients as if they were cars needing tune-ups and replacement parts, and not human bodies, not so straightforwardly, bloodlessly or, unfortunately, always repairable.

I shook her hand. "I'm Alice Levitt, Chloe's cousin."

Dr. Benedict was young, early thirties I guessed, with highlighted blond hair, rectangular copper-coloured glasses. She was short, slim and wearing a crème sheath with a strand of pearls peeking out from under her lab coat.

"Chloe's pregnant. Nearly two months I suspect, but I will know for sure after the blood work comes back. That leaves us a month for a first trimester abortion."

Abortion in the first trimester, up to eleven weeks, she explained, involved a less invasive technique called vacuum aspiration; while a second trimester, up to twenty weeks, was performed with a more complicated surgical procedure called a dilation and evacuation.

My heart skipped, though why I was surprised was a surprise. Stupid, faint hope had crashed and burned once again.

"I don't want an abortion. I want to have the baby," Chloe said defiantly.

Dr. Benedict just gave a big exasperated sigh, and then looked over at me as if she expected me to be the sane, reasonable one to make clear the so-called facts of life to Chloe. They must have been having this "discussion" while I'd been doing my inventory of the waiting area.

I glanced over at Chloe. She was dressed as if she was meeting

Kevin instead of a gynie. She had on a cropped V-neck crimson T-shirt, a pleated white miniskirt, wedged flip-flops and lots of makeup.

Not, by appearance, the picture of ready-for-prime-time motherhood – especially to someone like Benedict. But what did she know?

Leslea had looked the part, and look what kind of nonparent she had turned out to be. I'd seen three-year-olds handle their Barbies with more tenderness.

I didn't know whether Chloe should have the baby or an abortion. I did know that she had lots of potential to become a good mother. She'd been so caring with my mother, feeding her, washing her, diapering her, giving her meds, comforting her. She'd been way more handy and efficient than I. I'd always been so hesitant, out of my clumsiness and fear.

I didn't say a word. What I had to say to Chloe I would say in private, not in front of Benedict so she could use it to browbeat Chloe into what she blatantly considered the only sane, reasonable, responsible decision – abortion.

Benedict edged towards Chloe with an expression on her face that said she wanted to give Chloe a good shake, and say, "Smarten up, girl!" But when she reached Chloe's side, all she said was "I'm telling you this like I was your mother."

Hearing that, I had to fight with all my strength not to snort with disgust. First, that approach might have worked coming from a forty-plus gynie, not one barely over thirty. Secondy, the last thing Chloe wanted to be reminded of at this point was what her lousy mother was going to be hysterically blathering to her. One thing for sure though – the blather would serve only one end – making Leslea's life smoother, not Chloe's.

Chloe shook Benedict's hand off and turned her back.

Benedict looked towards me, pleading with me to do something. That was her job, not mine, I thought resentfully. Then I cooled down. Chloe had to hear and understand all the alternatives. Otherwise, she'd be eating herself up the rest of her life, just as I did every time I recalled my lack of understanding of the last option left for my mother.

"Chloe, you need to listen to make a decision you can live with," I said, going over to her side.

"I made up my mind. I'm having the baby," Chloe said in a hostile tone of voice, wanting to turn away from me too, but she had no room to manoeuvre with me on one side and Benedict on the other.

"More information can only help," I said. "No one is asking you to do anything but listen."

Chloe swivelled around. She stood there with her arms crossed in front of her and rolled her eyes. Benedict shot me a grateful look.

"You're only seventeen, Chloe," Benedict began. "To be a good mother involves not just taking care of your child, but giving your child the advantages of your life experience. And to do that as best you can, you need to have lived more of your life."

Benedict was right. Years down the road, there was the chance that Chloe might come to feel that having a baby so young had cheated her of living her own life. Which it just had to, in one manner or another. That was another fact of life.

Benedict was wrong though too. All you had to do to see how wrong was to cross over to the other side of the floor, to the fertility clinic.

"I'm not an idiot," Chloe spat out. "I don't think it's going to be like playing with Miss Pink baby doll. I know it's going to change my life."

"Chloe, I'm sorry to sound hard, but you have no idea of what is in store for you. How are you going to support yourself and the baby? What about school? What about a career? You are not prepared; you are not ready to be a mother yet. No one your age is."

Chloe gave Benedict a disgusted look and Benedict sighed.

Birth, death. *Who* was ever prepared?

chapter**thirty-one**

Chloe said she wanted to move in with me, and we could live together, including the baby, happily ever after.

I'd seen eight basement apartments. Dingy, reeking with mildew, tiny, dark as the far side of the moon with hideously high rent was the name of the game. Rent alone would eat up almost every cent I earned, not leaving much for food, bus and subway fares, phone bills and everyday unexpected expenses.

Each time John and I had descended into the bowels of the next basement apartment on the list, he'd mocked, "What fresh hellhole is this?" Though after the fourth hellhole, even John had been too disheartened to joke. Plus, every landlord of every dump made a huge deal about my age and how I might deface, even destroy, their dumps. John had told them he would sign the lease and be responsible for any back rent or damages I made. That was, if we ever found a hellhole for me to rent and damage.

Chloe insisted on coming with John and me this morning. Between Chloe's barfing and primping, we were fifteen minutes late. John was doing me a huge favour, coming before opening the bookstore.

"Sorry we're late," I said. "And sorry you have to hear me apologize for being late again. I really appreciate . . ."

"I know, Alice," he said. "We have to hurry through this, and return later, if this is to be your home beautiful for the time being."

"Here? This house? It's on a main street, it's going to be noisy," Chloe said as we headed for the front door.

"Houses on main streets do tend to be noisy," John said. "That's why the rents are more affordable."

A woman in her early thirties opened the door. As she did, two young boys tried to make a run for it, but she quickly shut the screen door. "Brian, Henry, what did I tell you! You can't go outside."

I heard one of them give this wheezy cough that led into terrible heaving. His mother took an inhaler out of her pocket and handed it to him. He took a few puffs, and his breathing relaxed.

"The boys both have asthma and it takes them awhile to recover from colds. I keep them home to keep an eye on them."

We followed her downstairs to the apartment.

"We'd have to keep the light on all the time here. Look at those windows! Cruise ship portholes are bigger," Chloe said in a whisper shrill enough for John and the woman to hear too.

"It's a basement, Chloe. What do you expect, floor to ceiling windows?" I whispered.

Though the apartment was tiny, it was a lot cleaner and a lot better maintained than the ones I'd seen. It was a studio apartment. Against one wall was the kitchen area, with a fridge, stove and sink and a few cupboards.

"If you're wondering where you sleep, the couch is a pullout."

"A pullout? We're going to sleep on a pullout?" Chloe muttered.

Two armchairs flanked it. The floral slipcovers on them were new, and the walls were freshly painted.

There was a loud, lurching mechanical sound and Chloe jumped. "What's that?"

"The furnace is in the next room," the woman said.

The ceiling began to shake, followed by the sound of jumping and yelling.

"Brian, Henry! Please keep it down!"

"Are we going to hear that all the time?" Chloe muttered, again loud enough for everyone to hear.

"It's an old house, Chloe," I whispered. "It's not going to have the concrete soundproofing of a luxury condo."

Chloe kept up her commentary as the woman showed us the kitchen appliances which, while old, were clean, and then the bathroom, which consisted of a toilet, pedestal sink and shower stall.

"I like to take baths," Chloe said.

"If you want to move, it's not going to be the same anymore," I said. "Get used to it!"

Her slumming socialite routine, gasps and sneering comments were grating on my nerves, and John's too. He was visibly annoyed.

The kind of place Chloe would consider acceptable to live in would cost two thousand dollars a month, at least. Impossible on my earnings, and it would drain the savings she had before long, and that wasn't even factoring in the expense of taking care of a child.

The rent was seven hundred and fifty dollars, more than I could afford. Still, it was the best place I'd seen yet. I thanked the woman for showing us the apartment, and John.

I was supposed to go to work with John, but outside on the street Chloe's head started to spin and she looked as if she was going to faint. John drove us to Chloe's and told me to stay with her. He gave Randy a call on his cell and Randy said he would come to cover for me.

"You're not going to take that place, are you?" Chloe said in the elevator up to her apartment.

"I'm thinking about it, if I can come up with the rent!"

"We can find something better than that!" she said

"On what money? Tell me that." I barked.

"I'll get a job," she said.

"What about school? What about Caleb and Parnell? You have talent. Are you going to give that up to work at Starbucks or the Gap? You think some minimum wage job is going to support you and a baby? You need to call your dad and tell him!"

She ignored my plea, again. Whatever Uncle Samuel advised her to do, whether it was something she wanted to hear or not, he would have Chloe's best interests in mind.

"Call him!"

Inside the vestibule she swayed, then sprinted toward the bathroom, but didn't make it, barfing on herself and the carpet.

While she took a bath, I cleaned up the carpet. As I sprayed and scrubbed, it finally sunk in that Chloe was afraid to tell Uncle Samuel.

She was edgy about telling Leslea, primarily because of the scene and screaming that would follow. However, that was nothing compared to the threat of losing her father's high opinion of her.

She'd been so proud to email him photos of her collages and relate what Caleb and Parnell said about her artwork and potential. And thrilled beyond belief by her father's praise and encouragement. He'd asked her to send him a collage, and if I could make him a memory genie shadow box containing my mother's keepsakes too. He said he would love to have something to remember my mother by.

Not for the first time, I wondered what it would have been like if they had somehow met and married each other. Without

Uncle Samuel's loving buffer, Chloe and I would never have made it through my mother's funeral service.

There had been no shiva though; that was too retro for the non-practicing non-Judaism of the Levitt clan. And it was the source of the most acid shouting match between Leslea, Eric and Uncle Samuel that I had been *privileged* to witness. When Eric and Leslea had refused, he'd threatened to hold the shiva in his hotel room at the Park Plaza, thinking that might shame Eric into holding it. And he would have, had the rabbi from my mother's congregation not talked him out of it. I wished he had. I wished I had been supportive and urged him on. But I'd been such a basket case, so groggy and so enervated I had done nothing.

Afterwards Uncle Samuel had looked as if he was having a heart attack; he'd been so red in the face, sweaty and struggling for breath, likely from restraining himself from punching out my father, and/or clunking his and Leslea's heads together.

Watching him fight with Eric and Leslea about the shiva, I'd remembered the seder dinner we'd had in the banquet room of the Marco Polo Hotel in Miami Beach. We were seated at a table with two other families. Uncle Samuel had led the Passover service, chit-chatting that he'd become an expert, given that he and the handful of other Jews living in Hong Kong had a short rotation on the holiday prayer-leading schedule. During the seder dinner, he and my mother, heads bent close together, had talked and laughed. Then, out of the blue, he'd reached over and run his fingers along my mother's cheek with such unmistakable affection.

Had he loved her? Was that another reason for his self-imposed exile in Hong Kong?

Who knew for sure? I sure didn't, even after countless replays of that memory, like some store surveillance tape.

I stood up from the carpet. That, at least, was clear. Completely spotless. Maybe I could supplement my income with housecleaning. It would be dry when Leslea got home, so Chloe would avoid having to explain about barfing. Until she was really going to have to explain.

chapter**thirty-two**

So what do you really think I should do?" Chloe asked, as we brought out the food and began setting up a buffet on Leslea's dining room table.

My throat was already parched from running through my speech several times, so I was sucking a lozenge. I cracked it into pieces, swallowed it and then answered. If I had been in Chloe's position, I would be doing the same thing. Wanting reassurance, wanting support, wanting a fairy godmother to fly over, wave her magic wand and make everything work out.

"Chloe," I said, "we've gone over this and over this. Right now we need to get everything on the table and ready before your mother and my father show up."

And silently added "for the showdown." The tables were being turned on Eric and Leslea. At the start of the summer, Chloe and I had received the buffet dinner before Leslea and Eric laid out their cases against us.

Since their indignation would inevitably leave them with indigestion, I'd suggested that it was a waste of money to spend a fortune on gourmet food. Why not buy a barbequed chicken, baked potatoes and coleslaw from Swiss Chalet instead? Chloe had refused, saying it would set Eric and Leslea off from the get-go. They would get all huffy and insulted that we didn't think highly enough of them to feed them well. Even more reason, to my thinking, to buy fast-food chicken dinners. It was Chloe's money though, so off I'd gone to Delano's gourmet food shop as per her instructions.

On the way there, I'd passed by Kaplan's Deli. The odour of corned beef and knishes corralled me with an invisible lasso, and I'd gone in telling myself I would just pick up a few things for Chloe and me to snack on later.

Three bags later with blintzes, borscht, chopped liver, potato kugel, tzimmes, krepachs, farfarel, apple strudel and more, I'd left. Chloe was the one who was pregnant, yet it was me who had the craving for food that had flavour, taste and memories of my mom's cooking. Kaplan's wasn't nearly as delicious as my mom's food, but it was yummy enough that I would have ordered everything on the menu.

Fortunately, Delano's was just down the street. Chloe had pre-ordered; all I had to do was pick it up, which was not so easy when already carrying three bags from Kaplan's. One of the cashiers called a cab for me and helped me load the food.

Too bad if they wouldn't deign to eat the food from Kaplan's. I would, and Chloe too, if she wasn't too nauseated.

I glanced over at Chloe. She didn't look well. In between our non-stop conversation, she'd been throwing up. "Why don't you lie down? I'll do the rest."

"Thanks," she said, and stretched out on the couch.

I went back to setting out the trays from Delano's. An assortment of "artisan breads" which consisted of sourdough, multigrain, flatbreads and bread sticks with oil and butter. A "Vegetarian Rhapsody" platter, which consisted of grilled Asian vegetable spring rolls, spiced potato samosas and panko-crusted avocado wedges. And an "Ocean Delight" platter, which consisted of grilled tiger shrimp, calamari satays and flash-seared tuna with a mint salsa. And for dessert, carrot cake.

Then I brought out the bags from Kaplan's. I was going to segregate the food on the far left side of the table like dairy from meat, but then I thought, what the heck, go wild and mix them up. I wasn't big on fancy layouts of food on the plates. Nonetheless, I tried as much as I could to arrange the food I'd gotten from Kaplan's "artfully," mimicking the trays. When I finished, it was impossible to tell which was gourmet, and which was from Kaplan's.

Except by the mouth-watering odours. I would have to stick my nose right into the "Ocean Delight" and "Vegetarian Rhapsody" platters to detect any smell, not there was much of any to detect on Delano's deodorized food.

I brought Chloe more ginger ale and saltines to settle her stomach. When she felt less queasy, she sat up, and I sat down beside her, feeling more than a bit queasy myself.

I squeezed Chloe's hand for reassurance. "You look great!" I told her. She was dressed pretty sedately for Chloe – sedately meaning a saffron-coloured cotton sweater set and a floral A-line skirt almost to her knees. I was wearing a yellow daisy print sundress of my mom's.

I don't know what kind of inner pep talk Chloe was giving herself as I held her hand, but I was warning myself that whatever Eric or Leslea said or did, I was to maintain a Mona Lisa-like composure, no matter how loud and strong my inner Edvard Munch screamer wanted to let loose some choice, blood-curdling sarcasm.

Who was going to come up on top? Mona Lisa or the screamer? I was going to be put to the test this very second. Leslea came through the door, carrying what looked to be a shopping bag from every high-end store on Bloor Street. I spotted bags from Holt Renfrew, Tiffany, Chanel and coming in the rear, Lothario Len, carrying his booty.

Len, an actor who mostly "acted" in commercials, was perpetually tanned. His dark wavy hair was slicked back and styled with a salon-worthy selection of hair products, his forehead was as frozen in place with Botox as was Leslea's, and I could see the washboard abs he manically excercised to maintain rippling beneath his tight black T-shirt. Leslea had met him on the set of one of the movies she was finding props for. Len had a part, a part that had more to do with American production companies needing to meet the quota of Canadians the companies had to hire to qualify for tax breaks than his "talent."

"My favourite treats – those will really hit the spot," Leslea gushed, coming over to air kiss me (she wouldn't dare touch me . . . she had learned that much) and plant a real smacker on Chloe.

Len was new enough as live-in boyfriend material not to be sure how welcoming he could be with Chloe or me. I got a "Hi" and a nod, Chloe, a squeeze on the upper arm, followed by "What's new?" If he only knew . . . he'd be racing out the door for a nice hibernation bout in a tanning bed.

"We'll just drop our bags and be out in a minute," Leslea sang out.

Shock of shocks, then Eric showed up, almost on time.

"A family dinner, how nice. The girls didn't tell me," Leslea said, setting down the bags and going over to Eric to give him a quick peck on the cheek.

"Yes, we did, Mother," Chloe dragged out. "You weren't listening, as usual."

"No matter," she said. "Let me just freshen up and then we can start eating." She picked up the bags and left the living room.

"I'm starving," Len said.

"When aren't you?" Chloe said with a groan. "It's a good thing you work out like crazy. The way you eat you should be a porker by now."

Len quickly glanced down at his stomach as if to make sure he hadn't suddenly sprouted a middle-aged beer belly, and then scurried after Leslea.

I snickered. I knew I shouldn't, but I couldn't stop myself.

I wasn't the only one with a slice and dice tongue. As much as I enjoyed Chloe's snarky comments, this wasn't the way to set up the mood for the evening. I pinched Chloe on the thigh and hissed, "Save it, okay?"

She shot me a look. I knew that look. I had that same look on my face too often, so Chloe told me. That smash-mouth look that said *Scram suckers, I'm this far from being out of control so don't push me!*

My father came over and sat down in the armchair at a right angle from the couch. He smoothly got Chloe talking about Caleb and the collage she was working on.

It was wonderful to see how working on her collages gave her so much joy. I didn't want her to lose that.

That little reprieve concluded when Eric glanced over at me and said, "That dress suits you. It looks familiar."

I sighed. "You've seen it before, that's why."

"That's right, you've seen it before. Your late wife, Ellen Levitt, she loved that dress. There used to be a picture in your front hallway of you and Aunt Ellen, and she was wearing that dress. You wouldn't remember, would you?" Chloe sneered.

How could I not think, you go, girl! Still, that satisfaction, I knew, would be another in my long list of pyrrhic victories over Eric.

"I forgot. Sorry Chloe. Sorry, Alice," he said, and actually looked as if he was.

"Old story," Chloe muttered.

"We're back," Leslea said.

"Mrs. Robinson and Canadian Gigolo," Chloe mocked.

I coughed, choked, tried to swallow, sounding like I was gargling mouthwash.

"We watch a lot of old movies," I said. Inept, inane, I knew. But what else was there to say? "I liked *The Graduate* more than *American Gigolo*."

No surprise, my little movie critique did nothing to change the vibes.

"Let's eat!" Never had I looked forward to the sounds of chewing, slurping, and swallowing quite so much. It would give Chloe and me time to regroup.

I went over to the dining room table and piled my plate with two blueberry blintzes, a slice of potato kugel, a couple krepachs, a scoop of tzimmes and a hunk of apple strudel, needing to fortify myself for the forthcoming title bout.

In my chair, I amused myself watching Eric, Len and even Leslea fill their plates with the food from Kaplan's.

"God, this pâté de fois gras is good," Len said, with a full mouth of, not pâté, but chopped liver. "And these cannolis, I could eat a dozen of them." Yes, I had to agree with Len on that, having eaten three. Little did he know they weren't cannolis, but blintzes.

Leslea, of course, despite all her claims that she could eat whatever she wanted to, never seemed to do so. However, unlike most mealtimes when she picked at her food as if she was doing a mental calorie count of each bite, she was now doing some major scarfing. She guzzled down her bowl of borscht, and returned to the table twice for refills of krepach, farfarel and tzimmes.

My father was cleaning his plate too. Only Chloe wasn't. She had a piece of flatbread and a couple of breadsticks between several exits from the room.

Not that anyone ever seemed to take note – why would this night be any different?

When she came back after her third trip, Len was shovelling down the remaining blintzes, and Leslea was slurping the dregs of borscht and scraping the last bits of chopped liver in the bowl onto a piece of flatbread.

"This gazpacho is so rich, and Len, you're right, the pâté, never better, as is that vegetarian quiche and those gnocchis," Leslea said.

I ran my tongue over my teeth, not merely to loosen the food bits stuck between my teeth, but also to stop myself from grinning as widely as a clown. If Leslea only knew, she'd just consumed her calorie quota for two days, at the very least.

"Mother," Chloe ground out. "That wasn't gazpacho; it was borscht. And that delicious quiche you thought you were eating, it was potato kugel. The gnocchis weren't. They were krepachs. All from Kaplan's Deli. You were all eating Jewish deli food, not Delano's gourmet platters."

Leslea looked ready to spit out her last bites as if she'd just consumed radioactive waste.

"Jewish food," Len said to Leslea. "This stuff is great. You're Jewish, Leslea. Can you make any of this stuff?"

From the livid glare Leslea gave Len, he wasn't going to get any tonight from Leslea.

"How could you?" Leslea screeched at Chloe.

I stood up. "Don't blame Chloe. I bought it. I was walking past and I couldn't resist. Neither could you, from the looks of your plate."

If that plate hadn't been Royal Crown Derby rimmed with twenty-two carat gold, I bet she would have hurled it at me.

"Leslea!" Eric said, startling me by coming to my defence.

"Where is Kaplan's?" Len asked, the fact that Leslea was not going to chop up some liver and fry a couple of blintzes for him anytime soon sinking in.

"Here, I'll give you the bill. It has the address and phone number. They deliver, too!" I told him.

Revved up by all that Jewish home-style food from Kaplan's, Len started talking a mile a minute about the movie he was "acting" in. Leslea continued to mope for a while, but then regrouped when Len began his name-dropping orgy of all the stars he and Leslea had met lately (and at what telescopic distances, I snidely speculated). Renee Zellweger, what a sweetie. Russell Crowe, what a hunk. And on and on it went until I swear I was ready to grab the tomatoes off the untouched "Vegetarian Rhapsody" platter and start doing some Leslea-style hurling. But I let them enjoy their "last supper" in peace.

The Len factor had me worried, but it was needless. The guy ate, then the guy exercised. He excused himself to go for a run.

While clearing the dishes with Chloe, I made her promise to keep to the agenda. My news first, then hers. And could she please keep her commentary to herself? Not that I didn't love it, not that I didn't completely agree, but in the end, I warned her, those verbal grenades creamed you along with your target.

Chloe was saving her strength – plus her head was spinning as well as her stomach – so she was now sitting in the living room. Theoretically, she was keeping Leslea and Eric company; really, though, she was a ticking time bomb seated on the settee, mere minutes from detonation.

Eric and Leslea remained blissfully ignorant and blissfully immersed in their discussion of who was staying at the superior luxury lodge in Muskoka over the Labour Day weekend. Ignorance was truly bliss in this case, and a pretty short-lived bliss.

I continued going back and forth to the kitchen as I cleaned up. I caught bits and pieces of the Muskoka lodge competition, and the tail end of it when I sat down beside Chloe on the settee. I waited for it to peter out to its pathetic end. Only then, did I say, "We need to talk."

Eric and Leslea looked at each other, then at us.

My hands clasped together in my lap, I announced. "I've decided I don't want to go to Regent's Academy. I don't agree that I need to go to Kingston to have a fresh start. I can have a fresh start right here."

I expected Eric to start in with his arsenal of arguments, but he didn't say a word.

"Alice, think of all the new friends you will make; friends that you will come to with no baggage; friends who will be contacts you can always turn to in the future." Loyal little sister Leslea jumped right in, unable to restrain herself from adding her two cents.

The screamer was screaming inside: you are such a brown-nosing social climber. The death of my mother, my grief, my rage, my withdrawal from my old friends, my cutting, all baggage, but they were as much a part of me as anything else. "Baggage" I should burn and forget. I didn't think so.

And contacts, give me a break! I hated when people did calculated use assessments of others.

"I've been making new friends this summer," I said, softly because I was afraid if I spoke any louder my contempt would be unmistakable even to clueless Leslea.

"I'm going to have a fresh start right here," I said. "I'm going to move out into my own place. I've been checking out some basement apartments and rooming houses with the help of John Atticus and his wife Eileen." I steeled myself for the coming pyrotechnics.

Leslea gasped, but Eric remained mute.

"A basement apartment, when you could live at the Prince Arthur," Leslea said.

"I wasn't going to be living there . . . except during holidays. I was going to be in a school dorm, remember?"

"Who do those people think they are? They're not your parents," Leslea whined.

"How would you know what a parent does?" Chloe piped in. "You've never been one. And don't give me the replay of your fifteen hours of labour. That was the first and last time you ever did anything resembling being a parent. If you can't remember, I do. Aunt Ellen took care of me like she was my mother. Not you; not ever!"

That shut Leslea up, but Eric still wasn't talking . . . which was making me edgy.

Only when Chloe had stopped to catch her breath, and I'd brought another glass of ginger ale for her from the kitchen, did Eric begin to speak.

"I know how hard the last few years have been for you," he said.

How would he?

"I thought that Regent's Academy would be a new place with no unhappy memories," he continued.

Unhappy memories were memories just as happy ones were. Just as inescapable, just as much a part of you. What was memory for, but for remembering? Did he really think if he shipped me off to a new place I would be as blank of memories as a sheet of white paper?

"I'll remember there just like I'll remember here," I said.

He shifted, and then rubbed the side of his face. "Alice, you've never gotten a chance to be a teenager," he finally said. "I wanted to give you that opportunity. These past two years, you've not had much time for a life of your own."

Well, I didn't get thrown for a loop often, especially with Eric, but I did now. Could his motives be not completely selfish? He was right. I hadn't had much of a "typical" teen life. Was I sorry? How could you miss what you never had?

I inhaled, not wanting to sound shrill, hostile, accusatory and confused . . . all the things I was, in fact, feeling.

"Do you really think that's possible? That if I put on a cheer-leader outfit, I'll become a rah-rah team type? That if I put on a Regent's Academy uniform, I'll become a cliquey private school type, giggling in the corridors, stealing smokes in the bathroom, hiking up my skirt waistband to show how hot I am, even in a plaid wool kilt. I don't think so."

Okay, when pressed, I invariably trotted out teen stereotypes that even I didn't consider the norm. Whatever that was.

"I suppose you're right, Alice," he said. "That's not what I meant, and that's not what I want for you, even if you think so. But if that's what you want to think, go ahead."

I felt a surge of baffled guilt. Was I just as guilty of pigeonhol-ing him as I so self-righteously (and maybe even wrongly) pre-sumed he was always pigeonholing me?

"Regent's Academy is one of the top private schools in the country. Your teachers consider you exceptionally bright. The school will stimulate you; give you a focus for your future professional life. You can be anything you want, Alice. Your potential is unlimited."

He put a stake through my guilt, killing it off and resurrecting my simmering anger and resentment with that canned, dead air speech. Where had he dragged that in from? From some Regent's Academy sales pitch? You mean anything *you* want, I thought but swallowed that down with a big gulp.

I sat there, carefully crafting as neutral a response as I could.

Not so easy. "I think I can realize 'my potential' at whatever high school I go to. You're right. I do need a fresh start. Though not in the way you think. I need to be on my own. I need to do this. I need a time-out."

From you. From all of this. I just wanted some peace of mind. No arguments. No tension.

And then there was Chloe's situation. Whatever her decision, the next months were not going to be a cakewalk. She would only have me. The effect of Chloe having the baby on my life suddenly dawned on me.

Before Eric could say anything more, Chloe stood up and announced, "I need Alice to be here, to help me out. I'm pregnant, and I'm going to have the baby."

"Pregnant?" Leslea gasped. "How is that possible?"

"You and Len should know . . ." Chloe left the rest unsaid.

"You don't look too far gone," Leslea said, staring at Chloe. "But it's hard to tell . . ."

"Because I'm already fat around the middle, like you're always pointing out to me," Chloe muttered. "I'm nearly two months along."

"Chloe, you're young. You have your life ahead of you," Eric interrupted, taking on the role he loved best – the voice of logic and reason. "There's plenty of time, years from now, to have a child when you are in a stable relationship, established in your career, have financial security."

Chloe hooted loudly at that, then looked over at me and broadly rolled her eyes. "You think that's what makes a good parent. That's the problem with both you and your sister as 'parents.' Love and caring have nothing to do with it . . . all you need is to be established, to have financial security. You and my mother have all that, and look what kind of parents you are."

Though it was great to have Chloe speak her mind, and the

truth as I saw it too, I knew that route led only to the ever-lurking pyrrhic victory. Whatever I could whisper to Chloe about cooling it, she would (and I would in her place, too) see as disloyalty, abandonment. Yet to let her go on wouldn't help.

"Chloe, Chloe," Eric said, sighing. "Tell us the reasons you want this baby right now."

"I want to have the baby, period, so live with it. I'm not giving you a list of reasons for you to rip apart one by one," Chloe said, looking back and forth at Leslea and Eric, belligerent and defiant.

Leslea lost it. She jumped up from the couch and circled the room, yelling, mad enough to pull out her hair, but too vain even when completely deranged by rage. "You're ruining your life!" Translation: you're ruining my life. "What do you know about taking care of a baby?"

"What do you know about taking care of a baby?" Chloe yelled back. "Who changed my diapers? Who fed me? Who took me to school, made me lunches, read me books, took me to the doctor, took care of me when I was sick and took me to movies, museums, on vacations? Remember. AUNT ELLEN did."

"Look at you. You're fat already," Leslea sneered. "And who is going to want you with a kid?"

Those words hit the mark. I could tell from the flush creeping up Chloe's face.

"I'll have my baby," Chloe said, her voice cracking.

"You'll have me too," I said. "Don't forget Auntie Alice."

Chloe gave me a little smile, but it was apparent that she was running out of the rage rush that kept her fighting back.

Leslea let out a half-screech. "Me, a grandmother! I won't allow it. We're making arrangements for the abortion. I won't take no for an answer."

That was the elephant in the room. What was the use of lying about her age and subjecting herself to Botox, if she became Bubbe Levitt?

"You'll have to. It's my body, it's my life, and I'm having the baby."

"Don't you think the father should have a say in this? The baby is his, too," Eric threw in, Mister so-called Reasonable to the rescue.

Hearing the word father, for a second I assumed Eric was talking about Uncle Samuel.

Naturally, given the antipathy between the Levitt siblings and Uncle Samuel, Leslea and Eric didn't even consider Uncle Samuel's say in the matter. Probably didn't want to consider it. Probably because he would be handling this with common sense and Chloe's welfare utmost in mind. I should have forced Chloe to call Uncle Samuel already, or done it myself.

And in regards to the "biological father," as I saw it, Kevin was no more than the sperm donor. Inform him? That was a nightmare scenario Chloe and I hadn't had the guts even to think about. Jeez. Kevin. Another parental disaster in the making. I wouldn't tell him if I was Chloe. Why? For child support? Who'd want him involved? Like he would want to be. Right.

"Keep your options open," Eric said. "Think about it."

On that one point, we were all agreed. All of us would be thinking about little else.

chapter**thirty-three**

Think about it."

In between, and even during, all the things I did throughout the day *not* to think, I thought about *it*.

Should Chloe have the baby or not?

Yes, I thought while typing patient data like a demon, the pile of patients' files to be inputted finally shrinking.

No, I thought while counting cash at the register at the end of my shift as I watched Randy joking with two sisters buying books for their first year at Ryerson University. Chloe would miss out on all that with a baby.

She and Randy had been going out, and it had been fun, she'd said. Randy was the first decent guy she'd ever dated. That didn't prevent me from worrying, though, about how would he react, along with everyone else, to Chloe's pregnancy.

Chloe was much more sociable than I was. She needed to be around lots of people. The more friends she had, the more people she knew, the merrier. That didn't apply to me. A couple of good friends that I could trust, share stuff with, go out with, and I was content. So having a baby would isolate Chloe in ways that would be tough for her to handle.

That was supposing she could even have much of a social life, having to squeeze it in along with baby care, school work and working on her art.

No, I thought after Chloe called me, happy, excited, pregnancy worries forgotten for a moment, to tell me that a collector, who had come to Caleb's to buy another shadow box to add to his collection, had seen one of Chloe's collages, and had offered to buy it. For three hundred dollars! I was thrilled; she was thrilled. Even Caleb had shown excitement.

Yes, I thought after speaking to Lindy, who despite her best efforts not to sound depressed as hell, sounded depressed as hell. If there *was* anything I could recognize that was it. Her speech was slow, kind of slurred; she kept drifting off, losing her train of thought while in the middle of saying something.

There was another option, and maybe it was just an option in my universe of wishful thinking. Chloe could have the baby, and give the baby up for adoption to Lindy and Don. She would be giving up the baby, yes, but giving her or him to loving, caring parents.

Well, I'd find out at the barbeque at Elaine's on Sunday whether this was a possibility or merely a rosy fantasy never to live outside my brain, I thought, as I scribbled down Lindy's driving directions to Oakville and Elaine's house.

If Chloe did decide to keep the baby and to move out, she wouldn't be living in the same manner that she was accustomed to. Where was the money going to come from? Likely Uncle Samuel, but she hadn't called him yet. That was supposing he agreed she should keep the baby. And even if he did, I suspected he wasn't about to support Chloe in Leslea's high style.

It would be years, if ever, before she could support herself from her artwork, which was a dicey deal at the best of times unless you'd achieved the recognition Caleb had.

When I'd gone to view his artwork at the gallery again, the owner of the gallery, who also had written the exhibit catalogue, had chatted with me about Caleb and his work. She'd said Caleb had struggled just to make a living until about ten years earlier when he'd seemed to have floored his creative gas pedal after the death of Artie.

According to her, Caleb had taken care of Artie with love and devotion. But that care and devotion, especially as Artie's health deteriorated, had to have sapped Caleb – time-wise and creativity-wise. I wondered if all the keepsakes and collages Caleb made of the things Artie had loved weren't just his mode of re-membering and honouring Artie, but also his means of working through his guilt. If you loved someone who was ill or dying, you never felt you were doing enough for them. Did Caleb feel regret and guilt over the time he'd devoted to his art, all taking away time from Artie?

Perhaps. He was never going to say. Though if he'd been able to have that kind of conversation with Chloe, she would get a bet-ter picture of what lay in store for her if she kept the baby.

Yes, no, yes, no, no, no. This was all on my mind, which never seemed to take a rest, as I spooned up Special K cereal for breakfast while reading a book. I was so immersed that I nearly choked on my cereal when I looked up and saw my father standing beside the table.

"We never finished our discussion," he said.

He glanced at the book, then at the Boston Red Sox cap on my head with a baffled look that said (before he made his face go defence lawyer inscrutable) who is this person, the sports hater wearing a baseball cap, reading a book about a fifties TV series?

I touched the cap with my hand. "A gift from Luke. He gave me the choice of a Howard Dean beanie or this, his two favourites.

From the photos he emailed, I chose the cap. The orange beanie was too ugly to wear. And the book, *The Honeymooners Companion,* it belongs to John. He got me hooked on *The Honeymooners.*"

The implied message, though it didn't come to me until I finished my explanation, was that my father never bothered to share any of his interests ever but, perversely, his work had gotten me hooked on crime shows. We both got that, and the all too common deadly awkward silence descended.

This led me to babble. "I'm getting Luke one of those red and white Roots toques with a little Canadian flag on it."

Continued silence – caused by bewilderment, disinterest, who knew?

He glanced at his watch. Now that I knew too well – the gesture signalling it was past time to cut to the chase.

"You said you wanted to finish our talk," I said, though it was the last thing I wanted to do. What I wanted to do was just eat my cereal and my strawberries with cream, and read in peace. I pushed the food away from me and folded my hands on the table.

Mistake. His gaze fixed on my hands, which looked the worse for wear. There were cuts on the top of my right hand, bruises on the left and my left index finger was bandaged.

Before he could accuse me of what he was thinking, that I had gone back to my "self-destructive behaviours," I beat him to the punch. I waved my hands. "A mess, huh? The marks of my pathetic hammering and sawing. Some carpenter I'd make. Got these at Caleb's. He's helping me build a miniature curio for Mom's collectibles. It's just a basic oak cabinet with glass doors, but I wanted to show off Mom's things in something I made."

"You could have asked me. We could have bought a new one for the apartment. I'm certain we could have found something you'd like at the Art Shoppe or Ethan Allen."

He was selling off all the furniture my mother had so lovingly selected. Now suddenly he was into displaying my mother's collectibles in a new curio in the new apartment?

I feigned what I hoped was a convincingly nonchalant shrug. "I wanted mom's things to be housed in something I made especially for them." A home for them. Like he was capable of getting that.

Of course, I did have to have a home for me first before I could have a home for the curio and shadow boxes.

He rested his briefcase on the tabletop. I couldn't tell whether it was because he was about to dash out the door or settle in.

"About Regent's Academy," he said, clearing his throat. "You don't have to go if you don't want to go."

To say it any other way would be to admit he'd changed his mind, or had made a bad decision.

Just be thankful, I told myself. At least I got to avoid any and all future arguments over that.

For a minute, I thought his resolve not to ship me out was his acknowledgment that I was in better shape, moving closer towards "normal" on the dial, and less of a social embarrassment and liability. I had made new friends, was no longer covered up burka-style and was less like a grenade ready to detonate at any second.

Maybe that was some of it. Then the primary reason came to me. By now Leslea and Eric had realized that whatever Chloe did, she was going to need a caregiver. And I was a proven caregiver, and they sure as heck weren't. I recalled how reluctant Leslea had always been even to touch my mother, even her hand, as if my mother's dying was contagious.

"I don't want to go," I said softly, and left it at that.

"So it's unnecessary for you to look for a place to live. You can move into your new bedroom," he said. "I really would like you to help me set up the place, if you'd like to. I have a meeting scheduled tomorrow evening with Francesca DiCarlo, the interior designer I've hired. If you are free then, please come. It is going to be your home too, Alice."

Was this the famous Eric Levitt rope-a-dope trick? God knows he'd had enough practice roping my mother in with some heartwarming action, only to soon resume his heartbreaking ways.

I didn't answer until I'd acquired some self-control. "I appreciate your offer, but I think it would be . . . good for me, and for you, if I moved out. Let's see how it goes for a while."

I could see he was struggling not to say something sarcastic or cutting about me living in some rathole basement apartment instead of the tony Prince Arthur.

"It will be disruptive for you," he said.

Choice. It wasn't "disruptive" when I was about to be shipped to Regent's Academy, but when I wanted to move out it was.

"Nothing disrupts my studies," I said quietly and he got it. Not even my mother's dying had. I had continued to plug away, my ability to escape by concentrating scary sometimes even to me.

He took a breath, searching no doubt for a new tack. "Living with me doesn't mean you can't continue working part-time at Atticus's Attic either. I know how attached you are to the job and to John Atticus," he said.

I could hear the inflection in his voice when he said "attached."

Was that his not so subtle needling of me about how much I liked John? Poor little Alice, I could imagine him thinking right now. Always getting so attached. Morbidly and otherwise.

I had the impulse to shout out, yes I am attached to John – why shouldn't I be, he's been like a good father.

This torturous reading, and possible misreading, of everything my father did and said . . . Would I ever get past it?

I had been positive, well almost sure I was positive, that moving out was the right thing, but I was back to being unsure all over again.

I had to eye my cereal, now disintegrated into a bowl of brown speckled milk. At the moment I wasn't up to eyeing my father.

"Alice?"

I made myself look up. "Thank you for the offer. I need to think about it."

I watched his face, wondering what he would do and say next. Would he continue to try to persuade me not to move out? Would he forbid it? Would he give in and offer me financial support? The longer he said nothing, the longer he mulled it over, furrowing his forehead, his eyes darting about, the more confused I got.

He sighed. "Don't make your life harder than it has to be, just to get back at me, Alice. Your life has been hard enough these past two years. "

I didn't know what to say, and he obviously didn't either. I couldn't recall him ever being at a loss for words before.

"I know . . . ," he said. "I know I wasn't much help to your mother. All those surgeries, all those treatments. She took everything in her stride, no complaints, just did her best, and went on with her life, despite the pain. I couldn't believe she wouldn't do that somehow again. And when she couldn't at the end . . . I couldn't deal with seeing your mother like that."

I looked over at him, and I had to look away . . . for his sake. He looked so uncomfortable, and almost embarrassed to have revealed that, and staring at him would just make him more uncomfortable.

As if I should care what my staring at him would make him feel like, but I did.

Some words the social worker leading that bereavement group had said to this widower came back to me. He'd been fuming over why so many relatives and friends hadn't been there for his wife when she was dying of breast cancer.

The social worker had explained how everybody handles death the way they can, or the way they can't.

Some, like lousy Leslea, avoided the dying as much as they could. If they didn't see death, it meant there wasn't death to be seen and experienced.

Some were awkward, ill at ease, as my father had been, unable to face the death of the person they loved.

The bottom line was that some people passed a cemetery and it said to them, live your life. Others passed a cemetery and it said to them, you're going to die sooner or later. And always sooner than you think.

I heard both, but lots of people, obviously including my father and Leslea, only heard the latter.

"I wasn't there for your mother. But I did love her, Alice," he said, stuttering it out.

Now I did stare him straight in the eye like a detective in an interrogation room. Had he loved her then? Even if he had still loved her, love was more than words; it was deeds and actions and responsibilities. It was easy to say you loved somebody, but love was a lot more.

I'd known that for what felt like forever, and he didn't yet? Then, viewing the embarrassment that still gripped him, I realized, he did know.

"Afterwards, I wasn't much help to you either, I know. So I sent you to therapists, and called Merle, thinking you might listen to her." He sighed loudly. "Your mother wouldn't want you to ruin your life, Alice. Consider what your mother would want you to do. We'll talk more later. I've got to run. 'What can I do? The client pays the bills.' Isn't that what I always say?" he said, mocking himself.

He lifted his briefcase off the table, and began tapping it.

"And try to talk some sense, will you, into Chloe!" he said wearily, and left the kitchen.

Talk some sense. Code words for talking Chloe into having an abortion.

That was "good" sense for Eric and Leslea, but was that good sense for Chloe and the baby?

And I began thinking about it again.

chapter**thirty-four**

Chloe was in her bedroom. At long last she was about to call her dad. I was on sentry duty in the living room. She wanted me there as support, and as a lookout on the off chance Leslea and Len came back early from their regular Sunday brunch at the Four Seasons Hotel.

I reassured her that, on that front, she had nothing to worry about. It was an all-you-can-eat brunch, and that meant Len wouldn't leave until he'd vacuumed in a couple of returns trips to the buffet table.

Mostly, I was here to make sure that Chloe didn't chicken out and postpone the call for another supposedly ideal time.

All I was hearing, though, was the sound of Chloe putting the receiver back down into the phone cradle. I tried to be patient. Gargantuan struggle for me. After listening to another lengthy stretch of silence, I called out, "Just do it, Chloe!"

This time I said it pleadingly and supportively, rather than with my earlier exasperation and irritation.

"I am doing it right now," Chloe said shakily.

I listened, kind of holding my breath, willing Chloe to do it. I exhaled when I heard her talking rapidly to her dad.

As much as I believed that Uncle Samuel wouldn't go ballistic at the news, I was anxious too, wondering how he would react, and how his reaction would affect Chloe.

So I did what I always did when I didn't want to think about something. I looked for work to do. I got up from the couch, glanced around and went over the coffee and end tables. I re-arranged the coffee-table books (ornamental, unread props) by subject matter. I put the travel books on one end table, the decorative art books on another, and spread out the ones on classic movies and famous stars on the coffee table. The only bookcases with books that were really read were in Chloe's bedroom.

That done, sighting the magazine rack, I alphabetized the magazines, and next arranged the issues in chronological order. I neared the spot on the carpet where Chloe had barfed. I studied it. Immaculate. Previously carpet cleaner, now librarian. Was there any other job for me to tackle as Chloe continued to talk to her dad?

Didn't look to be, so I grabbed one of the decorative art books and leafed through it, my fingers likely the first even to touch the pages.

A while later, still in her pyjamas, Chloe came out. She sank down beside me on the couch. She appeared calmer and relieved, so it couldn't have gone badly.

I bit down all the questions I wanted to ask, telling myself again to be patient, to allow Chloe to tell me when she was ready.

"My dad said he couldn't advise me what I should do. That I had to decide myself, and that whatever I decided, I'd have his support."

Not that I had expected Uncle Samuel to say or do anything but that, yet I felt calmer, and relieved too.

"He told me, though, that I should book the abortion at the clinic, in case it came to me that I didn't want to have the baby after all, 'cause I have only three weeks to go in my first trimester."

"Good advice!" I said

She nodded. "And my dad told me to research what the first few years of taking care of a baby involve, so I know what I am getting into. He wants me to write it all down and email him a strategy."

"More good advice, huh?"

"Yeah," she said, sounding a bit overwhelmed and tired suddenly. "Before he hung up, he said he hated to bring this up, but since I might not be able to count on my mom, I would have to depend on you for help. After what you went through with your mom, he said I had to ask myself whether that was a fair thing to do to you."

She looked at me beseechingly. I knew she wanted me to declare that it wouldn't be a burden; I'd be there for her, no matter what.

I would be, but that didn't mean, as I'd been slowly realizing, that it wouldn't be hard, it wouldn't be a burden.

I didn't know what to say, so I simply grabbed her hand and squeezed it.

All that Uncle Samuel had assumed was true, but hello, what about the fact he couldn't be counted on either, not really, not with him off in Hong Kong, and Chloe and her baby in Toronto? Didn't he get it that phone calls, emails and text messages just wouldn't cut it in a crisis?

To raise the baby, Chloe would need all the assistance she could get. And that meant more than just me. It meant a father there in person and a mother who was into parenting – non-starters, it would seem.

Though with Grandfather and Grandmother Levitt as their models, it was no wonder Eric and Leslea had major deficiencies in the parenting department. Given what cold stiffs Grandfather and Grandmother Levitt were, only really concerned about themselves,

Eric and Leslea hadn't gotten much warmth or attention from them while growing up. Predictably, growing up, neither had Chloe and me.

Granted, Eric had his moments, had tried more, especially when I was a kid. I thought of how he'd taken me with him to the occasional hockey game, tennis match or law firm event. Even then, we only did what interested him, not me.

Admittedly, it didn't help that I always couldn't wait to get back to my mother, and it was super obvious I loved her most.

Leslea hadn't shown much interest in Chloe until Chloe was old enough to be a companion, and a handy one at that.

At least Uncle Samuel had supplied useful advice – but then so could have an advice columnist.

No, that was too snarky. From what I could figure out from Chloe's rundown he seemed very distressed, as if a lot of this was his fault for not being around.

Which it likely was. Nevertheless, his advice was sound, and that was a first step.

"You up to going with me to Lindy's?" I asked.

"Yeah," she said, then shifted over and hugged me. "I love you."

"I love you too!" I said. "Now get dressed and make yourself even more beautiful, and we'll head off!"

chapter**thirty-five**

"Chloe will hold Rachel for you!"

Rocking newborn Rachel in her arms, Caitlin had come over to Chloe and me. We were sitting on lawn chairs near the garden.

"Caitlin, will you hurry up! It's feeding time!" Elaine called out in mock desperation. She was standing near a picnic table surrounded by six kids shoving and pushing.

Chloe shot me a look, and it wasn't the one of gratitude I expected.

I shrugged, feeling a twinge of remorse. I was only trying to help Caitlin and Chloe. I figured since Chloe was so gung-ho on keeping her baby, she'd jump at the chance to cuddle Rachel while Caitlin went to the rescue of Elaine.

Wrong. Again.

"Thanks!" she said, putting Rachel into Chloe's outstretched arms, then gave us a few instructions.

Chloe held Rachel awkwardly, making her squirm. Every few minutes her head slipped off Chloe's forearm and dangled in the air, making her turn red and yelp like a driver hitting a horn in warning.

"Chloe!" I said, as I bent over and shifted Rachel back into a safer and more comfortable position.

"Sorry!" she said. Yet her gaze kept drifting away from Rachel and towards the patio, where all the action was.

Today was the first day in nearly a week that Chloe wasn't vomiting, dizzy, nauseated or so fatigued that she could barely do anything without wanting to lie down and take a nap.

She actually had an appetite. We'd stopped on the drive here at Dairy Queen to down chocolate milkshakes.

"I'll hold Rachel," I said.

"Thanks, I'm starving," she said, her tone grateful and sheepish at the same time as she rose.

I gently placed Rachel's head against my upper arm as I cradled her. She took a few quick breaths, seemingly gearing up to start crying any second soon. I panicked, whirling through Caitlin's list of instructions. Then I noticed Rachel's pacifier had fallen out of her mouth.

What had Caitlin said about that?

"If her pacifier falls out, just push it into her mouth, like so." She'd pushed her middle finger into the pacifier. "Until she starts sucking again."

I did as she'd instructed and it worked like a charm; Rachel instantly settled down. I had no experience with babies. The only babies and toddlers I'd had contact with were babies and toddlers when I was a baby and toddler – not exactly experiences I had much memory of.

The Levitt siblings kept their distance from their handful of Toronto cousins (probably by mutual design) and my mother's relatives lived in Montreal and Chicago. I had had trouble even recognizing the majority of my relatives, on both sides, who had attended my mother's funeral service and burial. That limited the access to the children of my second cousins, who were mostly older than Chloe and I, to extremely rare family get-togethers, basically bar mitzvahs, weddings and funerals.

The backyard was overflowing with family and neighbours. On the patio, Elaine's husband Peter remained at the barbeque grilling hamburgers, veggie burgers and chicken breasts for the guests going for seconds and thirds.

The toddlers were shrieking with laughter as they jumped in and out of a large wading pool, splashing each other and everyone nearby. Revved up hamburgers and hot dogs just served to them by Elaine and Caitlin, the older kids were chasing each other, tossing bits of bun and potato chips.

Lindy's family looked to be, lucky for them, nothing like mine. They appeared close. Lindy and her sisters all lived within a few blocks of each other, and were in and out of each other's houses. Not that there weren't fights and resentments from what Lindy had told me; however, the blow-ups blew over fast.

I tried to imagine what it would have been like to grow up like this instead of in the Levitt family isolation chamber. Sure looked like it would have been nice. "You okay with Rachel?" Lindy asked, sitting down in the lawn chair beside me, still plainly sore from the surgery. She looked weary and pale, her long blond hair a tad greasy and sloppily tied back in a ponytail. "She's a cutie, isn't she? Yes you are," she said, bending her head down to kiss Rachel on the forehead. There was such longing on her face that I shut my eyes for a moment; it was too intimate to view.

"Yeah, I am," I said, and I was. At seven weeks, Rachel was just beginning to look around, show interest in what was happening around her. She would follow any loud noise, and when her pacifier threatened to fall out of her mouth, I tapped it back in place. I felt this kind of maternal thrill every time I managed, for now at least, to stop her from crying, and make her content in my arms.

"Thanks for inviting Chloe and me," I said. "You've got a great family. I'm having a good time."

And so was Chloe. I glanced up. She was now standing with two couples on the patio.

"I'm glad you both could come," Lindy said. "Chloe's pretty friendly."

I nodded, watching how hyped up Chloe was as she talked to Caitlin and her husband. I guessed she was releasing all the stored nervous energy she'd built up worrying about how her dad was going to take finding out she was pregnant.

I caught Chloe's gaze and waved, and she came over, grabbing a nearby lawn chair.

"Alice says your collages are amazing," Lindy said. "What are you are working on now?"

Chloe looked over at me with uncertainty, remembering, as I did, Leslea's reaction to a collage Chloe had brought home to show her two days ago.

"Oh, so that's what you're working on," she'd said. She had then made some superficial comment. When Chloe started talking excitedly about the collage, Leslea had cut her short, saying, "I get it, Chloe. No need to tell me more."

Standing there beside Chloe listening, I'd felt so badly for her.

Hesitantly at first, Chloe began describing her latest collage, and then, encouraged by Lindy's questioning, chattered away with enthusiasm and ease.

Lindy was being polite, yes, but her politeness was more than merely good manners. From my conversations with her I knew it came from her genuine interest in people and her thoughtfulness. Lindy made me, and now Chloe too, I could tell, feel heard and understood.

"Lindy, save me. I'm going under!" Elaine shouted.

We all looked over. Elaine was surrounded by wet toddlers shouting, "I'm hungry!" "I wanna eat, I wanna eat!" Laughing, she raised her arms and moved them back and forth in a distress signal.

Lindy rolled her eyes and gingerly raised herself out of the chair. "Elaine, I'm coming!" Turning to face us again, she asked, "Do you want me to bring you something to eat?"

I shook my head no, full from the milkshake.

"No thank you, I'm going back over to Peter for another veggie burger in a sec," Chloe replied.

As Lindy went towards Elaine, Chloe murmured, "She's so nice."

"She is, isn't she?"

"Too bad about everything. Her husband Don is nice too!"

On the drive over I had told Chloe about Lindy, how we'd met and about Lindy's surgery, and left it at that for the time being, waiting to see how they would get along.

Chloe leaned back, as if she didn't know whether she should stay with me or go back over to the patio.

"Go eat and enjoy yourself!" I said. "I'm good here."

I kept an eye on Chloe all afternoon, wanting to see how she got on with Lindy and with her family. In that regard, things were fine. She clearly liked them and they appeared to like her back. She was as relaxed and happy as I'd seen her since she'd told me the news at the fertility clinic.

Observing her with their children was a whole other ball game, however.

It didn't take long for her to get antsy with their stories, and with their showing off of their dolls and toys. I had yet to notice her take more than a few minutes to play with any of them. That was how she was with Frederick too, never carrying him down to the basement, never playing with him, and only sometimes quickly patting him, too wrapped up in her work, too wrapped up in herself period, to be honest. I hated even to admit this to myself, but her behaviour reminded me of my father.

If I remembered anything from being a kid, it was just how much attention I'd wanted.

I had that in mind when Elaine's two oldest daughters, Sophie and Lianne, came over, asking me to choose which outfits their Barbie dolls should wear to a movie premiere. I played Hollywood stylist, putting together various outfits for them to select from.

When they didn't let their youngest sister Holly join in because earlier she'd accidentally ripped the train on one of the Barbie's gowns, I whispered in her ear that once her sisters left to dress their Barbies, we could read together.

In a little knapsack slung over her shoulders, I saw several picture books. I supposed she was used to being excluded and her books were companions, at the ready whenever necessary. I knew the feeling.

As Rachel dozed, I asked Holly if she could read me a story. Sweet kid; she took care to read the first two *Olivia the Pig* books in a low voice so as not to awaken Rachel. Most excellent books; I liked them just as much as Holly did.

A few minutes after Holly left, Lindy came back over.

"That's so great that Chloe plans to be an artist," Lindy said, as she eased carefully into the lawn chair.

"Yeah, she's really gifted," I said, keeping one eye on Chloe and the other on Rachel, who was stirring. Chloe was, yet would she be able to develop that talent if she kept the baby?

"You are too," Lindy said. "Everyone that comes to my house admires the shadow box. I love it. You must miss your mother so much."

"I do," I said softly. Lindy looked over at me as I shifted Rachel in my arms and rocked her, her eyes closing as if she was dozing off again. I saw Lindy glance at the scars on my forearms. From the sad-for-me look she gave me, it seemed as if she'd figured out how I'd gotten them.

"What was your mother like?" Lindy asked, playing with Rachel's foot.

I was quiet for a moment, all the adjectives I usually trotted out to describe her feeling so inadequate. "Like you. A very caring person."

Lindy flushed. "Thanks."

Even with Lindy, I found it painful to talk much about my mother, and she got that. She had tact in spades – a key ingredient in any friend of mine.

"How are you doing?" I asked.

She hummed. "Getting used to not being able to lift anything. and still a bit sore. Otherwise, I guess better. At work, they made me a customer service rep. No lifting, just complaint solving."

"If anyone can do that, you can!"

"What about you? You find a place yet?" she asked.

I shrugged, not knowing what to say about reconsidering my scheme to move out. What Eric had said to me was reverberating, in my own version of jury deliberations. Having to agree with his arguments didn't come easy. The pièce de resistance of his argument – that my mother wouldn't want me to move out, have no contact with him, and undermine, or as Eric had said ruin, my future prospects, maybe my life – was impossible to disagree with.

Of course, the reality that the apartments John and I continued to see were either dumps or, if even passable, out of my budget, just braced up what Eric was saying.

And if I wasn't already spinning with indecision, there was the call I'd gotten from Parnell yesterday to tell me I'd been accepted for an internship at the Royal Ontario Museum. It was awesome, and I was thrilled until I started picturing how I was going to do it while going to school part-time and working almost full-time, watching every penny. That was a thrill killer.

Talk about Chloe being indecisive!

"My art teacher called yesterday," I said, doing the only thing I could do, considering my confusion: detour the conversation. "I'm going to be an intern at the Royal Ontario Museum for a credit. Once I'm settled in at the ROM, I'll give you an insider's tour."

"You better!" she said, smiling.

I didn't want to press her on her future. I had learned from Caitlin that everyone in Lindy's extended family was contributing money for Lindy as a birthday present. Money she could use for either one more try at IVF, once she had completely recovered, or towards an international adoption. Lindy and Don had already been on the Ontario adoption waiting list for a year and a half. Typically it took years to get an infant or a toddler. That was why so many couples went the international adoption route.

I looked around the backyard. Grandparents, parents, uncles, aunts, cousins, siblings – if my rosy fantasy played out, Chloe's baby certainly would grow up with a whole different experience of family than Chloe and me had.

Suddenly Rachel started to wail and kick her feet. Flustered, I glanced over at Lindy.

She smiled. "She's wet or hungry, or both," she said, leaning close and taking Rachel out of my arms.

"Certainly wet," she said, patting Rachel's bottom. Rachel dribbled the pacifier out of her mouth each time Lindy tried to tap it in. "And hungry too. It's time for a feeding. Caitlin left some bottles in the fridge." Cradling Rachel, who was now wailing with all her strength, she went towards the kitchen.

My arms suddenly felt empty without her, I had gotten so used to her resting against me.

I sighed. It would be really hard to give up your own child, even if it was for the best. Or to give up on having your own child.

chapter**thirty-six**

I decided to walk from Atticus's to Caleb's. On that hour-long walk, I thought over what my father had said about me moving out, and what my mother would have wanted me to do. My mother wouldn't have wanted me to; he was right about that.

She had loved him, she had accepted him, though to be honest, part of that was likely resignation. And forgiveness too. I had never heard her say a word of complaint about him. But there must have been enough not to complain about too; at least I hoped there had been enough.

I didn't have to like a lot of the things he'd done and how he could be sometimes; all the same, I didn't want to be caught up in hating him full-time either. It was just too much of an energy vampire.

My mother would have wanted me to work at having a better relationship with my father.

And I wanted to be able to enjoy what there was to enjoy in my life. Being with Chloe, John, Lindy and, even at long distance, Luke. The internship, school, working at Atticus's Attic. And that would be pretty near impossible to do running myself into the ground, trying to get by. I wanted my life to be more than just that.

So while making this legal-style closing argument to myself, jury of one, I reached my verdict by the time I reached Caleb's. I wasn't going to move out. I was going to tell my father later and Chloe now.

When I got to Caleb's, the tension between Caleb and Chloe was as visible as lightning. Even Frederick, aboard Air Alice on his journey down the rickety stairs to the basement, seemed aware of it. He stopped his frantic nosing into my backpack to get at his ham on whole-wheat roll for his in-flight snack, and began whimpering, manoeuvring his head to rest under my chin, his cold, wet nose in the hollow of my neck, his horrific doggy breath fouling the air supply to my nostrils.

When I put him down at the bottom of the stairs, instead of moseying over to Caleb, he plopped himself down on my feet.

"Hi folks!" I said. Dumb, lame greeting.

I was getting tense myself standing there with a basset hound who had just hooked his front paws around my ankles like they were the flesh and blood equivalent of Linus's security blanket.

Caleb and Chloe were equally frozen in place, without having Frederick as an anchor. Chloe was gluing something on a collage, a gluing that looked and sounded like she was pounding iron on an anvil rather than smoothing down something papery with glue on its back. And Caleb was measuring a plank of wood loudly, the metal tape measure making a tap-shoe ping on the plank.

"Oh . . . Alice," Caleb said, bent down over the plank.

"Alice . . ." Chloe breathed out, my name hissed more than enunciated.

"What's up?" Even dumber than my greeting. And to tell the truth, I didn't want to know what was up.

Then Chloe unfroze and pirouetted over to me, a leap of liberating fury, and like it or not, I was about to find out what was up.

"I asked . . . *him* . . . if we could move in. He's got plenty of space. Two empty bedrooms upstairs," Chloe said loudly.

Her referring to Caleb by the pronouns "him" and "he" told me all I needed to know about what Caleb's response had been.

"He said NO!"

Shout at me and, like Caleb, I shut down, in resistance. And from the tightness of Caleb's lips, the strained deepening of the lines around his mouth, his stare that seemed to be taking in nothing, his shop was closed for business. Then he turned on the power saw and started sawing the plank into strips.

"Can you believe that?" Chloe said, a bit softer as if she was slowly deflating, beginning that slide I knew so well from wrath to misery.

Actually, I could. Actually, I wouldn't have believed my ears had Chloe told me Caleb had agreed.

But I could also get why Chloe had asked, and why she had clung to the hope that Caleb would go along . . . despite all she knew about him.

I was embarrassed to recall that when I'd told John I was going to move out I was fantasizing that he would say to me, "Eileen and I have spare rooms. Why don't you move in?" Of course, he hadn't said that, but that hadn't stopped me from still grasping onto the stupid, faint hope that he would reconsider when he came with me and saw how dumpy the basement apartments were.

He never had though. I was hurt, but I also got why he and Eileen wouldn't. They had a life, a home, a peace and quiet routine they were comfortable with, and I would be one big major disturbance – especially to a couple that had never had kids. And there were probably tons of other reasons out of my sightline. So I got over it . . . mostly.

And Caleb, his reasons for not wanting Chloe, me, and possibly a baby were as obvious to me as the saw in his hands. And hidden from Chloe by the concrete curtain of stupid, faint hopes.

From what I could tell, he had made a life alone for himself that worked for him.

Sure, he wanted company, but he wanted company that came and went, and left him to live his life the way he wanted to.

Sure, he'd been nice enough to store my mother's keepsakes upstairs in one of the bedrooms, but things he could handle in his house, not people.

People who would disturb his routine, people who would make noise and, worst of all, make demands on him when all he wanted to do was what he wanted to do.

Sure, he cared for Chloe, but he was who he was, and he gave Chloe what he could give her. And he had given her a lot. In fact, he'd thrown her a lifesaver, and shown her how to keep afloat with it.

People gave you what they could. Sure, lots of times you wanted more. But that was like asking a cold-water facet to spout hot water. Were you going to punish them for not giving what they didn't have in them to give?

Frederick gave a mournful howl, as if he sensed all the unhappiness in the basement. I knelt down, scratched behind his ears and rested my head on the top of his. I would have liked nothing more than to give my own mournful howl.

"You and that . . . dog!" Chloe said, with disgust.

I guess she expected, hoped, that I would come to her defence and convince Caleb that the argument over this wasn't finished yet.

It was, though.

"Chloe, cool it, okay!" I shushed. "Don't wreck everything!"

As I got myself upright, Chloe stomped back over to her collage and returned to gluing with force loud enough to be heard.

After refilling Frederick's bowl with a bottle of water, I went over to Chloe, who was clutching the sides of the table as if she was dizzy. Next out of my Mary Poppins-style backpack (one of my favourite bits in the movie was how Mary Poppins seemed magically to have everything anyone needed inside her carpetbag purse) was a can of ginger ale and a roll of Ritz crackers. I handed them to Chloe.

She mumbled her thanks, popped the can open and started drinking. I leaned against her.

"Don't be mad at Caleb," I whispered. "He's done a lot for you. You know that."

She nodded, looking beat.

"You know him; you know how he's lived . . ."

She sighed, and then sagged against me. "I know. I just hoped . . ."

Don't we all.

"I decided not to move out," I whispered. "I'll give you the details later. So we don't need a place here anyhow."

"Like I would have gotten one for us anyway," she said, sounding sulky and weary at the same time.

After Chloe's blow-up at Caleb, we all went into pretend everything was the same as always mode. Chloe went back to work on her collage, but whenever I glanced over at her she had this dazed look on her face.

Caleb continued sawing and sanding planks of wood, occasionally coming over to help me get the shelves for the curio I was making into the grooves inside.

Just a couple of millimetres off and I could shove until the proverbial cows came home, and forget about it. You've got to watch out for the millimetres as much as for the avalanches – my newest motto to live by.

The afternoon passed with the sounds of sawing, sanding, shoving and the occasional melancholy howl from Frederick. Gradually I felt the atmosphere clear, like humidity out of the air after a thunderstorm, as if things were, close enough anyway for today, going back to how they'd been between Chloe and Caleb. She needed him; she needed what he had given her, and what he could give her. And he needed her in all kinds of ways too.

And I thought he knew that, even if Chloe had breeched his boundaries, big time. But Caleb was a man after my own heart. Not only was he a devoted dog lover, he was devoted to repressing what had to be repressed if you didn't want to end up suicidal or homicidal.

By the time Chloe and I had cleaned up our work areas, and I had lugged Frederick back up the stairs, and we were all on the porch ready to say our good-byes, Caleb was acting as if nothing had happened, and Chloe was going along. So was I, and so was Frederick, who was barking at each passing car and squirrel, and then gazing at me and Caleb with pride and triumph and a show of yellow doggy teeth, as if to say, *I did this for you, I chased away those wicked cars and squirrels with my barking.*

Thank goodness because Chloe was going to need what Caleb was giving her more than ever in the months to come.

chapter**thirty-seven**

I was back at the fertility clinic. Today not to work; instead I was here to tell Elizabeth Rainey that I was returning to school after all.

She nodded brusquely at my explanation. I no longer took her brusqueness personally. It was part of her efficiency policy – everything, along with every word and motion, to be said and done as swiftly and economically as possible. As I was about to leave, she called out, "You have a standing offer for a job next summer."

I flexed my fingers and performed as if I was typing away like a piano maestro at a computer keyboard.

She smiled at me. "See you next summer then."

Just outside her cubicle, I ran into Joan Lansing who was taking a patient to an examining room. She told me to hold tight for a minute because she wanted to talk to me.

I sat, having plenty of time before meeting up with Chloe on the other side of the floor. She had an appointment with a new gynie, Dr. Dinah Sonnenberg. Uncle Samuel had made the arrangements after Chloe had complained about Dr. Benedict. Uncle Samuel and Dr. Sonnenberg were old friends.

Relief of relief, Uncle Samuel was meeting us there too. He'd flown in late last night. Good for him and even better for Chloe. She was still insisting on having and keeping the baby. We were all getting together with Dr. Sonnenberg to talk it over.

I'd asked Chloe to meet me a half hour before. I wanted to bring up the option of her giving up her baby for adoption to Lindy, in private, so she wouldn't feel ganged up on.

Yet, yet, yet.

I could really get why Chloe didn't want to give up the baby. All the wisest reasons in the world didn't stop you from believing that somehow your love, your care, what you had to give, what you wanted to give, counted most of all, no matter what the circumstances were.

Plus, and what a Mount Everest of a plus it was, just like Chloe, I wasn't good at letting go of anyone and anything I loved. Even if it was better for them. Even if it was better for me.

I didn't notice that Joan was waving her fingers in front of my eyes until the two women sitting next to me started giggling.

"Joan! Sorry," I said sheepishly.

"Any more lost in thought and I'd have to send a search and rescue team," she teased. "Listen, I wanted to ask you how things were going with Chloe."

I gave her an update, finishing with the Lindy option. Joan bobbed her head enthusiastically at that possibility. She knew Lindy, and like everyone who knew Lindy, liked her enormously.

"Do you know about open adoptions?"

I shook my head.

Joan explained that, unlike in closed adoptions, where the birth mother never knows who the adoptive parents are and vice versa, in open adoptions, the birth mother and the adoptive parents get to know each other, and after the birth of baby have as much or as little contact as they all mutually want. In some open adoptions, the contact over the years is in the form of calls, letters and pictures. In others, the birth mother has an ongoing relationship with her child, like any close relative would.

Joan left me for a moment and came back with a handful of pamphlets on open adoption. I thanked her. I skimmed through them, getting excited as I did. This could work for Chloe.

I got up and took a deep breath. Now to make the prospect appealing. I wasn't Eric Levitt's daughter for nothing. If anyone could do it, I could. Right. Sometimes self-delusion was the best motivator you could come up, and if that was going to make me sound assured and confident, so be it.

I saw Chloe in the last seat in a row.

"Hey," I said, and sat down beside her.

"Hey yourself," she said, looking extremely fidgety. Who wouldn't be?

"So what do you think you want to do?" I asked.

"You know already," she said defiantly. "I'm going to have the baby."

"Having the baby doesn't mean you have to keep the baby," I said.

"You want me to give up my baby? The baby's mine," Chloe said, half yelling and sobbing that out. "You think I won't be a good mother. You think I can't take care of my baby."

"Of course you'll be a good mom, Chloe," I said. "But consider how hard it is going to be having to juggle care of the baby, going to school, your artwork, having a social life. Look how difficult that is for lots of women who work, women who have husbands and everything. Look how fried they get, and they have money and support."

"My dad will give me money; he'll take care of us. We can live together, and you can help me take care of the baby," Chloe said, reaching over to grab hold of my arm.

I knew this was going to hurt Chloe, and that she might get as mad as anything at me for saying this, but I had to say it. "I don't think that would work out for you, the baby or me. With the internship at the ROM, school, working for John, I won't be able to handle it, and I don't want to have to. You won't be able to do it all either, Chloe, even with your father's money. Do you really want that kind of a life for you and the baby? "

She sat huddled in the seat, crying softly.

I felt just awful. I didn't know what to say or do next.

"Hear me out," I said, pleading with her. "One of the nurses was telling me about this kind of adoption called open adoption where the birth mother can stay a part of her baby's life. Lindy and Don could adopt your baby. You met them, you know they would be loving parents, and you met their family. Picture the family life your baby could have with them."

Chloe continued to sob softly, not answering me for a while. "If I give up the baby, I'll be just like my mom, tossing my baby over to somebody else to take care of," she mumbled.

If anything was a sign of Chloe not being anything like Leslea, it was that worry.

"Don't even think that! If you decide to give up the baby, you're doing it because it is best for the baby."

"How are my girls?"

I looked up and so did Chloe, and there was Uncle Samuel barrelling towards us, his unbuttoned suit jacket practically flapping like wings he moved with such zoom power.

Before we could stand, bundle of energy that he was, he was there in front of us. We both rose and he enveloped us in a bear hug.

Chloe started to sob again. "Daddy, Daddy!"

Uncle Samuel hugged us tighter, holding on until Chloe stopped, then let us go.

I glanced over at them, so alike in appearance, and yet so different. If only Uncle Samuel had been here for Chloe, she could have been more like him in the ways that mattered.

Well, maybe now, way overdue, he could start administering his antidote to Leslea's poisoned parenting.

"So they cornered the market on beige synthetics here," he joked, pointing to the beige plastic chairs, beige berber carpet, the dingy beige-painted walls, beige cubicle dividers and beige metal desks. "Enough to turn you green, even the son of greenies like me," he continued.

Even Chloe smiled at that.

Greenie was a nickname given to immigrant Jews, like Uncle Samuel's and my mother's parents had been.

"Enough to turn you all natural," he quipped.

"You already are all natural." And he was. That was one of the things I loved about Uncle Samuel. He was who he was. There wasn't a phoney or false cell in him.

"All natural," he said, patting his stomach. "There's too much of the all natural, so my doctor keeps telling me. 'When are you going to lose that gut, Samuel?' is what he said so elegantly to me in my last checkup."

He looked down at his stomach. "Still here?"

We both nodded and then laughed.

He shrugged. "It loves me, what can I say? It doesn't want to leave me. I sit up, I push up, and still it hangs around."

"Samuel, the jokes, *still* the bad jokes." That had to be Dr. Sonnenberg speaking. A tall woman with straight shoulder-length white hair came towards us. Noticeably dressed for comfort, Dr. Sonnenberg was wearing black pants, a red cotton turtleneck and black flats.

Much taller than Uncle Samuel, she bent over and kissed him on the cheek.

"Dinnie, here's Chloe, all grown up, and this is my niece, Alice."

She shook our hands firmly. "Follow me to my office."

As we entered her office, we had to step carefully around the stacks of tottering files and books on the floor. Uncle Samuel called out, "Dinnie, the mess, *still* the mess."

She turned and made a face at him.

"You should have seen Dinnie's dorm room," Uncle Samuel said. "You could see nothing for the piles. Only the bed, and as I remember, it had piles of papers, books, notebooks on it too."

"I know where everything is," Dr. Sonnenberg said, a bit defensively.

"I've heard that story before," Uncle Samuel said, with a groan.

Dr. Sonnenberg sat behind her desk, and Chloe and I sat in the two chairs in front of it. "I'll get my secretary to bring another chair for you, Samuel."

"No, no, I need the exercise. Does standing count as exercise? It burns more calories than sitting, so it does count."

We all groaned loudly at that, and Uncle Samuel shrugged dramatically.

While Dr. Sonnenberg searched the top of her desk for Chloe's file, I peeked over at Chloe. What a difference just these past ten minutes with Uncle Samuel had made. She looked almost relaxed. No doubt that was behind Uncle Samuel's clowning around.

"Found it!" Dr. Sonnenberg announced, waving it at us.

"Took you long enough," Uncle Samuel said, pretending to grumble.

"All right," she said, looking at us, but most of all at Chloe, waiting for her to say what she had to say. Another pleasant change from the put-my-words-in-your-mouth approach of Dr. Benedict.

"Alice just told me about open adoptions," Chloe gushed out, startling me. "What do you know about them? What do you think about them? I can't abort my baby. I can't do that."

Chloe looked at us, one by one, then her gaze settled on her father pleadingly, as if she wanted him to make the choice for her.

"I know some about open adoptions," Uncle Samuel said slowly. "If you decided that was for you, you would select the parents and work out between you how much communication you would have in the future. Am I correct about that, Dinnie?"

Dr. Sonnenberg nodded and outlined how the process worked. The prospective parents went through the standard social agency background checks, interviews and home studies, and once they were approved, then all the other arrangements were made between the birth mother and the adoptive parents.

"From my experience," Dr. Sonnenberg said cautiously, as if she didn't want to make it sound like she was endorsing it, "it can work very well for everyone concerned. Chloe, it's a difficult decision you have to make, and as much as every one of us in the room would like to make it easier for you, you have to make it yourself because you will be the one living with the consequences."

Chloe twirled a piece of hair around her finger and sat there, looking around. "I met a couple, Lindy and Don McConnell, friends of Alice. Lindy, she's gone through a couple IVF treatments here at the clinic, and she hasn't gotten pregnant. They're extremely nice and so is their family. What do you think, Daddy?" Chloe said, her voice squeaking with nerves.

I caught Uncle Samuel pass a glance at Dr. Sonnenberg and she gave him this kind of look that said watch what you say.

He shifted from foot to foot, shifting into a pile of files on the floor which slid down like a row of dominoes.

"Dinnie, what did I tell you about the piles? You're going to have to switch to orthopaedic surgery because I tell you that's what your patients are going to need after tripping on the files."

"Maybe it's you, Samuel. I've danced with you, and if I didn't require orthopaedic surgery after that, I never will."

"Ha, ha," Uncle Samuel said. "Agreed, a suave ballroom dancer I'm not. Clumsy I may be, but the piles, they make getting through your office an obstacle course. Do you give your patients award medals if they make it safely over to your desk?"

We laughed hard at that.

Then Chloe said, "So, Daddy?"

"It sounds promising. Good people, Alice?" he asked.

"Terrific," I said quickly.

Chloe was quiet for a while. All I could hear in the room was breathing and paper shifting like a pile was about to do its own version of a rock slide.

"You don't think that . . . you don't think that . . . this makes me like Mom?" If Chloe twirled that strand of hair around her finger any tighter, her finger would be purple from lack of circulation.

"No Chloe, it doesn't," Uncle Samuel said, sighing.

"Let me tell you a story," he said, taking in a big breath. "Dinnie knows it; I should have told it to you already. You and I had been apart for so long, and when we got back together, you had spent all those years thinking what a schmuck you had for a father, and I didn't want to send you right back to thinking that. When your mother and I married, I wanted a family right away. Your mother got pregnant. We hadn't been married long, and she wasn't ready yet to be a mother. Not that she didn't love you. Once she had you, she did. I adored you too. Who wouldn't? You were a cutie, a heartbreaker, remember Dinnie? I adored you, but did I help your mother? Hardly. I'd just gotten promoted and was on business trips for half the week. I loved being a father, and I took care of you when I was around, but I wasn't around much. Your aunt Ellen, she made up the slack, taking care of you, loving you, even though she was going through a rough pregnancy carrying Alice. She'd already miscarried twice."

Chloe, stunned by all this, was listening raptly, as I was. I hadn't known anything about my mother miscarrying.

"Your mother and I fought about this. This, combined with the other problems, made things come to an end between us in a big bang. Leslea convinced me that she should have sole custody of you because of all the travelling I did. I gave in. I hated coming back to Toronto, and I did it less and less. By then, you weren't glad to see me anymore, and who could blame you. So to the point. I love you, but I've been self-centred too – when you were born, and even these last few years when I've been asking you to live with me in Hong Kong. Did I change my life? Did I move here? No, I asked you to move. You understand the point I'm making? I hope you do. I think I lost it back there somewhere," he joked nervously.

I got it. I also got something else. Uncle Samuel's voice had quavered with such tenderness and grief when he'd said my mother's name. Now I was a hundred percent sure he had loved her, and that had to be some of the reason why it had been so painful for him to come back to Toronto. Had my mother known, and loved him in her way? And had that way been a little romantic, too, or more than just a little?

I watched Chloe's face anxiously, as did Uncle Samuel and Dr. Sonnenberg.

"Hey Daddy," Chloe said, and stretched out her arm towards him. Tiptoeing around the piles like an awkward ballet dancer, he made it over to Chloe's side and took her hand.

"I'm going to give up the baby to Lindy and her husband," she said, her voice breaking. "But I will still be the mom?"

"Always," Uncle Samuel said softly.

Tears starting running down Chloe's face, and then Uncle Samuel started getting teary.

Even if a choice was the right thing to do, that didn't make it any easier.

chapter**thirty-eight**

An oddball and more than a little ill-at-ease gathering, consisting of my father, Leslea, Uncle Samuel, Chloe, Merle Adler and I, were standing in a semi-circle surrounding my mother's gravesite, waiting for the rabbi to show up.

The unveiling of my mother's tombstone had occurred in mid-March. Toronto had been hit then by a fierce late-winter blizzard. That had cut the number of mourners who had said they were coming to the service to only a dozen or so. Even the rabbi had almost not made it. Driving to the cemetery, his old Toyota Tercel had slid off the road twice on the hilly, two-lane road leading to the cemetery.

By the time the flustered rabbi had showed up half an hour late, covered with snow and sleet, the mourners had all resembled snowmen, and my mother's snow-coated gravestone, as those in the row beside hers, miniature igloos.

The rabbi's prayers could hardly be heard through the pounding of the wind. When he'd cut off the cloth covering the inscription on the tombstone, it had whirled up striking him in the face, then had fluttered away.

Every time I recalled how horrific the unveiling had been from start to finish, I felt sick with grief. After the appointment with Dr. Sonnenberg when Uncle Samuel had questioned me about it, I'd started weeping like a monsoon. By that time we were in his hotel room. That had gotten Uncle Samuel all remorseful as he'd kept apologizing for not being there.

Then Chloe had come up with the idea of holding a second unveiling. Not even waiting to pull myself together, I'd called Eric and blubbered into the phone as I'd asked him if we could. The combination of my totally out of character blubbering with the knowledge that Uncle Samuel was sitting next to me listening to every word I was saying, had made him give his consent immediately.

So here we were, waiting for the rabbi again. Another one though. This one was a rent-a-rabbi. Since Eric had never been a member of the synagogue congregation my mother had belonged to, and the rabbi only conducted services on behalf of congregation members, he'd had to hire a rabbi to conduct this unveiling. The rent-a-rabbis were usually rabbis who had just graduated from the yeshiva. The majority had yet to be retained by a synagogue congregation, and thus were available to conduct weddings, funerals and services at shivas.

Unlike that gruesome day in March, the weather today was as perfect as weather could get. The sky was a cloudless blue, the temperature hovering near thirty Celsius was pleasantly hot and soothing and there was a light breeze causing the two wind chimes Chloe had hung in a maple nearby to tinkle melodically.

Leslea had arrived with Eric, decked out as if she was attending a late-afternoon cocktail party instead of a late-afternoon unveiling. She was wearing a strapless print dress with a pearl and diamond choker with matching earrings and bracelet, and Jimmy Choo stiletto heels.

Was she dressed this way to show Uncle Samuel what hot stuff he was missing out on? Or was she dressed this way to raise his blood pressure when he saw where his alimony money was going? Probably both.

As Leslea had tottered forward to kiss Chloe, Chloe had stepped back. It was a good thing Eric had been working on his biceps because he'd needed that upper-body strength to grab hold of Leslea as she'd nearly done a yoga-worthy split on the roadway.

"Dressed to kill, mother," Chloe had sneered. "Any males in the area are dead already."

That was a bad pun worthy of Uncle Samuel, whom Chloe was staying with at the Park Plaza. He certainly had seemed to enjoy it; I could see him struggling not to laugh.

He, Merle, Eric and Leslea had then shaken hands as if they were gripping a slimy cod; afterwards all looking as if like they'd like nothing better than a fast bout with a hand sanitizer.

As we'd walked towards my mom's gravesite, Leslea had trouble keeping up. With each step her stilettos pierced the damp grass, forcing her to struggle to free her foot until in a final, losing battle one of her heels had remained in the ground permanently.

Merle had offered to go back to her car to get a pair of flip-flops she had in her gym bag. She'd just come from swimming at the Bathurst JCC. Neon purple, they made quite the fashion statement, though probably not quite the fashion statement Leslea had had in mind.

At the gravesite, the breeze had turned gusty, picking up in the process Eric's yarmulke. He had to sprint after it before it blew away. When he'd returned from catching it, Uncle Samuel, taking pity on him, had silently handed him one of the bobby pins he'd used to anchor his into his curly mop of hair, naturally having more experience with the anchoring of yarmulkes since he was an observant Jew. Thanking him, Eric had pinned his yarmulke down.

On seeing the glorious blooming flower bed in front of my mother's gravestone, Leslea had grumbled to Eric, "What are the girls complaining about? Look at those flowers. Magnificent, aren't they?"

"No thanks to you, Mother," Chloe had muttered. "It's thanks to Alice and me. We replanted the whole flower bed."

"We had to."

"Your cut-rate gardeners' motto must be: Dead flowers for the dead."

Leslea had stared at Eric, imploring him to do or say something. Then I had stared at him, daring him to defend her.

"Stop it!" he'd said perfunctorily, as if he knew he had to say something to appease her.

By then, all of us were praying for the rent-a-rabbi to arrive already. Five minutes later, he did. We had all quieted down and were just staring at the gravestone, thinking and remembering (excluding Leslea who kept looking down at her feet to stare at the damage the flip-flops and muddy grass had done to her French pedicure and then all around, as if she couldn't bear even to glance at the tombstones).

Eric didn't appear any more comfortable either, surrounded by all these inescapable reminders of mortality.

The rabbi, the really young rabbi – he seemed to be the age of an undergraduate student with his boyish round face and longish wavy brown hair – hurried towards us. "My apologies," he said. "I got trapped in the middle of a funeral procession and had problems finding a roadway to reach this section."

"This *is* the place *that* is going to happen to you," Merle said dryly, as she stepped forward to shake his hand. "I'm Merle Adler. Ellen was my best friend."

"Rabbi Feinberg," he said, introducing himself to her and us.

Standing next to Merle, Uncle Samuel was so rapt in memory staring at my mother's gravestone that the arrival of the rabbi didn't even register on him. His eyes were shiny, and his cheeks stained with tears.

"My deepest condolences on the loss of your wife, Ellen," Rabbi Feinberg said, grasping Uncle Samuel's hand, breaking through his reverie. Our collective gasp helped with that.

"No, no, I'm not the husband," he stuttered out. "The gentleman over there, Eric Levitt, Ellen was his wife."

If the earth could have opened and swallowed him up, the very red-faced and very embarrassed Rabbi Feinberg would have gone willingly. Though we all, excluding the pedicure examiner, could see how the rabbi had made the mistake.

Uncle Samuel gave the impression of being overcome by grief, while Eric was, as ever, self-contained. The rabbi rushed over to Eric and apologized, and Eric accepted it graciously. Still it was obvious, at least to me, from the way his gaze rapidly shifted from person to person, as if he was checking out their reactions, that the rabbi had just activated one of his guilt buttons.

All these weird, blackly comic moments would have freaked me out in the past. Rather than upsetting me though, I thought of how all this would have amused my mother. Mehitabel the cat's favourite all-purpose motto came to mind, and I could hear my mom's voice singing out, "*toujours gai, tourjours gai.*"

I had mostly forgotten what a mischievous, sly sense of humour my mother had had. I had mostly forgotten how much she laughed and how startled people would be when my demure-looking mother would let loose one of her deadpan zingers.

I saw Merle watching me, and I mouthed "*toujours gai, toujours gai.*" She laughed softly and winked at me.

Rabbi Feinberg quickly shook the rest of our hands as we made our introductions, and then began the prayer service in Hebrew. Uncle Samuel and Merle chanted along with him in Hebrew the first section of the *Eil Malei Rachamim,* while Chloe and I, after months of weekly visits, were able to chant it by heart in English. Eric and Leslea stood silently, Eric at least having the decency to look more and more discomfited. Leslea just looked bored . . . to death, an Uncle Samuel type pun if there ever was one.

After that the Rabbi asked us all to join hands. "I would like each of you to share a favourite memory you have of Ellen."

Usually this touchy-feely sharing stuff made me squirm. Right now, though, it seemed to be the right thing to do.

Definitely the next right and kind thing to do was to thank the rabbi, who still had a hangdog expression on his face, in all probability for his lateness, and of course, for mistaking Uncle Samuel for the husband. "That's a really nice idea, isn't it? Thank you for suggesting it," I said looking around at everybody, who added their thanks.

The rabbi smiled with relief.

"I'll start," said Chloe. "I was, like, so nervous about performing in this figure skating competition. I thought I would fall; I thought everyone would laugh at me; I thought I would come in last and wanted to cross my name off the list. But Aunt Ellen ordered me not to cross my name off because none of those things were going to happen because I was going to be wearing a magical figure skating sweater guaranteed to shield me against any and all *einhorehs.* The skating competition was two days away and Aunt Ellen spent most of those two days knitting to finish that magical sweater for me. I didn't fall, nobody laughed and I placed third. When they announced my name, I could hear Aunt Ellen and Alice cheering and clapping. And I wore that sweater so much that the wool was worn as thin as cotton. It's in my bottom dresser drawer and pinned on it are five ribbons I won for placing in the top three in several competitions."

I had completely forgotten that.

"Can I go next?" Uncle Samuel asked, his head bent down as if he didn't want us to be able to see his expression, raising it when he'd gotten a grip on the feelings evoked by Chloe's story.

"The girls, Ellen and I were visiting the Parrot Jungle in Miami. Must have been four years ago. After the parrot show, we were standing around and one of the star parrots – granted, it could have been a co-star, they all looked the same to me – landed on Ellen's shoulder and squawked, I'm guessing this, 'Polly wants a cracker' into her ear. When Polly didn't get her cracker, she nipped the first button off Ellen's blouse, then the second. Before Polly could eat off all the buttons, Ellen, laughing so much she could scarcely open her shoulder bag, took out a bag of mixed nuts. She always carried around a supply of drinks and snacks for the girls. Alice yelled out, 'Is there ever not a grocery store in that purse, Mom? Mom, you're such a mother!' Polly the Parrot thought so too. She started squawking orders like General Patton and in a second, a swarm of green and yellow parrots were flying in fighter-pilot formation right towards us, like in that Hitchcock movie *The Birds*. We had to run for cover to the gift shop and the owner gave Ellen a couple of safety pins to fasten her blouse. I would have taken a picture, but Ellen threatened to break the camera, then my arm, if I tried. So the only picture I have," he said, tapping his forehead, "is in here."

The memory made me really laugh, as it did Chloe and Merle.

It took some staring at Eric to sort out the jigsaw puzzle of emotions which that story had provoked. Coupled with affection for my mom was also strong resentment towards Uncle Samuel.

Rabbi Feinberg faced me. "Would you like to go next and tell us a favourite memory?"

Instead of all the sad ones shoving their way to the front of the line and blocking from view the happy ones, a happy one elbowed its way through.

"My mom and I used to go the movies once a week, sometimes twice. She loved Meg Ryan, ever since Meg started off on TV in this soap opera. She was all excited about me seeing her favourite Meg Ryan movie, *Sleepless in Seattle*. It was playing at a second-run movie place. Like she did during all movies, my mom leaned against me, so she could whisper stuff about the movie in my ear, telling me what she liked, what was so, so dumb or so, so bad, and grip my hand during the scary and suspenseful parts. It made going to the movies, even terrible movies, fun. She really got involved. That was why she always chose seats for us away from everyone else, so she could whisper all she wanted to me without being shushed or thrown out of the theatre."

"Such a good memory," Rabbi Feinberg said, then gestured towards Leslea that it was her turn.

She gave an exasperated sigh, and then Eric gave her this threatening look. "Passover, last year, no two years ago, Ellen made that seder dinner. She cooked everything herself. The food was good."

She paused, and we waited for her to say more, but she didn't. She just went back to fiddling with the choker, which if there had been any justice and supernatural magic in the world, would have strangled her in a chokehold.

She couldn't even bother to exert herself to come up with more than that generic memory. My mother had always held the Passover seders, had always done all the cooking. The food was good. No kidding. Thanks for the non-memory, Leslea.

"Alice was born premature," Eric said vehemently, like he had to assert himself, like he was getting forgotten, as if it was being forgotten that he was the husband who had lost his wife. "She weighed just five pounds at birth so she had to stay in an incubator for two weeks. When Ellen was released from the hospital, she cried and cried, saying 'all the other mothers, they get to go home with their babies, but I can't.' Every evening after work, I met Ellen in the hospital, and we would take two chairs, sit by the glass surrounding the room with the preemies, and hold hands as we watched you through the window. You hardly gained any weight those two weeks, and after your mother begged the doctor, he let us bring you home. And in a month, when Ellen and I brought Alice in for a checkup, the doctor said he could hardly recognize Alice as the same baby. She'd gained six pounds."

Eric then took hold of my hand and squeezed it. I squeezed it back. I had thought I always knew most of what there was to know (and wished wasn't there to know) about my parents' relationship, but I was being proven wrong again. Maybe they had been happy and in love, on both sides, for longer than I thought.

"My turn," Merle said lightheartedly. "I knew Ellen before any of you did. Since our days at Hebrew school where we were always being made to sit apart in our classes because we never shut up. On Friday and Saturday evenings, after ironing our long hair straight, and I do mean with an iron, Ellen and I dressed up in our hippie best – halter tops, bell-bottoms, leather sandals, love beads, dangling earrings – and hung out in Yorkville, back when it was a hippie hangout and not an enclave of pricey boutiques. Us imitation hippy girls, we went to the Riverboat, ordered one espresso after another and listened to folk music. Gordon Lightfoot and Joni Mitchell performed there before they became famous. And we met our share of hippie boys too. Some we dated. Some we dumped. Some dumped us too. Fools. You don't know what you missed out on. Those were the days, my friends, *toujours gai, toujours gai.*"

Eric hadn't let go of my hand, and I glanced over at his face and he had kind of a half smile, like he was remembering my mother, not only as my mother, but as herself.

"I would like to end with the personal meditation concluding *Eil Malei Rachamim,*" Rabbi Feinberg said. This time, instead of chanting in Hebrew, he said each line in English and asked us to repeat after him, so we could all pray together in memory of my mother.

Accompanied by the tinkling sounds of the wind chimes, we did.

chapter**thirty-nine**

I was on the terrace stretched out on a Muskoka chair. It was early evening, cool edging toward crisp; the faint honking of cars was the only constant sound, along with the occasional protective growl from Frederick, who firmly believed he was babysitting me.

My father had gone to see a play at the Royal Alexandra Theatre with Suzette, and Chloe had left an hour earlier with Caleb to go to a gallery opening.

I was glad for the quiet, glad to have the chance to sit outside staring at the night sky with only Frederick and a hazy sliver of moon and freckling of faint stars for company.

It had been a crazy, hectic couple of days in a crazy, hectic September – but good in ways unexpected.

The week before school and my internship started had been taken up with moving into the condo at the Prince Arthur. What my father had planned to be a slick bachelor pad (albeit a mighty big bachelor pad with three bedrooms, a den, a solarium and a terrace large enough for a helicopter to land on), was anything but.

Most of the furnishings were new. Naturally his bedroom was. Sleekly decorated with black modern furniture, it was all minimalist straight lines and angles; the walls were a deep aqua blue that matched the colour of the satin bed covering and blinds. Stylish as it was, it looked so much like an aquarium at Niagara's *MarineLand* that each time I entered I felt like I should be donning a wetsuit and flippers.

My bedroom had been transported complete, as had the guest bedroom. Chloe was going to be camped out there whenever Uncle Samuel was away on his frequent business trips.

Uncle Samuel, better late than never, a truism never truer, was returning to Toronto to be a father to Chloe in person. He'd already rented a three-bedroom condo where Chloe was going to be living with him.

From the moment Chloe had made up her mind to give her baby up for adoption to Lindy and Don, Leslea had not shut up. She'd been ragging Chloe relentlessly about why, if she was giving up the baby, she just couldn't go ahead and have an abortion. Not only was it driving Chloe around the bend, it was doing likewise even for Len. Chloe reported he headed for the front door with the speed of an Olympic track star the second he heard Leslea restart her abortion rant. Even her bro had told her he didn't want to hear a single word about it ever again.

Yet she couldn't shut up, having become the designer-dressed version of one of those street preachers standing on the corner outside the Toronto Eaton Centre ranting about hell and damnation for all unsaved shoppers and browsers. The undisputed fact of the matter was that Chloe giving birth to her grandchild made her a grandmother, cryonic beauty regimen and all. And she just couldn't face it, pun or not.

Leslea going ballistic had its upside though. It had firmed up Uncle Samuel's resolve and had finally put something of a dent between little sis and her big bro.

After moving in, I got this bug in my head about commemorating Rosh Hashanah in this new place, celebrating it exactly as my mother would have done when she'd been well enough to do so.

So alongside the movers, the Molly Maids, the unpackers (yes, there is such a profession as professional unpacker), I had worked like the dedicated (a pleasanter word than obsessive though both applied, the latter more than the former) fiend I could be when it came to work, to get the condo into semi-decent order.

And voila! The guests I had over for Rosh Hashanah dinner on the evening of September 15 were able to eat at the dining room table with china plates and silver cutlery and roam around the condo without stubbing their toes on boxes.

The people my mother loved were there – my father, Chloe and Uncle Samuel (I had invited Merle but she was with her family in Montreal). Lindy and Don, John and Eileen, whom she would have liked as much as I did, were there too.

Caleb had declined my invitation with an expression of dismay on his face, as if I'd asked him to crowd into a phone booth with a bunch of college students attempting to make it into the Guinness World Records.

And Leslea? My father didn't say boo when I'd told him I wasn't inviting her, almost certainly craving as much peace as was humanly possible with Uncle Samuel at the same table.

The morning of the holiday Uncle Samuel had driven Chloe and me to Pardes Shalom because one of the traditions of Rosh Hashanah was to visit the graves of loved ones so that the prayers and good wishes of the dead could help the living. While we prayed for my mother, it was nice to think that she could be praying for us too.

A TTC bus engine backfired and Frederick growled, licking my hand when the noise stopped, assuming he'd done it again, kept me safe.

"Yes, you're such a brave boy, yes you are," I said, massaging his head the way I knew he liked it, and then under his drooping chin. With all seventy pounds plus of Frederick spread out on my lap and legs, I needed no blanket against the crisp chill of the air.

The terrace was bare except for two Muskoka chairs and a small table. Chloe had already diagrammed the terrace garden she'd create next spring with flower boxes, planters and miniature trees. Well, it wasn't completely barren. Off to my left was a pine birdhouse in the shape of a folk-tale chalet that Caleb had made for me as a very surprising housewarming gift.

The wish that Chloe had made that summer afternoon at Harbourfront on the propeller plane taking off had come true in a weird fashion. Who would have figured – not me, not in a million years – that our Noah's ark would be my father's new condo?

A sparrow suddenly swooped into the feeder jutting out from the birdhouse like a front porch. Good thing Frederick had poor night vision; otherwise, he might have injured himself (and me!) in his effort to protect me from any encroachment. The sparrow had departed by the time he'd opened his other eye.

The visiting birds would be the only animal occupants of this Noah's ark . . . for the foreseeable future. I would have loved to have a dog of my own, but I thought that would be pushing my luck with my father.

So I would have to continue to get my dog fix from Frederick and from Emma. Whether it was the scent of Frederick on me, or the memory of all those glorious scents wafting off me in the summer, Emma no longer sped past me like a non-stop commuter train. Instead she parked herself at my feet during Parnell's lectures, lifting her head once in a while for a big sniff, like she was waiting for a resurgence of my smelly ripeness, and then she would give a long howl, and lay down in obvious disappointment. One of these days, I was going to roll around in Emerson's football field until I was completely filthy and stinky, then go to class and make her day.

See, Luke did have some competition for my attentions; I'd told him so a couple of days ago in an email. I remained the undisputed babe magnet of the geriatric dog set.

Frederick gave a little snort, or was it a sneeze, against my stomach, then snuggled closer as if to affirm that. Though if he kept burrowing closer, he was soon going to be in my intestines.

Luke's housewarming gift was taped to my bedroom door. It was an autographed poster from the Kerry/Edwards presidential campaign. He was coming to visit for a long weekend in mid-October.

My bedroom, a keepsake itself, had become a veritable haven of keepsakes. Uncle Samuel had hammered a mezuzah he'd selected for me into the frame of my door. A gorgeous crocheted afghan, as brightly streaked with colour as a Jackson Pollack drip painting, knitted by Lindy, was draped over my bed. A small collage of Chloe's hung next to a vintage-framed movie poster of *Harry & Tonto* starring the great Art Carney of *The Honeymooners,* given to me last week by John and Eileen.

My own memory genie box hung across from the bed; it was the first thing I saw when I woke up every morning. It would be good to be able to say that I remembered some happy memory each time I saw the box, but remembering was still dredge work, requiring will and concentration.

Sometimes they came unbidden though, an unexpected gift. Like two days ago when I'd glanced out the window at the Royal Ontario Museum while on a guided tour led by the curator supervising my internship, and caught sight of Philosopher's Walk, a park-like walkway behind the museum leading to the University of Toronto campus.

I recalled how my mother and I would go there, plop down on a bench and pass the time talking and people-watching.

I was still hit by surges of memories of my mother lying curled up listless in bed, her cries for help, that last anguished look, recollections that sometimes made my knees feel like they were about to buckle, forcing me to sit down immediately.

As painful as those memories were, I didn't want to forget them. I just wished that more of the happy ones would come back to life for me. Now that her keepsakes, my memory genies, were freed from their cardboard box-bottles, maybe they would.

I missed her so much. Sometimes the longing to hear her voice, to hug her, have her hold me, to simply know she was there for me, was so sharp.

The night sky had cleared and the sliver of the moon and the scattering of stars suddenly became luminous, and I thought of Caleb's night-sky shadow boxes, haunted by ghostly glimpses of elusive dreams, longings, memories.

Before some clouds floated in and hid the moon and stars again from view, I gazed up at the night sky and wished.

I wished I could have one more ordinary day with my mother. I would make sure to memorize everything we said and did. No memory fragments, but instead a whole day of doing everyday, ordinary things together to replay the rest of my life, whenever I wanted and needed to. I wished for the chance to say goodbye to her and tell her how much I loved her. Just because a wish could never happen didn't stop the wishing, not one bit.